The Playbook

NEW YORK TIMES & USA TODAY BESTSELLING AUTHOR

KELLY ELLIOTT

Copyright © 2016 by Kelly Elliott
Published by K. Elliott Enterprises

Cover photo and design by Sara Eirew Photographer
Editing and Proofing by Erin Noelle
Proofing by Holly Malgieri with Holly's Red Hot Reviews – Proofing
Interior design and formatting by JT Formatting

First Edition: July 2016
Library of Congress Cataloging-in-Publication Data
The Playbook – 1st ed
ISBN-13: 978-1-943633-21-0

www.kellyelliottauthor.com

For exclusive releases and giveaways signup for Kelly's newsletter at
http://eepurl.com/JoKyL

Prologue

Brett

"**W**HAT PLAY COACH?"

Forcing myself to look away from the brown-haired beauty standing next to Joe Evans, I turned to my quarterback. "X22OE."

Mitch nodded and pulled his helmet back on. Pulling the mic closer to my mouth, I glanced over to her again. When my stare caught hers, she grinned and it felt like the ground shook. Returning the smile, I watched as her face blushed. I could feel the heat of Joe's stare but I didn't give two shits. It was probably his fucking girlfriend. Pinching my eyebrows together at the thought, I tried to look away again. Something about her drew me in and caused me to lose all focus. She was the one who finally broke the stare-down when she looked away.

Fucking hell. Get it together Owens. You don't lose focus.
Ever.

With my attention back on the game, I watched as Mitch called out the play and then executed it perfectly.

First down. Fuck yes!

I followed the chains as I watched her walk. *Lord almighty, she has a nice ass.*

Clearing my throat, I tried to keep my dick from growing hard during a fucking game.

Covering my mouth with my paper, I asked one of the coaches in the box, "Pete, who's the girl with Joe Evans?"

Hearing his sigh, I couldn't help but chuckle as I pushed up the sleeves on my University of Austin shirt.

"Jesus Christ, Owens. We're in the middle of the fucking championship game, and you want to know who the broad is next to Evans?"

With a chuckle, I replied, "That's what I asked."

Troy was yelling another offensive play to Mitch as I made my way next to him.

Turning my head to the side, I probed Troy. "Who's the chick with dickhead Evans?"

"You didn't even give me a chance to find out!" Pete responded in my ears.

"You're too fucking slow," I replied as I covered my mouth

Troy glanced around, trying to find where Joe was. Once he saw them, he smiled.

"Ah yes … Aubrey Cain. She works for ESPN as an analyst. Works under Joe."

Lifting my brow. "Under him, huh?"

Shooting me a look, Troy shook his head. "From what I hear, she's not that type of girl."

With a smirk, I replied, "That sucks for me."

"Focus on the damn game, guys. Owens, you can have your pick of women to fuck in a few hours." Pete grunts from up in the booth.

That was the truth. I would have my pick of women. But I wanted the one standing next to her boss. The one dressed in the white top and dress slacks that hugged her body in all the right ways. The one who smiled and made me lose complete focus.

I watched as my top-ranked quarterback ran down the field for a touchdown. The extra point was good and we had this championship nailed with less than two minutes to go.

Smiling, I slapped all my guys and congratulated them as they came off the field. With another chance look, I caught her eye-fucking the hell out of me. My dick pressed against my cotton pants, leaving no doubt in my mind that this woman would rock my world in bed. I couldn't help but imagine what it would be like to have her under me. Naked and screaming out my name.

With a hard slap on the back, I turned to see Pat Stevenson, the athletic director and one of my dearest friends, standing there with one hell of a smile on his face.

"You did it again, Owens."

I returned the gesture with a slap of my own on the side of his arm and laughed. "Took the whole team, but I never doubted we couldn't do it."

As we headed out across the field, I looked back through the crowd for another glimpse of Ms. Cain. The way she was drawing my attention to her caught me off guard. I loved a beautiful woman, but she was different. I'd never had a woman pull my focus from a game.

Never.

My heart dropped when I couldn't see her anymore, and if I hadn't known any better, I would have sworn I felt a slight ache in my chest.

What in the fuck is that feeling?

Snapping my head back to the front, I shook my head. The quicker I forgot about her the better.

Pat leaned in and yelled into my ear, "You okay?"

With a quick nod, I answered, "Yep. Perfectly fine."

Little did I know that one simple exchange would rock my entire world.

Chapter One

Aubrey

A few months later...

PLACING THE GLASS to my lips, I took a sip of wine and gazed around the room. My parents had gone all-out hiring caterers and servers. When it came to their kids, they spared no expense.

"So where's the dick?"

Turning to my sister, Nelly, I sighed. "That seems to be the million-dollar question. If one more person asks me where Cliff is, I'm going to jump off one."

Nelly giggled then licked her lips and gave the waiter her practiced seductive stare as she took a wine glass. "Damn, what I wouldn't do to crawl on top of that."

Rolling my eyes, I made a gagging motion. "You're disgusting, do you know that?"

With a shrug, she kept her focus on the poor guy's retreating ass. "Why? Because I like to look at men?"

"No, because you like them between your legs every chance you get," I whispered while leaning in closer to her.

She gave me a befuddled look. "And, what's the point you're trying to make with that statement?"

"Ugh, never mind," I replied, waving her off with my hand. My once quiet-as-a-mouse sister was now hell-bent on proving to her ex-husband that she could get any guy she wanted. After five years of marriage, the bastard told her he was having an affair with his secretary. Nelly broke down and went off to some yoga resort with one of our other sisters, Marie. When she came back, she was totally different. She ate right, exercised every day, and dropped fifty pounds. She looked amazing.

"You know, you don't have to prove to anyone you're sexy as hell, Nelly."

Her head snapped over and the look she wore on her face should have dropped me to my knees. "I'm not trying to prove anything to anyone."

Marie, the second to oldest out of all four of us, walked up and draped her arms around both our shoulders. "Don't fight. It's your special day, Bree. You got the job you've been working so hard for! Sideline reporter in the house!" She called out while doing some weird movement that looked like something close to the chicken dance.

"What are you doing?" Nelly questioned while attempting to hide her grim.

Marie stopped and smirked. "I'm dancing in celebration of Bree's new job! She is finally on the sideline like she's always wanted."

"Let's not forget she also turned thirty today," Nelly said with a smirk.

Curling my lip up at her, I went to say something sarcastic when our mother walked up.

"Aubrey, darling, where is Cliff?"

2

Hearing his name filled me with anger. "I guess he's not coming, Mom."

Her smile faded as she laced her arm with mine and dragged me off to the side. Heaven forbid we cause an unnecessary scene. "What do you mean he isn't coming? Why in the world not? How could he miss such an important day in your life?"

Taking another sip of wine, this time a much longer one, I swallowed the heavenly delight and replied, "Oh, I don't know, Mom. Maybe because he thinks my job is stupid. That women don't belong in sports, let alone on the sideline of football games."

"Nonsense, he's an asshole then."

Covering my mouth to hide my giggle, I felt my face burn hot. It was rare for my mother to swear, but when she did, it tickled me so. My father on the other hand, he could drop the F-bomb at least once in every sentence if he thought he could get away with it. Six years of being groomed to be the husband of a US senator and to always be on his best behavior took some of the fun out of him. It was hard for him at times, but he supported mom one hundred percent.

My mother gave me a wink. "Don't let him ruin your evening. And don't look so sad. You got what you wanted."

My head pulled back in shock as a part of me burned on the inside. *I got what I wanted? What the hell?*

I could feel my body begin to tremble as I set my wine glass down and looked directly into my mother's eyes. "Is that what you think, really? Because let me tell you something, Mom."

She grabbed my arm and dragged me into her office, shutting the door behind her. "Oh, Aubrey, you know I didn't—"

The threat of tears was strong, but I wouldn't let them win. My shoulders slumped while I walked over to the chair. Making a very dramatic sigh, I flopped down.

Holding up her hands, my mother said, "Stop. That is not what I meant, and you know it. You're angry, Aubrey Cain, and don't you dare take it out on me."

"Mom, why do I have to keep proving myself over and over?"

"Because you're a woman, and that's what we have to do."

Dropping my head back, I let out a gruff laugh. "I'm so ready for the NFL, but Joe thinks my knowledge of college football is too great to let slip by. Just a couple of years sidelining college games and *then,* maybe the NFL he said."

The couch moved as my mother sat next to me. Taking my hand in hers, I felt that familiar calming effect. "I know you expected yourself to be further along in your career, sweetheart, but you knew what this was going to be like. Take a deep breath and look at this opportunity to prove to Joe that you have more than what it takes. Go out there and *show* him you're ready for the NFL."

Turning to face her, a weak smile formed at my mouth. "I feel like I'm starting completely over and trying to prove my worth all over again. I figured by now, I'd have been on the sidelines for a few years. I'd be talking marriage. Maybe thinking of kids." A frustrated sigh pushed from my mouth as a memory hit me.

My father's fork stopped right at his mouth while his eyes bulged out in shock. "Bree, did I hear you right?"

With a slow nod, I cleared my throat and sat up taller. "You did, Daddy. I've accepted an internship with ESPN as a research-assistant. It's for their ... um ... for their college football program."

I was sure his head was about to explode. "You can't be serious. Sports? You want to work in sports?"

Why was that so hard to understand? I was athletic all through high school. From running cross-country, to going to state in golf.

"You know how much I love sports. This is like a dream opportunity for me."

He pushed the pasta-wrapped fork into his mouth and chewed while staring at me. I took the moment of silence to glance around the restaurant. It was lunchtime and mostly businessmen and women surrounded us. Like clockwork, my father ate at the club twice a week—Monday and Thursday. It never failed; he was here at twelve sharp.

Dabbing the corner of his mouth with his napkin, I held my breath and waited for him to speak.

First, he nodded. I grabbed my napkin and wrung it in my sweaty hands under the table.

"Yes, Aubrey, I know how much you love sports. We couldn't seem to keep you out of them."

"Here I thought it was because it kept me busy and out of your hair," I joked with a smirk.

Pinching his brows, he gave me that look that said he didn't find my joke funny.

Inhaling deeply, he slowly let it out and asked, "What about law school?"

"That was your dream, Daddy. Not mine. I'm doing what I want to do, not what you want me to do."

The muscle in his neck jumped, causing me to fidget in my seat like a small child getting ready to be punished. I knew better, though. My father didn't have a mean bone in his body.

He tossed the napkin onto the table. "Last I checked, I was paying for your college."

My brow lifted. "I'll pay for it myself. It might take me longer to get through because I'll have to get a job, but I'm sure I can manage on my own. Mother did it." There was no way I was going to let my father strong-arm me into doing something I didn't want to do.

I couldn't help the small smile that spread across my face. My mother was smart, beautiful, full of life, and one of the best lawyers in the state of Connecticut. Of course, now she was running for senator, which meant all attention would be on everything we did as a family. Probably why my father was pushing hard for law school.

"Your mother was different, Aubrey. She came from nothing. Worked her tail off to get through college."

My blood boiled as I dropped back against my chair and folded my arms across my chest.

Rolling his eyes, my father sighed and whispered, "Oh, here we go."

"You're saying I don't work my tail off? Is that what you're saying? Last time I checked, I had a job at fourteen, bought my own car at seventeen, all the while managing to keep straight A's and grace the honor roll each semester. Oh, and excelled at sports along the way."

"You're the most stubborn child of the bunch. I want you to be able to do what you want to do, darling. Even if that means no law school. What in the world are you hoping to get out of this, though?"

A wide grin grew across my face. "Sideline reporter for the NFL."

His face fell. "Wh-what?"

With a confident nod, I sat up even straighter. "I know I can do it, Daddy."

He continued to stare at me like I'd grown two heads. "You do realize that most men mute the TV when the women start talking."

"Daddy! I can't believe you of all people would say that. You have four girls!" I gasped as he started laughing.

Holding up his hands, he shook his head. "I'm kidding! My goodness, take it easy. Give me a moment to let this soak in. First you tell me no law school, and now you hit me with sideline reporting." His face fell as he gave me a serious look. "I need you to know this isn't going to be an easy career. You know that, right?"

The waiter walked over and asked if we needed anything. My father lifted his gaze to him. "No, thank you, we're good. If you'll put this on my tab please."

With a quick glance in my direction, the waiter winked before excusing himself. If my father had seen him do that, he'd rip him a new one.

Ugh. Men.

"Back to what I was saying. This is going to be hard work, Bree. You're going to have to work a hundred times harder to prove you belong on the sidelines. Being a woman in this field is not going to be easy."

I nodded. "I know I can do this, Daddy. This is what I want."

He reached for my hand and kissed the back of it. "Then you know your mother and I will support your decision."

With a sly grin, I inquired, "Does this mean you're still paying for college?"

Throwing his head back, he laughed like I had said the funniest thing in the world. We both stood and my father motioned for me to lead the way. "Yes. Even though you'll be changing your mind about this career decision in a year. I guarantee it."

With pure determination in my voice I announced to him and practically the whole country club, "I'll be an ESPN sideline reporter before the ink is dry on the last college tuition check."

My mother's voice drew me from my thoughts.

"You do know you can be a working mom, right?"

With a shrug, I chuckled. A part of me longed to be the type of mom who stayed home with her kids. Not one that traveled most of the time. "I know. I'm feeling sorry for myself because I haven't met my own crazy goals and my piece of shit boyfriend isn't even at my damn party."

My mother stood and peered at me. "Now that is the first thing you've said that I completely agree with."

Standing, I followed her to the office door. "Which part?"

She opened the door and looked over her shoulder at me. "The piece of shit boyfriend."

I couldn't help myself; I let the laugh roll out like I'd been holding it in for months. Years probably.

As I walked back into the party crowd, I decided on two things. First thing was to break up with Cliff. The second, prove to Joe he made a huge mistake by not putting me in the NFL and keeping me in college football. If I had to do college first, though, I was going to be the best damn college sideline reporter in the history of sideline reporters!

I sat in Joe's office with a dumbfounded expression on my face.

"Did you hear me, Aubrey? We want you to do an article for the magazine on the University of Austin and, more importantly, Brett Owens."

Closing my eyes, I shook my head to try and rattle out the words that were still bouncing around in there.

"Wait. I need a moment to process this." I let out a chuckle. *Is he for real?* "You can't be serious." I swallowed hard. "An article? A month? Why a month?"

Joe leaned back in his chair and rested his chin on his fingers. With a smug look he replied, "You've done interviews before for the magazine so that can't be why you're so unsure. Are you afraid of him?"

Rage instantly raced through my veins. *How dare he think I'd be afraid of some stupid playboy college coach who acts like his shit doesn't stink? Who cares that he has a smile that rocked my world a few months ago. Or the fact that I couldn't sleep that night thinking about how he kept looking over at me.*

I let out a gruff laugh. "I'm neither unsure or afraid? Why would I be afraid of Brett Owens?"

The smirk on Joe's face spoke volumes. He knew exactly what he was doing. He had caught me staring at Brett during the championship game and made a smart ass comment about it. This was my do-or-die moment. Brett Owens had a reputation. A few of them really. He was a ladies' man, he didn't like female reporters in his locker room, and he thought he was the best football coach on the planet. Needless to say, he had taken the University of Austin to three straight national championships over the past three consecutive years. So yeah, maybe that last one was somewhat true. The others were rumors.

"Well, the main reason would be his dislike of women sports reporters. I'm not sure how he's going to feel about you following his every move for an entire month."

Narrowing my eyes, I took a few moments to let my heartrate settle back down. Joe was setting me up for failure. He didn't think I could handle this. He thinks I'll sleep with Owens.

Asshole.

"Then it looks like I'm the perfect reporter to get him over that. I'm sure Mr. Owens and I will be able to forge a good working relationship together."

Joe lifted his brows. It was obvious the bastard was attempting to hide his smile. "That's the attitude to have, Aubrey."

Standing, I smoothed out my pencil skirt and flashed my famous "I've got this smile" at him. "When do I leave?"

"Tomorrow."

Now, I was positive my mouth hit the floor. "Tomorrow?! Joe, you're giving me no time to research my subject. You're throwing me into the ring without even a warm up."

He stood. "Calm down, Aubrey. I want you in Austin early to get familiar with his turf. Research the shit out of him all you want. You have two weeks before the first meeting will be set up." So now my month turned into a month-and-a-half.

Pulling my lower lip in, I chewed on it before realizing what I was doing. *Don't show fear, Aubrey!*

"Should I introduce myself to him early?"

Joe's smirk grew wide. "Oh, he hasn't been told yet. The university will tell him a few days before you're set to meet him."

I groaned internally. Great. They were springing it on him and that would for sure piss him off.

"Perfect," I replied, trying to keep the nerves out of my voice. "I'll let you know when I'm settled in."

Spinning on my heels, I sprinted out of his office and straight to the ladies' room.

Michelle Brown, my best friend and co-worker, was hot on my heels as she followed me inside.

I placed my hands on the sink and inhaled a few deep breaths.

"So? What was that all about?"

Lifting my gaze to the mirror, I got a good look at myself. My light brown hair was worn in a French twist with a few loose tendrils hanging. Moving in closer, I looked into my brown eyes.

Is that fear I see? Hell no! Brett Owens is not going to be the one to bring my career down before it even gets started.

"Brett Owens. I have to do a piece on him," I mumbled.

Michelle leaned against the other sink. "He's an asshole. I covered his first national championship win. He actually asked me off camera if I wanted to go back to his hotel room and celebrate with him."

My head jerked to the side to look at her. That auburn hair of hers fell just below her shoulders and her green eyes sparkled. Almost as if the memory of Owens gave her a small thrill. "What?"

"Yep. I tell ya, for a few seconds, I sure as hell was tempted to take him up on it."

Turning my body to face her, I crossed my arms over my chest and stared at her in disbelief. "Michelle!"

She chuckled and waved off my surprised reaction off. "Never in my life have I been that close to a guy as handsome as he is."

I huffed. "Please, he's not *that* good-looking."

"Oh, you'll find out soon enough. You only saw him that one time. From a distance. Up close, girl, it is totally different when you are standing in front of him. Good thing you have a boyfriend to keep the temptation at bay."

With a frown, I replied, "I broke up with Cliff."

"What? Why?"

With a shrug of my shoulders, I attempted to push away the sick feelings in my stomach. I'd dated Cliff since my last year of college. He'd promised me the moon and never delivered. I was the stupid one who hung around and waited.

"Cliff never showed up for my birthday celebration with my family. Turns out, he had other plans. That night, I told him I was done and he didn't even argue with me. He packed up a bag of stuff and said he'd make arrangements for the rest of his things to be picked up."

Michelle snarled her lip. "Just like that, the jerk walked away?"

"Yep. Like it wasn't a big deal at all. I can't even cry over him because I think I've known it was over for awhile now."

"Well, I say good riddance. He was an ass anyway. He didn't even come to the winter gala. He never did support your career."

I nodded in agreement, but the words still hurt to hear. I'd give anything to have a man actually support my career choice and me. Cliff thought it was ridiculous to be working in sports.

Taking in a deep breath, I sighed and leaned against the sink. "You know what Joe is doing, right?"

She frowned. "Setting you up to fail. We've all been through it, Aubrey. The big boys don't like it when the girls come play in their sandbox. Especially when we can build the castle bigger and stronger."

My eyes closed and I shook my head "My father warned me, and there are days I wish I had listened. But I love my job, and I can tell you right now, I won't fail."

"Hell no, you won't. What is it, a one-on-one interview?"

With a groan, I turned to face her. She had been there for me since I first started my internship. Everyone whispered about how we all don't get along, but I work with some of the most amazing women I'd ever met. We all supported and cheered each other on. Michelle was no exception. Career-wise, I had a few years to go to get to where she was, but every Sunday, when I watched her on the sidelines of an NFL game, I beamed with pride. Her guidance helped me more than she would ever know.

"A full spread on him. What makes him one of college's best coaches is what they want me to focus on. Also, what he does in his spare time, right down to his playboy ways. I'm spending an entire month following him around for an exclusive college edition on the great Brett Owens and the University of Austin."

I'd never seen Michelle wear a look of dread like she was.

"You have to spend a whole month getting into the life of Brett Owens?"

With a nervous laugh, I replied, "Yes ma'am."

Michelle pushed off the sink and stood in front of me. Placing her hands on my shoulders she slowly shook her head.

"Aubrey. You. Are. So. Screwed."

Chapter Two

Brett

PAT STEVENSON SAT on the other side of the desk and grinned at me like he had just given me the best gift ever. I swear, if he wasn't the athletic director and my boss, I'd tell him to go fuck himself.

"You want me to let some reporter follow me around for a month for an *ESPN: The Magazine* article?" I let out a laugh. "No wait … let me clarify that. You want me to let some chick follow me around for a month. Are you insane, Pat?"

Clearing his throat, he leaned forward. "They're doing a special college football edition and you're the featured coach. And that *chick* is a reporter for ESPN and has been with them for some time. Brett, this is more than an article. You've damn near got the biggest magazine in sports doing a feature on you, along with the University of Austin."

"Then why is she covering college football? Why isn't she following around the head coach of the Dallas fucking Cowboys? Why me?"

"Because everyone wants to know something about you. Anything."

I laughed. "It's called privacy, Pat. I like it. A lot."

"Listen, Owens. I'm not beating around the bush here. I know you are loyal to the school and me. I appreciate that. I also know you're hiding here."

My blood boiled. "*Hiding*? What the fuck does that mean?"

He lifted his eyebrows and gave me a look as if I knew exactly what he was talking about. "It means we both know if you were to say you wanted to move up to coach in the NFL, you'd have a plethora of owners knocking at your door. Yet you choose to stay here."

"Are you saying you want me to leave?" I asked, giving him a questioning look. I knew Pat would never ask me to leave. He was like a second father to me. Had been since I played football here. I also knew he was a hundred percent right when he said I was hiding. This place was my safety net. The place I knew I could thrive in.

"You know I don't want you to leave. But, I think by doing this, giving the world a glimpse into your life, you're not only helping your career, but you're helping our college football program as well."

I grunted and combed my fingers through my hair. "What's her name?"

"Aubrey Cain."

My dick jumped. "No shit," I uttered with a wicked smile. I instantly thought back to a few months ago when she flashed me that sexy ass grin of hers at the championship game. She was all I thought about the rest of the fucking day… and night.

Pat rolled his eyes. "Don't even think about it, Owens. Keep your hands and, most importantly, your dick in your pants. I have a feeling Joe Evans is testing Ms. Cain."

My interest was piqued. "Testing her? Why? She's damn good at her job from what I can tell." That night, I spent the next three hours google searching the hell out of her. Reading anything I could find on her and looking at every damn picture out there. My dick was raw by the end of the night.

With a stunned look, Pat asked, "Was that a compliment to a female reporter?"

"Yes. I have nothing against female reporters. I just don't want them in my locker room. They're a distraction."

"For who? You or the team?"

"Both!"

Pat chortled. "I guess Ms. Cain has been pushing to sideline on Sundays. Joe feels like she's better in college and not ready to handle the NFL."

I had to admit, I wasn't surprised to hear that Joe was keeping back a female reporter. He acted as if he was okay with women in sports, but one drunken night at a bachelor party revealed how the asshole really felt. The last place he thought a woman should be was on the sideline of a NFL game.

"What makes him think she couldn't handle the NFL?"

"That's just it. I don't think he's sure if she can or not. What a better way to test her ability to stick it out with the tough stuff, than to throw her at you. If she can handle you, she might be ready to move up."

Holy fuck. I was being used. I didn't like being used.

"And if I say no?"

"You won't."

I stood and laughed. "Really? Why's that?"

"Because if you say no, I'll fire you."

My eyes widened. There was no way I'd get fired for not doing an interview. It pissed me off that Pat was trying to strong-arm me on this. Then again, if it was a huge special edition spread, the university would be all for it. Which meant, I was doing it whether I liked it or not. But that didn't mean I had to like it.

"Then fire me because I'm not doing it. That fucker is using me to test one of his damn reporters. He can use someone else. I'm not going to be a part of it." I spun around and headed to the door.

"Sit down, Brett."

Pat's voice was full of control and I knew he wasn't fucking around. Slowly turning around, I stared him down. "No thank you, sir. I'd rather stand."

"We need to show people you're more than a pretty face. I'm not sure if you happen to notice the signs all the girls hold up every Saturday claiming how hot you are."

I couldn't help the smirk that curled at the corners of my lips.

"People need to see the side of you that is driving this college program to what we hope is our fourth national championship. This girl, excuse me, this reporter is going to be the one to do that. She knows her stuff when it comes to college football and is probably the only person who could stand to be around you for a month."

I huffed. "Joe doesn't seem to think she'll be able to stick around."

Pat stood. He inhaled in a deep breath and exhaled out. "I don't want to have to force you. I want you to go into this with a positive attitude and see it for what it's really about. You. I don't give a shit what ESPN's reasons are for sending Aubrey Cain. That's not my problem. You're doing the piece and you'll invite Ms. Cain into your world with open arms."

My jaw was beginning to ache from clenching it. I'd never been so pissed off in my entire life. And it wasn't because I was being forced to do this. It was because I knew it needed to be done. "Fine. I'll do the piece. But I want you to know, I'm not changing anything about me. If something comes out in this piece that Ms. Cain decides to print, it's on your shoulders, not mine."

Pat nodded. "Agreed. That's why I need you to be on your best behavior, or at the very least attempt to be, or you could very well not be coaching next year."

Fuck. I can't believe this.

"When does this all take place?"

"Ms. Cain will be here tomorrow at ten in the morning. Be sure to get here early. I don't want her starting off with a negative opinion of you."

My stomach dropped. "Tomorrow morning?"

The only thing I got in return from my question was a blank stare. "Pat, tell me you didn't give me less than a day's notice for this." My heart started racing. I needed more time.

More time to prepare.

I need more time to prepare for that smile. That body. Those lips around my thick hard cock.

Shit. I was already losing focus and she wasn't even here yet.

"Go home and get a good night's sleep, Brett. You're going to need it."

He sat and lifted his phone. "Betty, will you please get me Joe Evans with ESPN."

Balling my fists up, I turned and left Pat's office.

Fuck sleep. What I needed was a drink. Or ten.

My hand slipped around the waist of the blonde standing next to me. She'd been hitting on me since I first walked into Moontower at one in the afternoon. It must have been written all over my face I needed a good lay.

"So, what do you do for a living?" she purred into my ear.

Turning to brush my lips against her neck, I replied, "My father owns a couple cattle ranches, so I live off his money." So maybe only half that statement was true.

Her body trembled. I never told people what I really did. If they didn't know, I wasn't about to offer up the information.

"How about we get out of here?" she softly spoke.

"My place or yours?"

Her face lit up. "Yours."

I dropped a few twenties on the bar and grabbed her by the hand, leading her out to my Dodge Hell Cat.

Stopping in front of my car, the blonde started clapping. "Oh, my. Look at that sexy muscle car!"

With a grin, I opened the passenger door. I wasn't going to argue with her. It was a badass car. And it also happened to be a fucking chick magnet.

She slid in and made sure her tiny little skirt didn't leave much to the imagination. My dick was throbbing. Rounding the front of the car, I got a text from an unknown number. Hitting ignore, I got in and started up the engine. Turning to the blonde next to me, I smiled and winked. "Maybe you should at least tell me your name before I sink my cock inside of you."

Her lips parted and she barely got the words out. "Tracy. Yours?"

"Brett. And I plan on hearing you scream it out a time or two."

"Jesus," she whispered as I floored it to my place.

The moment we walked into my condo, Tracy was ripping at my T-shirt to get it off.

Feisty. I like it.

"Oh. My. Gawd. Your body is so amazing," she whispered as she dropped to her knees and ran her tongue along my abs. Ten seconds later, my pants were down and her mouth was wrapped around my cock.

"Fuck yes," I hissed. I didn't normally let women give me a blowjob unless I was two sheets to the wind. I still trembled thinking about Patricia Harley's braces nearly cutting my dick off in high school.

Before she caused me to blow, I tugged her up. "Get undressed and get your ass on my bed."

It didn't take long for Tracy to start yelling out my name. She was like a fucking racehorse. The more I gave her, the more she wanted, until we both collapsed onto the bed.

"Holy shit. That was amazing!" she giggled.

My phone had gone off again. Getting up, I walked over to it. Tracy murmured something about my ass, but I couldn't hear what she said. Actually that wasn't true. I chose to ignore what she said. Picking up the phone, it was another text from an unknown number.

"Do you have any wine, Brett?" she called out as she made her way out of the bedroom.

I didn't like the way she was making herself right at home, but I figured I'd get another good fuck out of her, so if she wanted wine, I'd let her have some. We probably had time for one more round before I'd send her on her way and make my way out for a late dinner.

Swiping my finger over my phone, I opened up the text message.

Unknown: Hi, Mr. Owens. This is Aubrey Cain. Are you free this evening?

My heart damn near jumped to my throat as I stared at the message. Aubrey Cain sent me a text.

Why in the hell did that freak me out?

I knew why. That fucking smile. That goddamn body. I was going to be spending a lot of time in cold showers.

Trying to get a bit more information on her, I googled her again after I left Pat's office. This time it wasn't to jack off to her, but to learn something about her career at ESPN. If she was doing this article, I needed to make sure I knew who I was dealing with. She had been an analyst for ESPN for awhile and had been rumored to be making her way to sideline reporting. The few connections I had at ESPN all informed me of how good she was at her job and that she knew college football like the back of her hand.

Unknown: Shit. I hope I have the right number. I thought maybe if we could meet at Second Bar & Kitchen before tomorrow it might be easier. I'm having dinner with my boss there tonight at seven. Brett? If this is your number, we'd love to treat you to dinner.

How quickly I went from Mr. Owens to Brett. Interesting.

"Brett? I can't seem to find your wine opener?"

Rolling my eyes, I walked into the bathroom and grabbed a towel. Wrapping it around my waist, I made my way back through my bedroom and to the kitchen. My condo was fairly big, especially for being right in the middle of downtown Austin.

Tracy was leaning over, stark-ass naked, looking in a drawer. For a quick moment, I thought about going and grabbing a condom but then a strange feeling came over me as I thought about Aubrey's text.

My heartbeat increased. It felt like I had run up and down the bleachers at the stadium about ten times.

I stopped walking and stepped out of the kitchen like it was about to catch fire.

Glancing to my phone, I typed my reply.

Me: See you tomorrow.

Warm hands landed on my chest and moved ever so slowly. The towel dropped to the floor. "Looks like we're going to have to skip the wine. Seeing you standing here got me all worked up again."

For the first time in my life, I felt guilty for fucking a girl I picked up in a bar, and I had no clue why. Confusion swam around in my head along with mixed emotions about what I wanted to do right now. It took me less than thirty seconds to make my decision.

"I'm sorry, Tracy. I got a text. I need to leave, work emergency."

She dropped her arms and looked at me with a confused expression. "I thought you said you lived off your parents' money?"

I fake laughed. "It was a joke. I have a job at the University. I need to get going."

Her lips formed a pout. "Does your dad have two ranches, though?"

I headed to my bedroom and called out over my shoulder, "Yep!"

"When can I see you again?"

With a smirk, I mumbled, "Never."

Chapter Three

Aubrey

MICHELLE HAD BEEN talking for months about this restaurant. She often came to Austin. The guy she was dating was a doctor here. Joe and I sat at the table as the waiter handed us each a menu.

Joe took his napkin and folded it across his lap. "So, no word from our golden boy?"

I had to admit, when he mentioned meeting Brett before tomorrow, I was unsure. But if it meant getting the coldness I was sure to get from him over with, then maybe that was what I needed to do.

"He sent a text saying he had plans this evening," I replied with a polite grin. I wasn't about to tell him the jerk blew off my invite with not so much as a "No, thank you" or "I'm sorry, I have plans."

Dick.

"Yeah, his boss called me earlier today to tell me he dropped the bomb on Owens this morning."

My breath caught in my throat. *Oh. Shit.*

I tried to act casual as I asked, "And how did that go?" One day? They gave him one-day notice? No wonder I got the cold reply.

When the young waitress came over, Joe went into flirt mode.

"What can I get you two to drink?"

Joe spoke first, cutting me off before I could respond. "Well, my-oh-my. Do they breed all women in Austin to be as beautiful as you?"

I gave him a dumbfounded look. Was that the best he could come up with? No wonder the guy was still single.

When a giggle came from her lips, I turned to her and gave her the same look. *Please tell me you're not falling for that line of bullshit?*

"You're making me blush, sir."

I cleared my throat, getting both of their attention. "I'll take a water, please."

The girl smiled and turned back to Joe. "And for you?"

"A glass of Merlot, please."

Flashing us both a friendly look, she said, "I'll get those right out. Are we going to be doing appetizers?"

Glancing over to Joe, I shook my head. "I don't care for any, but if you do, don't let me stop you."

"No, I'm good. Maybe a few minutes to look at the menu."

The waitress nodded and quickly left to get the drinks.

Taking in a shallow breath, I opened the menu and looked for this great burger Michelle went on and on about.

"What are you in the mood for?" Joe probed.

"I'm getting the burger. Michelle raves about it."

With an absentminded nod, he continued to peruse the menu. I wondered if he even heard what I said. I figured he had simply gotten used to making small talk. Half the time, in meetings when I would speak, it was if he was staring right through me. I swore he never heard half the shit that came out of my mouth.

Glancing around the restaurant, a strange feeling came over me. It felt like someone was watching me. I quickly did a search of the place before I shook it off.

The waitress brought back our drinks and set them in front of us.

"Are we ready to order?" she questioned.

Joe motioned for me to go first without so much as looking in my direction.

I fake-smiled at him and then set my sights on the waitress and replied, "I'll have the congress burger with everything, and well done, please."

She turned to Joe. "And for the handsome gentleman?"

Gag me.

"I think I'll take the soba noodles and sprouts."

I internally rolled my eyes at my boss. Yep. The more I saw, the more I understood why he had never settled down.

"Got it. I'll put that order in now."

Folding my arms in front of me, I looked directly at Joe. "I know why you put me on this piece."

His head lifted. When the slow smirk spread across his face, he leaned back and looked at me like he knew something I didn't.

"Is that so? Enlighten me then."

"It's simple. You want me to fail so you can go back to your boss and tell him you made the right decision in keeping me on the college level."

He tried not to show that my words affected him, but I saw the twitch in his neck muscle. "Why would my boss care?"

"Because, he suggested I cover the NFL two years ago, and you chose to ignore his suggestions."

My gaze fell to Joe's throat as I watched him force a swallow. Now the ball was in my court. I knew it was risky to call him out, but I was pissed he put me in this situation.

"Who told you that?"

Leaning forward, I smirked. "Does it really matter, Joe? I can tell by your reaction it's true. Why you did it no longer concerns me. My goal now is doing this piece and making it the best goddamn feature in the history of ESPN. You want to know about Brett Owens on and off the football field? No problem. I'll make sure every high school football player decides the University of Austin is the place they want to play college football for. And when I'm done, every woman in America will be lusting after the hottest football coach in college football. Hell, in all of football!"

My body trembled. It wasn't from fear or being cold, it was that feeling of being watched again. I didn't dare take my attention off Joe, though. The last thing I could show was fear.

"I want to know if you've gone over my head with this thing, Aubrey?"

The left side of my mouth curled up and my heart pounded in my chest. Joe was pissed and I was treading on thin ice, but it was a chance I had to take. "You really think I'm that kind of person? To go running to the higher-ups because I didn't get my way? Your boss had a little too much to drink and shared his thoughts on how he really feels about your call on keeping me at the college level. Turns out he's second-guessed a few decisions you've made in the past."

He leaned forward. I could practically see the steam coming from his head. "Don't fuck with me, Aubrey. I've been doing this shit a lot longer than you, and if you push me, you'll be back to being a research assistant faster than you can say your name."

I lifted my eyebrow and shrugged. "Unlike you, I don't fuck colleagues."

Pushing my chair back, I dropped my napkin onto the table. "Thanks for flying in to see how I'm doing. As you can see, I think I've got it under control. I had a good warm-up session this evening. Have a safe flight back to Bristol, Joe."

Making my way through the restaurant, I fought to keep my feet walking forward, as well as keep my breathing under control.

Damn it. The burger.

Now I was going to have to come back and try the burger another night. My stomach instantly rumbled, alerting me of my bad decision to wait and go off on Joe until *after* dinner.

There went that feeling again. One quick glance over my shoulder, and his blue eyes caught mine. I stopped on a dime and stared at him.

25

I slowly turned around and faced him. Brett Owens stood at the bar watching my every move.

He lifted his bottle of beer to his lips and smiled before he took a drink. It was no ordinary smile. It was one that you read about in romance books where your knees get weak and your stomach does that stupid flip thing.

I'd just told off my boss, there was no way I was going to let Brett Owens throw me off my game plan. With a smile of my own, I walked over and stopped directly in front of him.

His intense gaze looked over my body before they landed on my lips. Deciding to play him at his own game, I slowly ran my tongue across my lower lip.

When Brett's eyes snapped up to mine, I couldn't help but notice his breath hitch. "Do you know how fucking hot it sounded hearing you put your boss in his place?"

I knew it. I knew someone was watching me. Sneaky little bastard.

With a quick peek over toward Joe, I saw he was in full-on flirt mode with the lady at the next table and not paying any attention to anything else around him but the blonde in the tight skirt. Placing my attention back on Brett, I reached for his beer and took a drink. Setting it down, I winked and answered him. "Funny how your plans landed you in the same restaurant as me this evening, Brett."

He laughed and it rumbled through my body. I had to focus on my breathing. Michelle was not lying when she said how good looking this guy was up close. Dark messy hair that looked like he ran his fingers through it one too many times. Eyes the color of the sky, and a body that, from where I was standing, looked like he worked out often. Oh yes, not to mention the fact that it appeared he hadn't shaved in a week. I see now why she was tempted by this man. Of course I knew all too well how Brett Owens could tempt a woman. I still could close my eyes and see that smile he flashed me on the sidelines and how it caused an instant ache between my thighs.

"Well, turns out I was free after all."

My head tilted. "Get stood up?"

His gaze burned with so much intensity, I had to take a step back. Another look in Joe's direction showed he was still lost in his conversation.

Brett took a step toward me and wrapped his arm around my waist, tugging me up against his body. The heat settled between my legs as he took control of the conversation in an instant. What I wouldn't give to feel his lips on my body.

No! Stop this, Aubrey. This is work. Do not let this guy get to you!

"Turns out my cock can only fuck a girl about three times in one afternoon before I'm spent. So I sent her home and came to see who my new buddy was going to be for the next month."

My mouth dropped. *Did he really just tell me that?* I'd never been stunned into silence before, but Brett Owens was able to do it. And that pissed me off.

Leaning in closer, he placed his mouth up against my ear. "Don't look so shocked, Aubrey. I'm sure in all of your research you have to know I love two things in life. Football and fucking. In that order…most of the time."

My hands landed on his chest. I tried like hell to ignore the zip of energy that raced through my body. Giving him a good push, I winked.

"Good evening, Mr. Owens."

Digging deep down in my gut, I focused on keeping my voice strong and even. I have had plenty of guys hit on me in locker rooms, on the sideline, hell, even at work. None of them ever affected me, though. None. But Brett Owens' mouth up against my neck and his dirty words whispered in my ear shook me to the core.

His smile grew bigger. "Good evening, Ms. Cain."

Warmth radiated through my body as I made my way through the restaurant. It was going to be a long night.

Dragging in a deep breath, I slowly blew it out.

"You've got this, Bree."

Jumping, I nodded. I'd just gotten back from my morning run when Michelle called. I filled her in on everything that went down last night with Joe and Brett.

"I've got this!" I exclaimed, stretching my sore limbs. I hadn't slept at all. Every time I closed my eyes, all I could see was Brett's piercing gaze and hear that silky smooth voice of his.

"He's gay! He's not even really interested in you."

I stopped hopping around. "What do you mean he's gay? He sure didn't seem gay."

Michelle groaned. "For goodness sake, I was trying to get your mind focused in the right place."

"It is! I'm not the least bit worried about Brett Owens. He caught me off guard last night. Now I know that was what his intentions were. I'll give him round one, but round two is going to me."

"What are you wearing?"

I looked into the closet of my corporate condo. "Well, I could go conservative. Dress slacks, a nice blouse, and simple heels. Or I could go sexy. Tight skirt, blouse that hints at cleavage, and killer high heels."

"Conservative. It will at least keep the pussy hound from sniffing around you."

My brows pinched together. "What did you call him?"

"A pussy hound."

I couldn't help but laugh. I yanked my T-shirt over my head and tossed it onto the floor. I knew the moment I walked back out it would drive me crazy seeing it on the floor, but for now, I was feeling daring.

"Did you make that up?" I asked.

"Yes, but you have to admit it fits him."

I couldn't argue with her on that one.

"Okay, I'm totally going conservative."

"Good choice. I'd play it very cool with this cat."

Knowing Michelle was right, I picked out a simple pair of dress pants and a light blue dress shirt. "I better get going if I want to be a little early. Thanks for your help, Michelle!"

With an evil laugh, she cackled, "Good luck! You're going to need it."

My stomach dropped and I was instantly filled with dread and fear. I knew she was right. Brett Owens rocked my core last night. That was last time that would ever happen to me. I wasn't about to lose my career over some jackass who thought he was God's gift to women and football.

After getting dressed, I stared at myself in the mirror. I looked cute, but not overly sexy. Dress pants and a nice shirt would surely keep Brett Owens at bay. I even pulled my hair up into a ponytail.

Chewing on my lower lip, I closed my eyes and allowed myself one more forbidden thought about Brett Owens before I pushed him from my thoughts and refocused on the one thing I lived for.

Reporting.

Chapter Four

Aubrey

AN HOUR AND a half later, I stood outside the athletic director's office trying to keep my nerves settled. In a way, I was glad I saw Brett last night. Now I could walk in and not be the least bit swayed by him.

"Ms. Cain?" My head popped up as I grinned at the receptionist. "They're ready for you?"

A quick glance at the clock showed they waited until exactly ten to call for me, even though I knew Brett was already in the office since the receptionist informed me when I first got here both Pat and Brett were in a quick meeting.

Standing, I grabbed my briefcase and purse and followed the older lady into the office.

The moment Brett glanced over to me, my breath caught and my heart spiked to record beats per minute.

He gave me a once-over quickly as I tried to drag mine off of him.

"Ms. Cain, what a pleasure meeting you." I quickly looked at Mr. Stevenson. He sat on the opposite side of the conference table that probably seated at least twenty-five people. He stood and Brett followed suit.

I reached my hand out to him and shook it with a slightly firm handshake. Just like my father taught me. I turned and did the same to Brett, trying like hell not to look too hard at him. I failed.

He was dressed in jeans, a University of Austin T-shirt, and a baseball cap that he wore backward.

Backward! What in the hell was it about a man in a damn baseball cap... turned around?

"Brett, it's a pleasure seeing you again."

The reaction from him caused me to smile slightly. I was positive he wouldn't have expected me to bring up our little encounter last night.

Mr. Stevenson looked at Brett for an explanation. "I ran into Ms. Cain at Second Street Bar."

When his boss nodded like it was no big deal, my small victory was quickly smashed into the ground. Brett must have noticed it because he felt the need to say something.

"I live across the street and go there for dinner a lot."

My heart dropped to my stomach.

Oh. No.

"You ... you, um ... live downtown?"

He was enjoying me being thrown off guard... again. "I do. Second Street condominiums."

Fuck. My. Life.

I flashed a wide grin. "Well this works out good then for me."

His smile faltered. "How so?"

"I'm staying in a corporate condo in the same building. It will make following you around... I mean, researching you easier." I turned to Mr. Stevenson and grinned. He gave me an awkward smile in return. "For the piece I'm doing on you."

Brett shook his head. Clearly he was not happy about this and neither was I. We were both going to have to suck it up and deal with it, though. We were dealt the same card, now we had to play it.

I cleared my throat, getting their attention. Reaching into my brief case, I took out my notebook that I had already filled with research on Brett and the university college program.

I flipped through the endless pages of notes until I found a blank page.

"So, I'm assuming since it's spring training, I'll be granted full access to the stadium." Peeking up at Brett, I added, "That includes the locker rooms."

His jaw muscles flexed and I couldn't help but smile. "I'd like to really observe you, Mr. Owens, for the first week or two here at work. Really get an understanding of your work habits and ethics with the team and, of course, your habits away from the team as well."

His lips parted to say something, but Mr. Stevenson coughed and Brett shut his mouth.

"This piece is going to be about getting to know Brett Owens. Three-time national championship winner. Youngest head football coach in college football, and rumored ladies' man."

"What?" Brett gasped, nearly chocking on his own spit.

I shrugged and flipped through my notes where I found a reference to picture in *People* magazine.

"Yes, here it is. A picture of you with two women on your arms exiting a bar in downtown Austin. I believe it was on New Year's Eve." I held it up for him to see.

His eyes narrowed and I swear they turned black. "What in the hell do you have written down in that book?"

I pointed to my notebook, while keeping my focus fixed on him. "This notebook?"

When his hand combed through his hair, I felt a tug in my lower stomach that I quickly pushed aside.

"Yes, that notebook, Aubrey! I don't see another notebook on the fucking table."

My head drew back with raised eyebrows. I quickly flipped back to the empty page and wrote a note.

Curses like a damn sailor.

"Wh-what are you writing?"

I couldn't help but feel giddy knowing I was getting to him. "Just taking some notes, that's all."

Brett leaned closer to me as I covered the note with my hand. "What did you say? I saw sailor written down!"

I flashed him an evil smile which only irritated him more, causing him to curse more under his breath.

Mr. Stevenson sighed heavily next to me. "Oh, for the love of God. The two of you are going to have to learn to play nice. Your boss, Ms. Cain, and the president of the university, want this thing to happen. Now I hope you will shine a more positive light on Mr. Owens and not focus on his… on his um—"

Brett and I both looked at him, anxiously waiting for him to finish his sentence.

"On my what?" Brett questioned.

With a roll of his eyes, Mr. Stevenson answered, "On the colorful lifestyle you lead outside of work."

"That was gently put," I mumbled.

"Ms. Cain," Mr. Stevenson started.

"Please, call me Aubrey."

He nodded. "Aubrey, you will have full access so getting in places will not be an issue. I advise you to stick close to Brett until you learn your way around."

"Thank you, Mr. Stevenson."

"Pat will be fine."

"Pat, it is."

"Now, I believe, Brett, you have a staff meeting at noon."

I swear it looked like Brett was sitting over there pouting. It probably killed him he had no safe-zone to hide in. I was going to be stuck to him like glue. Oh, this made me all kinds of happy right now.

"Yeah. It's at noon."

Pat stood. "Good, show Aubrey around and to the office she'll be using."

My heart skipped a beat in my chest. "Thank you, Pat. That means a lot to me to have a place to work while I'm here. That's very thoughtful of you."

He looked at Brett and then me. "Don't thank me, thank Brett. It was his idea."

My head snapped to the side as I looked at him. That was totally unexpected, and I couldn't hide the fact that it made my chest tighten some.

"Now, if you'll both excuse me, I've got my next meeting in a few minutes I need to prepare for."

Brett reached over and tried to grab my notebook, but I was too quick. "Ha!" I whispered as I shoved it in my briefcase and headed to the door.

"Thank you again, Mr. Steve—Pat."

He lifted his hand and grinned as he dropped into his seat and picked up his phone.

Making my way to the elevator, I heard Brett behind me. He said something to the receptionist, causing her to laugh. I groaned internally and hit the down arrow.

My body heated when Brett reached around me and hit the up button. "We're going up."

I simply nodded.

When the doors opened, I quickly walked in. The moment the elevator closed, Brett was next to me, his mouth near my ear. I totally lost my concentration when he began to speak. "I know another thing that is coming up—my cock. You look sexy as fuck. Dinner tonight? By the way, I love the ponytail. Gives me something to hold on to when I take you from behind."

My mouth fell open in shock.

I was in dress pants. And a button-down shirt that I practically had buttoned up to my neck. *How in the hell could I possibly look sexy?* I also made a note to myself to never wear a ponytail around him again.

Did he ask me out or did he ask for sex?

Reaching over, I hit the stop button, causing the elevator to come to a halt.

It was time to set Mr. Cocky Pants straight. Glancing down quickly, I had to keep my eyes from bugging out. Mr. Cocky Pants indeed.

Pointing my finger at him, I jabbed him in the chest, causing him to jerk back.

"All right, you listen here. There is no way in hell I would ever go out with you. Let along let you *take me from behind.*"

He lifted a single brow and gave me a panty-melting smile that caused my stomach to flip. "What about after your whole article piece bullshit is down? Then?"

I shook my head. "No! Not even then."

"How about a quick fuck then? Get it out of our system."

"Oh. My. God. Do you hear yourself speak? How have you not gotten fired?"

Tossing his head back, he laughed. "I don't talk like this to co-workers."

Anger zipped through my veins. "Newsflash asshole, we are working together for the next month and longer after that. I'll be covering your stupid games on Saturdays. That means interviewing you, your staff, and yes, your players in the damn locker room. I could slap you with a sexual harassment charge so fast your head would spin."

His stare dropped to my lips. In one brief moment, I wanted him to kiss me. Brief! Very brief.

I wonder how he tastes. Would he draw my lower lip in when he kisses? God, that is hot as hell.

His hands landed on my hips, plucking me from my daydream.

"So tell me, what were you thinking because your face is flush?"

My heart pounded in my chest as I frantically searched for an answer. "My boyfriend, and how much I'm going to miss him being stuck here with you."

His hands dropped from my waist, causing me to instantly miss the heat from his touch.

"You have a boyfriend?"

Oh my gosh. I found my golden ticket. Mr. Cocky Pants has a conscience. He won't touch me if he thinks I'm with someone.

Could I lie? The way he was looking at me and making my panties wet, I had no choice.

"Yes. His name is Cliff. We've been dating for over five years now."

36

Narrowing his brows, he slowly nodded. He reached around me, his body brushing up next to mine. I was positive he saw my reaction as my betraying body shivered.

"Let's get you to your office so you can settle in before the staff meeting."

And like that, it was as if someone had thrown cold water on Brett Owens. Bringing him to a screeching halt.

Nodding my head, I moved and stood next to him. The air in the elevator changed. The playfulness, excitement, whatever it was we shared between us was gone.

I should have been happy. I found a way to tame the bad boy. Instead, I felt sick to my stomach. Like I just pushed the one thing away from me I've wanted my entire life.

Peeking up at Brett, I noticed his jaw was clenched tight. My eyes dropped to his fists that were squeezed shut. I turned and faced the doors as they opened. Brett quickly stepped out first and walked down a long hall.

I couldn't help but notice how when he passed by women they all tried in some way to get his attention. He never faltered and stayed the course. Stopping outside an office, he pointed in through the open door. "This is your office. You're right next to mine. Patty is my assistant and she'll be more than happy to help you with anything you need. I handpicked her myself."

Ugh. Patty. She was probably twenty something with a rocking body and breasts that spilled out of her shirt. I bet he's already had sex with her.

"I go to lunch every day at twelve forty-five. If you're truly going to be following me around, take that into consideration. I also run every morning here at the stadium, three miles. I doubt you'll want to partake in that, though."

And like that, he turned and walked away. I slowly shook my head. "Asshole," I whispered.

"That he is, but he's a lovable asshole."

I jumped when the female voice behind me spoke.

Turning, I looked at a sweet older lady smiling at me. She had to be about sixty-five, maybe older. With a wink, she glanced into the office. "I tried to make sure you had everything in here you might need. Scanner, and printer on the desk over in the corner. If you need anything else, let me know. The name is Patty."

I let out a small laugh. "You're… I mean… you're Patty?"

She grinned and answered, "Last time I looked in the mirror. Why? What did you hear about me? I'll kick their ass if they said anything negative."

My hand came up to my mouth as I shook my head in disbelief. "You're Brett's assistant?"

Standing a little taller, she grinned. "I am indeed. Use to work for his daddy years ago before I moved to Austin with my husband. Once he passed, God rest his soul, I was bored out of my mind. Brett called me out of the blue one day after he got this job. Said he need-ed a kick-ass assistant and if I wanted it, the job was mine."

Damn it. Just when I have it set in my mind that he is an ass-hole, he does something to change my mind.

"Well, he spoke very highly of you."

She lifted her chin and stared me down. "You were thinking I was some blonde twenty-year old who had probably slept her way to the position."

I dropped my head in embarrassment. "Now that you mention it."

With a chuckle, she waved it off. "Don't even think twice about it. I keep that boy in check. You let me know if he does anything to upset you. I'll kick him in the ass."

Oh my. Patty has spunk.

"Yes ma'am. I'll remember that."

After Patty went to her desk, I got myself organized. Then it was off to the staff meeting and then lunch. Which was with the coaches. I took a ton of notes and really got to see a completely dif-ferent side to Brett Owens. There was a reason this guy was good at what he did. He may have been a lot younger than some of his secondary coaches, but they all respected him. That was easy to see.

The only time he talked to me or about me is when he introduced me. Other than that, it was if I didn't even exist. I don't even think he looked my way all day. I was bothered by that more than I wanted to admit. All the talk about football coming from his soft delicious looking lips had me moving about all day in my seat. The ache between my thighs only grew when he would glance up at me then quickly look away.

By the time I got to my condo, I dropped onto the couch and kicked off my heels. I dropped my head back and went over the day in my mind.

It was a productive day. I got a good amount of information on Brett and how he coached. Smiling, I thought back to how much the players really seemed to look up to him. I could tell he honestly cared for those guys. Writing the working piece of this article wouldn't be that hard. It was the personal side that I was dreading.

Sitting up, I sucked in a breath of air. My chest felt as if it was squeezing down on my lungs as I remembered Brett's face when I told him I had a boyfriend. *Why did that depress me?*

I know why. Brett Owens was no longer interested in me. That one word hung between us and I had no idea how I was going to take it back.

Closing my eyes, I thought back to the look on his face.
"You have a boyfriend?"

Reaching for the decorative pillow, I pushed it onto my face and screamed into it.

"What is wrong with me? First I don't want him to pay attention to me. And then when he doesn't, I want him to. What is this? What is this man doing to me?"

I paced back and forth. I needed advice.

Reaching into my purse, I brought up my sister Marie's number and hit call.

If anyone could help me sort this mess out, it was her.

Chapter Five

Brett

PULLING INTO MY parking spot, I stared out at the track. I had to drag my ass out of bed this morning after only getting about four hours of sleep.

Every time I closed my eyes, all I could picture was Aubrey and those brown eyes of hers. The golden specks floating in her irises lit up when she was excited and that was all I noticed yesterday. Every time someone started talking statistics or strategy, her eyes sparked with delight. She was in her comfort zone, there was no doubt. She knew football too. And not just college. I wanted to rip Bernie Hansen's goddamn head off when he started to talk to her about players in the NFL. I knew he was testing her and I'll be a son-of-bitch if she didn't get every single thing right. Even her prediction on who she thought would make it to the Super Bowl was the same exact team I was going for.

Aubrey Cain was smart as hell … and taken. The second she mentioned her boyfriend, I knew I had to back off. That was one thing I would never do is cheat. I'd been on the receiving end of it, and it was not something I would wish even on my worst enemy.

Scrubbing my hands over my face, I grunted. My head dropped back and I let out a "Fuck!"

"Aubrey Cain. You're going to be the damn death of me."

My phone rang and I knew who it was. Troy Rogers. He was the quarterback coach and was also a teammate of mine when I played college football at the University of Austin. When I got the head coaching job, I knew immediately I needed Troy on my staff. He was good. Really good. The only reason he didn't go to the NFL was because he got his college girlfriend pregnant. He wanted to be a hands-on dad. Their marriage only lasted two years.

"I'm on my way."

"Where in the hell are you?"

"Parking lot." The silence on the phone caused me to sigh. "I had a rough night."

"Aww dude, you know the rules. Girls on the weekend only. It's Tuesday!"

I shook my head. There was no way I was going to tell him I jacked off twice last night, once in bed and once in the shower. I tried like hell to get Aubrey out of my head. Problem was I couldn't stop thinking about her and that's what led to the damn lack of sleep. And a sore cock from the punishment I put it through.

"I wasn't with a girl, asshole."

Getting out of my Hell Cat, I slammed the door shut.

Right before I walked up to the gate, I heard another car driving up. Ignoring it, I pushed the gate open and made my way to the track. Troy was already jogging in place. I shook my head and dropped my gym bag next to his.

"You ready or do you need to take it easy today?"

I glared at him. "Fuck off."

Letting out a roar of laughter, he punched me on the arm. "Dude, why the hell are you in such a bad mood?"

"No sleep. I already told you. It's been a fucked-up last few days."

Troy glanced over my shoulder. "Well it's fixin' to either get better or worse. And from the way you were ignoring her yesterday, I'm betting worse."

I looked at him like he was crazy. "What in the hell are you going on about?"

Motioning with his head, he looked over my shoulder. I turned and felt my heart slam against my chest and my stomach dipped.

What. In. The. Fuck. Was. That?

I don't react to women like that. The only part of my body that should be reacting is my cock. And even he is too tired.

"Aubrey?" I asked as I watched her make her way over to us.

"Good morning, gentleman. Patty told me what time you start your morning run. I myself am a morning runner, so this works out great."

Why? Why is she doing this to me?

"Is this my life for the next month?" I questioned, making sure to not look at the way her tits looked in the University of Austin T-shirt she had on.

Aubrey gave me an innocent smile that had my stomach feeling like I hit a high-ass-roller-coaster dip going ninety miles an hour.

She has a boyfriend.

Off limits.

"Oh, come on. You surely can't be bothered by me running with you, Owens. That is, unless you guys have some secret thing going on."

Troy and I instantly stepped further away from each other. "Fuck no!" Troy replied before I had the chance to. "I like girls! Lots of girls. I'm a dad for Christ's sake."

Aubrey held up her hands and laughed. "I'm kidding. My gosh. I already know the history. Teammates in college."

Troy and I looked at each other. "She has a whole fucking notebook of shit about me. It's kind of creepy."

Aubrey placed her hands on her hips and grinned even bigger. "I even know what kind of underwear you buy."

My eyes widened in shock. "What?"

She nodded and said, "Yep," popping the *p*.

"How?" Troy asked for me since I was still in a somewhat state of utter shock.

Aubrey did a few stretches and took off jogging backward while she called out, "I have my sources!"

With an evil laugh, she turned and started running.

Troy and I stood there watching her as I tried to figure out ways to send her back to Connecticut.

Troy chuckled as he hit me on the back. "I'd be very afraid of that girl."

"Oh, trust me, I am."

In more ways than one.

The heat was getting to me for some reason today. Bob Strikes, my defensive line coach, happened to be the unlucky person to get the brunt of my foul mood.

"Son-of-a-bitch, Bob. Can you not coach your line? Get them the hell in there or I'm taking over."

Bob nodded like he was taking me serious, but we both knew I had a bug up my ass and I wasn't acting myself. It had been two weeks since Aubrey showed up and her fucked-up boss told her a month wasn't long enough. He wanted her here during spring training and three weeks after that.

Fucking asshole. I knew it was because of her telling him off that night. Now I was being punished.

I chanced a quick look over my shoulder and saw her talking to Michelle Brown. Another fucking female reporter, just what I needed.

Another ten minutes went by and I yelled and screamed some more.

"Long time no see, Owens. Something crawl up in your ass and die this morning or have you really become that much of an asshole."

Closing my eyes, I counted to five before turning around. "Hey, Michelle. How are you?"

Both Michelle and Aubrey seemed surprised by my lack of attitude back.

The two of them stood there and made a comment or two about a few of the players. I tried like hell to tune them out.

"He's fast," Michelle said.

Aubrey agreed. "First round draft pick for sure."

Michelle sighed as the tight end dropped the ball. "He can't handle the ball worth shit."

I spun around and glared at them. "Do you mind taking your commentary and moving it down the field?"

Michelle lifted her hands up in a defensive manner. "Sorry, Coach."

When they started walking off, Michelle kept on talking.

"So, have you gotten some Texas dick since you've been here?"

My stomach dropped as I focused back on the two of them walking way.

"Shut up, Michelle. Geesh."

I followed them as they kept on.

"Well, I figured since you've been single for over a month and all, you might have encountered some interested parties. Dust the cobwebs off the va-jay-jay. Oil the rusty can."

"Ugh. You talk like a guy do you know that?"

Stopping in my tracks, I tried like hell to keep my anger in.

She lied to me. She fucking lied to me about having a boyfriend.

Turning back to the field, I stole another look at Aubrey. Her brown hair was blowing lightly in the wind as she laughed. So she thought she could hold me off by telling me she had a boyfriend.

I can't stand liars.

The next hour had me growing more and more angry. I finally called it a day and headed to my office, letting Troy take over.

When I walked and sat at my desk, there was a letter addressed to me.

I picked it up and held it while looking out the window. I had no idea how to handle the situation with Aubrey, but I knew for sure I had to figure out a way. And soon. I wouldn't have someone I couldn't trust following my every fucking move.

The knock on the door caused me to yell out, "I came in here for a fucking reason!"

"Brett?"

Her voice made me both angry and happy.

"What is it, Aubrey?"

"Um, I was wondering if I could talk to you about something."

I sighed as I looked at the letter in my hand. "Can it wait?"

"Not really. After talking to Michelle, I realized I did something that I need to ask your forgiveness on."

I let out a small chuckle. She must know I overheard the two of them.

Spinning the chair around, I took every inch of her in. I wanted her, there was no denying it. Even if I could get a small taste of her. That's all I wanted. One taste.

"Why?"

She looked confused. "Why what?"

"Why did you lie to me?"

She shook her head. "I have no clue what you're talking about."

Now I was confused. "What did you need my forgiveness for?"

"The way the two of us stood there going over your players like that. It was unprofessional, and I apologize. If that's the reason you were so angry, then I'm truly sorry. I'd never want you to leave a practice on account of me."

She doesn't know I know.

Standing, I walked over to her slowly. "Do you want to know why I'm angry, Aubrey?"

Taking a step back, she stared at me. "Is that a trick question?"

"Shut the door."

Hesitating at first, Aubrey turned and slowly shut the door. When she spun back around, I was practically on top of her.

"Shit!" she gasped and fell back against the door. "I take it I'm the reason you're angry?"

I nodded my head as I traced her jawline with my fingers ever so lightly. Her body trembled under my touch. "Do you know how much I want to kiss you right now?"

She swallowed hard. "Kiss… kiss me?"

"So fucking bad. But I can't."

Her gaze dropped to my lips before looking back up at me. "Because, we have a um… a working relationship?"

"No."

Those beautiful brown eyes burned with desire. The gold flecks sparkled and I knew she wanted me as much as I wanted her.

"No?"

I lifted my hand and pushed a piece of her hair back that had fallen from her ponytail. "No. It's because you have a boyfriend. There are two things I can't stomach. A cheater and a liar."

Her lips parted and my heartbeat picked up.

Just. One. Taste.

Aubrey closed her eyes and took in a deep breath before opening them again. "Brett, I need you to take a couple of steps back please. I can't think straight with you this close to me."

"What's there to think about?"

"The only way I knew to keep you from hitting on me was to say I had a boyfriend." She shook her head and I watched as water pooled in her eyes. "My job is my everything. My entire life and the way you affect me scares me. If I thought I would be able to handle it, I'd ignore you and your advances, but I can't."

The tightness in my chest grew more and more as she spoke. "Why not?"

Her chin trembled and my knees about buckled.

"Because I'm attracted to you, Brett. And the way you make me feel when I'm around you is unlike anything I've ever experienced before, and it has shaken me to the core. So yes, I lied to you and if you can't forgive me, I understand."

A tear slipped from her eye and slowly rolled down her face, making my gut feel like someone had punched it about fifty times in a row.

I leaned in closer, holding my breath as Aubrey did the same. I kissed the tear away and whispered, "Please don't cry. I can't bear the thought of knowing I made you cry."

Her hand came up between us as she covered her mouth. Leaning my forehead against hers, she dropped her hand.

"I'd never do anything to put your career at risk, Aubrey."

The sob that slipped from her lips ripped through my body. The last thing I would ever want to do is put her job on the line. Stepping back, I went to turn away when she grabbed my arm.

"Please kiss me. Just once."

I would never forget how those words made me feel. Like the first time I saw her and she smiled at me.

Cupping her beautiful face within my hands, I brushed her tears away with my thumbs.

"Once," I whispered as I ran my lips over hers. Aubrey's hands came up to my waist as she held on.

I was scared to death if I kissed her, I wouldn't be able to stop. What I wanted to do was rip her clothes off and fuck her hard against the damn door, and I wouldn't give a shit who heard us.

My right hand slipped behind her neck, drawing her mouth closer to mine. Everything inside of me screamed to stop, but I couldn't. I didn't want to stop no matter how wrong I knew it was.

Smashing my lips to hers, it didn't take long for her to open up to me. I moaned as my cock throbbed in my pants. She tasted sweeter than honey.

Instead of pulling back, I deepened the kiss while our tongues danced in perfect harmony. I could only imagine what her pussy would taste like. It took everything out of me not to drop to my knees and take what I so desperately wanted.

The knock on the door jolted us both out of the kiss. I quickly took about ten steps away from her.

Aubrey's chest was heaving, and I knew the kiss affected her as much as it did me.

She quickly stepped aside and made her way over to the conference table and sat.

The door opened and Pat walked in. "Brett, what in the hell is going on with you?"

I looked over at Aubrey. *Where in the hell did she find the pad of paper?*

Glancing over her shoulder, she smiled. "Oh, hey Pat. How are you today?"

Only I could hear the shake in her voice as she tried to play off what had happened.

"Yeah, sorry, Pat. I haven't been getting very much sleep. This whole starting quarterback thing has been keeping me up."

Pat grinned and slapped me on the side of the arm. "You'll work it out. You always do. Don't forget that benefit dinner is tonight."

Facing Aubrey, Pat continued, "Aubrey, you should accompany Brett. You could get a look at a different side of him. The kinder gentler side."

My chest felt like it was clamping down as panic set in. "No. I'm sure Aubrey has plans and couldn't be bothered by something like this. It's Friday night, after all."

When her brown eyes pierced my blue, I knew I was fucked. Her smile spread from ear to ear. "Nope. I have no plans at all. Is it formal?"

"Yes, and I'm sure you didn't bring anything expecting to go to a formal dinner, so no worries if you have to decline."

With a smirk, she replied, "Nonsense." She looked back at Pat. "What time does the dinner start?"

"Eight," Pat answered with a triumphant look.

"That's perfect. I'd love to accompany Brett. I'm curious to see this other side of him he's been keeping a secret."

I rubbed my hand along the back of my neck. There was no way of getting out of this one.

Chapter Six

Aubrey

MY HEAD WAS going in a million different directions when I opened the door to my condo and walked in. Michelle was sitting in the middle of the living room on the floor in some weird yoga pose.

"I'm so screwed."

She scrunched her nose and stood up. "What happened? Your face is flushed."

I shook my head. "I need a formal dress for a benefit tonight that is honoring Brett."

Pulling her head back with a shocked expression, she asked, "Pussy hound, Brett? He's being honored for something? What? The most women to be fucked in his sexy Hell Cat this year?"

With a groan, I hit her on the arm. "I'm serious. I need a dress. How am I going to find a formal gown that will fit me within the next few hours?"

Michelle took out her phone. "I have a friend who owns a shop here. Matter of fact, she's in walking distance. Her place is right down on Second Street."

There was no way this would fall into place so easily. "Great. Can you call her?"

"I'm on it."

Heading into the kitchen, I grabbed a bottle of wine out of the refrigerator and opened it. I poured a glass and drank the whole thing in one gulp.

"You kissed him, didn't you?"

My heart jumped and I let out a small scream.

"Jesus, Michelle. You scared the piss out of me."

Her brows lifted and she crossed her arms. The stance she was in almost creeped me out. Like she was trying to read my mind. She looked pissed too.

"Did you get a hold of your friend?"

Damn! My voice is all over the place. I never was good at this kind of stuff.

"You broke." Shaking her head, she made a tsk-ing sound. "I thought you were stronger than that?"

My lips tingled thinking back to the kiss. It was the most amazing kiss of my life. Like something from Brett poured into my body and it was still on fire. My breathing picked up thinking about it.

Shit. Get it together, Aubrey.

"Yes. He kissed me."

Michelle's entire body sunk as she leaned against the wall. "No! Bree! Why? You went to the dark side, and now there is no coming back. Oh, what if Joe finds out?"

I frantically shook my head. The ramifications of what Brett and I did hit me like I had run into a brick wall.

"He won't find out because it's never happening again. We got it out of our system and now we can work without the tension there."

I smiled, but Michelle stood there staring at me like I had grown two heads. Ugh. I knew what just came out of my mouth was total bullshit. The moment he drew his lips away I wanted to beg for more.

"Oh, it's far from over, and I know you realize that."

"Brett said he would never do anything to put my job at risk."

"He's a pussy hound!" Michelle cried out.

Hearing that now caused a pain in my chest. The thought of Brett sleeping with other women after we shared that earth-shattering kiss did things to me that I wasn't sure I liked. I was feel-ing… jealousy. I don't get jealous. Ever.

My hands came up over my mouth as I sucked in a deep breath. "Oh, God. What did I do?"

"You have to make sure you don't do it again. If you do, you might not be able to stop at the kiss. By the way, how was the kiss?"

Dropping my hands to my side, I stared at her. "You told me I had to make sure I didn't do it again. If I talk about it, I'm going to want to do it again!"

She wiggled her brows and giggled. "That good huh? Can you imagine what else he could do with that mouth?"

"Stop!" I shouted, slamming my hands over my ears and sing-ing, "La! La! La! I don't hear you!"

Michelle reached for my hands and yanked them to my side. "Stop acting like a three-year-old. How was the kiss?"

Exhaling a breath, I barely smiled. "Unlike any kiss I've ever experienced before."

The grin that spread over Michelle's face made me giggle. "I knew it! His lips look so soft."

My fingers automatically touched my lips. "They are. And I would bet your right when you say that mouth is magical. I was practically melting on the spot."

"But you had the sense to stop it."

My chest tightened. If Pat hadn't knocked on the door, how far would Brett and I gone? I was internally begging him to touch my body.

"You were the one who stopped it… right?"

Lifting my shoulders, I gave her an indecisive expression. "Not really."

Her left eye narrowed and the look she gave me felt as if my mother was getting ready to scold me. "What do you mean, 'not really'?"

"Well, you see," I explained with a nervous laugh. "Pat knocked on the door and that broke the kiss."

Michelle gasped and took a few steps back while covering her mouth in total shock. "Oh, no! A third-party interruption? This is not good!"

Furrowing my brows, I leaned my head some as if I hadn't heard her right. "Where in the hell do you come up with this shit? Did you make that up just now?"

Her head shook frantically. "This is bad. This is really bad."

I wrung my hands together. "It's not that bad. I mean, it's not like I was begging him to rip my clothes off and take me right there on the spot." The thought made my insides quiver.

"Aubrey! I can tell by the way your face is flushed that is exactly what you wanted to happen! You can't go to the dinner tonight."

My lips parted as I was about to protest.

"No. If you show up looking all sexy and hot, Mr. Pussy Hound will be all over you and then, next thing you know you'll be at his place. Then there will be a conflict of interest with the piece you're writing and Joe will have the one thing he has been wanting, something to hold over you."

With a look of displeasure, I sighed. "Please. We are adults who understand that a relationship, sexual or more, is never going to happen. Geesh, can't a girl fantasy about a hot guy? I mean come on, if Brett Owens kissed you, tell me you wouldn't think about wanting more."

She waved me off and walked up to the wine. Pouring another glass, she handed it to me. "Please. I'd ripped my own clothes off, lock the damn door, and have my wicked way with that man."

With a chuckle, I took the glass and drank some of it. "You're going to need to stay focused tonight. Why are you going?"

"Pat said Brett needed a plus one."

"Oh, my gawd! Ugh." Michelle gave me a frustrated look. "No! You are going because Brett Owens is your assignment, that's all. The guy you're writing about for a huge spread for your job. You remember your job, right?"

My lip curled up as I answered, "Yes. I remember." Lifting the wine glass, I finished off the rest of it in one drink.

"Come on, we need to get to the store. I've already arranged to have a hair stylist there to fix your mop."

"Hey!" I said, touching my hair. Michelle grabbed both our purses and dragged me out the door.

"You look stunning," Michelle whispered.

I stared at myself in the mirror and grinned at the woman I barely recognized. "I forgot how fun it is to play dress up."

"Stella McCarthy is one of my favorite designers. The plunging sweetheart neckline will for sure catch the eye of every guy in the room."

My hand came up to my stomach and I couldn't help where my thoughts went. What would Brett do when he saw me in this dress? Would it affect him in any way or was the kiss from earlier enough to get it out of his system? He seemed to play it off pretty good when Pat walked in. He was so calm and collected and I was practically dying on the inside.

"Are you sure black is okay?" I questioned Lisa, the owner of the designer dress shop Michelle had brought me to.

"Honey, please, when is black not okay?"

Lifting the gown, I smiled as I looked at my latest promotion gift to myself. The four-and-a-half-inch suede Jimmy Choo heels. The crystal mesh added the perfect elegant touch. Too bad the dress had a long skirt and no one would ever see my expensive-ass shoes that I had buyer's remorse for weeks after I purchased them.

I blew out a deep cleansing breath. "So, I think I'm ready."

Michelle stood and walked over next to me, staring at me in the mirror. My hair was pulled up in a sloppy bun with curls framing my face. I went very light on my make-up. A slightly smoky eye with mascara only finished out my light brown eyes. A very light tint of pink graced my lips and was applied to bring out the almost same shade of blush on my cheeks.

"You look stunning, Aubrey. Only you could pull this off with only a few hours to do it."

My lips pressed together to keep my emotions in check. Turning to Michelle, I replied, "I couldn't have done this without you. Thank you for pulling strings and making me feel like a princess."

She fiddled with one of the curls and grinned. "Who knows, maybe you'll meet your prince charming tonight, then we'll both have boyfriends in Austin!"

I chortled at her comment. "You never know."

Michelle's smile faded as she took my hands. "Have fun and talk to other people besides Brett okay? Get out there and meet someone."

With a nod, I replied, "Yes, Mom!"

Michelle handed me a small clutch. "I put a recorder in there if you wanted to take notes."

"Thanks," I softly spoke. We made our way out of the store and I hugged Lisa before leaving. "Thank you again for helping me find the perfect dress."

"You're so welcome. I still can't believe we found one that fit you like a glove."

My hand ran over the silk fabric of the dress as I said, "It was meant to be!"

"We better get going. Brett's supposed to pick you up in a few minutes."

I carefully slid into Michelle's rental car as we made our way back to my condo. The drive was less than three minutes, but the entire time I stared out the window. I had no idea what tonight would bring. For all I knew, Brett had a date to this thing and his boss pushed me into her spot. That would suck.

Michelle was right. I needed to take tonight to mingle and meet new people. If Brett's reputation served him right, he'd be bringing home a girl tonight to screw around with. I needed to have my own plans.

"We're here."

My best friend's voice drew me out of my thoughts. It was settled. Brett was simply my assignment. I'd accompany him tonight, but I was not going to expect to be his date. The sooner I pushed that kiss from my memory, the better.

Business.

This was only business.

Chapter Seven

Brett

WHY IN THE hell are my hands shaking?

Dragging in a deep breath, I exhaled and stepped off the elevator. I told Aubrey I'd pick her up at seven forty-five. I never liked being right on time for things like this. If you showed up a little late, less attention was on your arrival because people were already deep into conversations.

I stopped at her door and stood there. Cracking my neck from side to side, I took in a few calming breaths.

We kissed. It was over and done with. I had a taste of her. It was time to move on.

I wanted more.

No. I promised Aubrey I wouldn't put her job on the line and I intended to keep my promise. That meant I needed to practice self-control. Hell, I jacked off before I got dressed in hopes my cock would play nice tonight.

Focus was the key. As soon as we got there, I'd make it my mission to find the first woman I saw and strike up a conversation with her.

This is not a date.

This is business.

Nothing more.

My hand came up and knocked.

"Coming!"

I closed my eyes. "Fuck," I whispered. The sound of her voice caused my heart to race.

Focus! Damn it. Shake it off... business only.

The door to Aubrey's condo opened and I almost fell back on my ass.

"Holy shit," I murmured, taking in the sight before me.

Aubrey stood there dressed in the most beautiful black gown I'd ever seen on a woman. The way it hugged her body had my betraying cock growing quickly in my pants. My eyes scanned her, nearly bulging out of my head when I saw the neckline.

Son-of-a-bitch. I bet her tits would fit perfectly in my hands.

I closed my eyes and re-focused. Opening them, I grinned and tried to act like I didn't want to press my lips against hers again. Or run my hand over that silky material to see if she was wearing anything underneath it.

Finally, able to get myself under control, I spoke. "You look beautiful, Aubrey."

With a smile so sweet the ground felt like it wobbled, she replied, "Thank you. And look at you. You give new meaning to the word handsome in that tux."

Her voice faltered and I knew she was just as affected by this as I was. My lips itched to feel hers. It didn't help when she ran her tongue along her bottom lip and sucked it in quickly before releasing it.

Fucking hell. This was going to be a long night.

The ride over to the W hotel seemed to last forever. Aubrey sat next to me with her body barely touching mine. The heat was almost too much and I forced myself to remain still. Fighting internally with the question to move closer to her or further away.

"So, what exactly is this we are going to?"

I hated talking about myself, especially to Aubrey. I knew everything I said would most likely end up in a magazine article.

"It's a benefit dinner for a kid's organization. Some of Austin's richest people are invited for the gala-type event with hopes of raising money. Tonight they happen to be paying special attention to me... unfortunately."

Feeling the heat of her stare on me, I turned to look at her. She was giving me the evil eye.

"No shit. I wouldn't be dressed in a formal gown if I didn't know that. What are they honoring you with and why did you say unfortunately?"

With a shrug, I answered, "I don't like the attention. I do it because it's something I'm passionate about, not for the attention."

Aubrey grinned. "What is the organization?"

"I started a group last year for young kids in the Austin area. The guys on the team spend time with the kids, helping them with everything from homework to teaching them how to throw a football. It's a way to give back to the community while keeping the guys' heads on straight. Plus, it hopefully helps the kids pick a path that leads to success."

The way Aubrey was looking at me made me feel uncomfortable. I wasn't sure why, but it was as if she was trying to look into my soul.

"That's wonderful, Brett. What made you decide to start the group?"

"Probably the fact that my parents always taught me to never take for granted the things in life we're blessed with. Giving back to the community was, and still is, huge for them. I simply followed in their footsteps."

Her mouth fell open and she slowly shook her head. "Just when I think I have you figured out, you do a one-eighty on me."

Flashing her a sexy smile and a wink, I leaned in closer and whispered, "Does that make your panties wet knowing I give back to the community, Aubrey? That I'm really one of the good guys?"

The way her eyes sparkled had my dick pressing hard against the fabric of my pants. She quickly looked away and sighed.

"Why do you always have to ruin it with your dirty mouth, Brett?"

I let out a laugh. "Most women like my dirty mouth. Especially when it's between their legs."

She turned back to me, her lips parted as if ready to say something. Her stare fell to my lips. Rolling her eyes, she looked straight ahead and didn't utter another word.

At least the questions stopped.

For now, anyway.

The moment we entered the room, I turned and walked to the bar. I could practically feel the daggers coming from Aubrey. After ordering my drink and downing it, I glanced over my shoulder to see if she waited for me or made her way deeper into the room. It didn't take long to find her. She was the only woman in the ballroom who looked beautiful beyond words.

My heart slammed against my chest as I watched Aubrey flash that innocent smile as she spoke to a small group of people. I'd never had a woman make me feel the way Aubrey did. It both pissed me off and excited me.

"Owens, how's it going?"

Turning to my left, I forced a smile when I saw Ryan Dryer standing next to me.

What I really wanted to do was punch the asshole and tell him to fuck off. He knew I wouldn't make a scene, though. "It's going. How are you, Dryer?"

Ryan flashed me that fake smile of his that he reserved for fucking politicians. It pissed me off he used it on me.

"It is going pretty damn good I must say."

With a slight nod, I looked back at the bartender. "I'll take another."

Slapping me on the back, Ryan laughed. "Better slow down there, Owens. We both know what happens when you drink too much."

Glaring at him, I forced a grin. "What do you want?"

He jerked his head back and laughed. "Can't an old college buddy come congratulate you on yet another success to check off your list?"

"You never do anything without having a reason behind it."

Lifting his whiskey filled glass to his mouth, he looked past me. I followed his gaze straight to Aubrey.

"Who's your date?"

I watched Aubrey glance our way and smile. She was beautiful, smart, and had a body that every man desired. Perfectly curvy. Just the type of woman who Dryer would be attracted to.

"Aubrey Cain."

Ryan looked at me when I didn't offer up any additional information. "You two a thing?"

With a laugh, I shook my head. "Hardly. She's a reporter for ESPN. They're doing a whole spread on the University of Austin's football program for an upcoming magazine."

With a nod, he replied, "Well no article on the school would be complete unless there was something about the great Brett Owens in there."

I took a drink and tried to keep my anger down. "Fuck you, Dryer," I muttered under my breath so only he would hear it.

Throwing his head back, he slapped my back again. "Since she's not your date, I think I'll go introduce myself."

Every part of me wanted to tell him no. Shout that she was mine and only mine, but the truth was, Aubrey wasn't mine. She belonged to no one. And if I did say that, it would only egg Ryan on.

For the next hour, I tried to focus on talking to people. My anger grew more and more as I watched Aubrey dance with Ryan. He was sticking to her like glue, that asshole.

"So, what big plans do you have for the kids this summer, Brett?"

Pulling my eyes off of Aubrey and Ryan, I turned back to Tara. She worked for the law firm that helped me get everything off the ground with *Bright Futures*.

"Not really sure yet. We are thinking one thing we might do is a dude ranch type thing with them."

Her eyebrows lifted. "Are you thinking of doing it at your dad's ranch?"

How this girl knew so much about me should bother me, but right now I was more focused on the way Ryan had his arm wrapped around Aubrey's waist, pulling her closer as they danced.

"Um… probably not since it's a good ways from Austin."

Ryan whispered something into Aubrey's ear, causing her to toss her head back and laugh.

"Looks like someone is stealing your date, Owens." Pat stood next to me and wore a smirk as he looked out toward where Aubrey and Ryan were dancing.

"She's not my date. If you remember, you pushed her on me tonight."

With a chuckle, he looked at me. "I'm sure that was such a hardship to escort such a beautiful woman this evening."

"No, but it was a pain in the ass when she interviewed me in the limo on the way here."

Pat shrugged as he carefully watched Aubrey and Ryan. He didn't trust Dryer any more than I did. "Well, that's why she's here."

The reality of his statement felt like someone punched me in the stomach.

Once the song was over, I watched as Ryan placed his hand on Aubrey's lower back and guided her over to another group. Introducing her like she was his date.

"Excuse me," I quickly said as I made my way over to them.

Aubrey laughed at something someone said and it vibrated through my entire body, causing my damn dick to jump.

"There you are," I said with a grin as I stepped between Aubrey and Ryan, making sure to give him a go to hell look. "I've been looking for you everywhere, Aubrey. I guess you've been dancing the night away with Mr. Dryer here."

Everyone looked at Aubrey and then me. I knew it appeared that Aubrey was with Ryan, and by me walking up and essentially acting like a goddamn caveman claiming his woman, it made it seem like Aubrey was giving more attention to Dryer than to the man she came with. The man who happened to be the one being honored tonight. It was a dick move, but I didn't care. I was pissed off. She was supposed to be here for me. This was my fucking piece she was working on, not Ryan dickhead Dryer.

Ryan held up his hands and laughed. "Whoa, settle down there, Owens. I was only getting to know Ms. Cain." He glanced over and smiled at her. "Turns out we have a lot in common."

Aubrey gave him a slight grin before looking at me. "How about a dance?" I asked, taking her by the arm gently and leading her away from the group.

With a huff, she replied, "Well it looks like you're not giving me much of a choice."

With a tight grin on my face, I replied, "You always have a choice, Ms. Cain."

"And if I'd rather not dance with you, would you be okay with that choice?"

My entire body trembled with rage. The thought of Ryan's hands on Aubrey almost brought out the monster I had worked so hard at burying deep inside.

Pulling her body closer to me, I placed my mouth to her lips and kissed her. Her mouth felt better than I remembered from the kiss earlier. The feel of her up against me instantly turned me on. "Is that what you want, Aubrey? For Ryan to take you to his fancy house and fuck you on his silk sheets?"

She tried to step away, but I held her closer to me. Close enough so she could feel my hard dick pressing into her stomach.

"The next time you dance with him, think about one thing."

Aubrey's breathing increased as she lifted her eyes to mine.

"What's that?" she barely spoke as she swallowed hard.

"My hard cock pressed against your body right now and how much I want to bury it deep inside of you. Or the fact that I could easily make you come by simply touching your body."

She frantically searched my face as she fought to keep her breathing under control.

"You certainly think highly of yourself, Mr. Owens. From the little I've talked to Mr. Dryer, I can tell you one thing for certain."

My jaws clenched together. "What's that?"

Pushing me away, Aubrey lifted her chin and smirked. "He's more of a gentleman than you'll ever be."

Turning on her heels, she started to walk off. Quickly walking up next to her, I took her arm and led her to the back door that went to the hallway. I knew it well because I'd escaped to it often at events like this to catch my breath.

In a low voice, Aubrey stated, "Let me go, Brett. Now!"

Ignoring her, I pushed the door open and walked into the hallway. The moment the door closed, I pushed her against the concrete wall and kissed her again.

At first she denied me the kiss, but soon she was opening her mouth to me. Both of us getting completely lost in each other. My hand wrapped around the back of her neck, pulling her in closer to me as I pushed my dick into her stomach.

The low moan from the back of her throat drove me mad. If I thought I could, I'd lift her dress and bury my cock inside her right now.

My hand moved down her body until I felt the slit on the side of her dress. Slipping my hand under the dress, I cupped her pussy. Aubrey grabbed onto my arms and squeezed them tightly. She wanted me as much as I wanted her.

One quick move had my hand down her panties as I gently rubbed her clit. I could feel her body trembling under my touch and knew it wouldn't take much too make her come. The urge to slip my fingers inside her pussy to see how wet she was was strong.

Aubrey's head fell back, breaking the kiss as she pushed herself into my hand. She wanted this too. Needed it.

"Brett," she gasped as I pushed harder and ran my tongue along her neck. "Oh, God, yes."

I couldn't deny myself any longer. One finger slipped between her lips and was instantly coated with her desire. Hissing against her neck, I gathered up every ounce of fucking strength I had and withdrew my hand from her panties.

Aubrey's chest rose and fell quickly as she stared at me with a confused look on her face.

I winked and took a step back. "He may be more of a gentleman than me, but he'd never be able to make your pussy pulse like that."

Reaching for the doorknob, I yanked it open and walked back into the ballroom. The sounds of Aubrey's labored breathing echoed in my mind while I walked further away from the one thing I desired more than anything in this world.

Chapter Eight

Aubrey

MY HEAD DROPPED back against the hard wall while I tried to make sense of what in the hell had just happened. Closing my eyes, I let out a frustrated moan. I did the one thing I said I wasn't going to do again. Let Brett Owens in.

My fingers brushed over my still tingling lips. My body still reeled over his touch and the looming build-up he left me hanging with.

Placing my hands over my flushed cheeks, I opened my eyes and took in a deep breath.

"That asshole," I whispered.

How dare he do this to me? No wait. How did I even let him do this to me? The man was my weakness, there was no doubt. But why did he bring me out here and—

Then it hit me why he did it. Brett had been jealous of the attention Ryan had given me.

I shook my head to clear my thoughts. Why in the hell would he be jealous of Ryan? It didn't make sense. He was the one who walked away from me the second we walked into the room. Did he really expect me to stand there and wait for him?

Fuck that.

Inhaling a deep breath in, I turned and headed back into the ball-room. Quickly scanning the room, I saw Brett. He was standing in a group of people with a few kids mixed in.

Looking past him, I saw Ryan. When I brought my eyes back to where Brett was, our gaze met.

I started making my way to him and couldn't help but notice the slight smirk he wore on his face. As I drew closer he turned to face me. Glancing over his shoulder, Ryan stood talking to an older couple.

"There she is," Pat said as I stopped directly in front of Brett. I was hoping the look of evil I was giving him spoke volumes. I plastered on a smile and turned to the group.

"This is Aubrey Cain, she is the reporter doing the ESPN article on college football at the University of Austin, specifically on Brett."

A little boy began jumping. "I want to be a college football player."

Smiling, I bent over and looked into his eyes. "Then if that's what you want to do, I'm sure you'll be amazing at it."

His face beamed with my words before he glanced up to Brett. "Coach Owens said if I want to play ball, I have to do really good in school, respect my parents, and work really hard at practicing my throws."

I stood and looked at Brett. He was peering down at the boy with the first genuine smile I'd seen on his face since I'd met him.

His hand went to the young boy's head where he ruffled up his hair and laughed. "You're going to come play for me aren't ya, Tim?"

With a peek back at Tim, I couldn't help but giggle when I saw his chest puff out. "I sure am. Coach! I'll be the best quarterback you've ever had."

Brett held up his hand and Tim hit it. "I'm sure you will be, buddy."

The whole exchange between Brett and Tim was short, but it was so powerful I fought to hold my tears back. It was clear this young boy looked up to Brett, and he obviously thought the boy hung the moon. In that moment, I wondered why Brett hadn't settled down with someone. Did he have the desire to get married and have kids? The idea that he maybe wasn't interested in that life made me feel… sad.

"Would you like to dance?"

Brett's hot breath on my neck caused goose bumps to pop up across my entire body.

Without saying a word, I gave him my hand and allowed him to lead me to the dance floor. It was hard not to notice Ryan watching our every move.

Brett pulled me in and tucked me into his body. I couldn't help but notice how I seemed to fit perfectly within his arms. I should have been pissed at him for what he did, but again, the man had some kind of power over me.

"Moonlight Crush" by Outshyne started and I was once again stunned by Mr. Owens. The way he danced was enough to swoon me right out of this dress and into his bed.

Stay. Strong. Aubrey.

His lips grazed against my cheek as he whispered, "You're the most beautiful woman in the room, Aubrey."

Confusion swept over my body. One minute he was talking dirty in my ear and the next he managed to cause my heart to stop and the ground to shake as he swooned me with compliments.

Gripping tighter onto his arm, I drew back and looked into blue eyes. "Thank you, Brett."

His smile made my stomach flutter. I was almost positive something moved between the two of us, and if we were alone, I wouldn't even try to stop him if he tried to kiss me. Or touch me. Or make love to me.

There was something about Brett Owens that felt dangerous. He made me want things I knew I shouldn't want, yet I didn't care. I felt daring when I was around him.

Oh, God. What would he be like in bed? Hot and dirty talking while he slowly brought out one orgasm after another. Everything a good girl desired but was too afraid to admit she wanted in a man.

Ugh. Stop thinking that way, you horny bitch!

My hand moved and pressed against his chest. I was positive his heart was beating as fast and hard as mine.

"Brett," I barely spoke.

He closed his eyes and quickly opened them again, this time they weren't filled with lust, but more like confusion. Guilt. Pain.

"I made you a promise, Aubrey and I intend on keeping it. As much as I want to bury myself deep inside you for days, I won't go back on my word."

And like that, my heart dropped and disappointment rushed over my body. I knew what he was doing was the smart thing... the right thing to do.

A part of me wanted to argue with him, and I might have if it hadn't been for Ryan.

"May I cut in?"

Brett turned and shot Ryan a dirty look. I couldn't pull my gaze off of Brett as I watched him take a few steps back and head over to the bar.

Ryan stepped in front of me, drawing me into his body with the start of the next song.

With one more look over his shoulder, Brett's eyes caught mine. I silently pleaded with him to come back. I didn't want to be in Ryan's arms, I wanted to be in Brett's. As wrong as we both knew that was, we both longed for it.

When the blonde walked up and stole his attention, my world quickly came to a stop.

"From the look on your face I'd say I saved you from a rather uncomfortable dance?"

Focusing in on Ryan, I tried to take in what he had said.

"I'm sorry, what was that?"

Motioning with his head back toward Brett, he repeated his words. "The look on your face when I walked up. You seemed like you were in need of saving."

I forced a smile. "No, not at all. Brett is a very interesting subject."

There was something between these two and I was not going to play into either hand. At least not until I found out what it was that made the two of them not like one another.

"How well do you know Brett?" I probed. The reporter in me clearly coming out.

Ryan chuckled. "Too well. We went to high school together, then college. We were even roommates at one point."

I was sure my face wore a surprised expression. *How in the hell did I not know this? What a shitty researcher I am.*

"Don't look so surprised. We didn't really announce to the world we shared a house. My parents bought a place and we rented it from them. We only lived on campus the first year when we were required to."

I made a mental note to dig a little deeper into Brett's past.

"Did you play football as well?"

His crooked smile was my answer. "Yes, but I wasn't nearly as good as the golden boy. He excelled at everything. Always one step ahead of me in everything, including women."

My eyebrow rose. "Is that a hint of bitterness in your voice, Mr. Dryer?"

His head jerked back and a loud laugh came from his mouth. "Hardly. In the end, I won, or at least, I always win."

His statement totally caught me off guard. I was about to ask him a question when an older woman called for everyone's attention.

Taking a chance look, I saw that the blonde was still standing next to Brett. I never was the jealous type, but something about her made my skin crawl. Even Brett seemed very uncomfortable standing next to her. She was young, maybe twenty-five, twenty-six at the oldest.

Ryan followed my stare. "Aww, I see Brett has found his girl for the night."

Snapping my attention to him, I asked, "What do you mean?"

With a casual shrug, Ryan continued speaking. "Brett doesn't like to be alone. He never has. He was always bringing home a different girl, I swear."

My stomach dropped at the idea as I looked back at Brett.

"Tonight we celebrate a man who has worked effortlessly in starting this program and helping it grow. Hundreds of kids have benefitted from Brett Owens' tireless work he has put into making this program such a huge success."

Brett turned and gave the blonde a look that honestly scared me so I was sure it had to have scared her. There was nothing but pure hate on his face. He quickly turned his back on her and continued to listen to the woman standing at the podium going on and on about what an amazing job he was doing with *Bright Futures*.

"Brett looks a bit upset, I wonder if everything is okay." Ryan examined.

My eyes drifted back to the blonde who was now heading out of the room. She appeared to be crying.

"I'm not sure," I absentmindedly said while watching the young woman leave. "But I intend on finding out."

We stood and waited for the car to come around in complete silence. Ryan had asked me if I wanted a ride home in front of Brett, and I thought a war was about to start so I quickly declined.

The car drove up and Brett took my hand in his as he opened the door for me. It didn't go unnoticed how my heart skipped a beat and my stomach clenched at the sweet gesture.

Before I went to get in, he lifted my hand to his mouth and gently kissed it. With a seductive smile, he practically purred the next words. "Will you need help getting out of your dress?"

Yes.

"No thank you, Mr. Owens. I'm very capable of undressing myself."

He pouted and I swear my heart melted. Brett Owens gave me a pout and I totally fell a bit more for him. I felt like a high school girl with her first crush.

The moment he dropped my hand, I missed the warmth of his touch. I needed to get a grip. There was no way anything could, or would for that matter, happen between us.

Brett let out a sigh and took off his tie as he asked the driver to go to Kerbey Lane Café.

"Kerbey Lane Café? Brett it's one in the morning."

He looked at me and winked. "And I'm hungry. Kerbey Lane has the best pancakes around."

My stomach growled and Brett laughed. "See, even your stomach agrees."

Before I knew it, I was being helped back out of the car and walking into a restaurant. I wished like hell I could strip out of this dress, but no bra and a pair of thong panties probably wouldn't go over well in public.

We weren't even sitting for two minutes when someone walked up and asked for a picture with Brett.

After the third request, Brett got up and took my hand. "Where are we going?" I inquired.

"To the corner."

I giggled. "Have I been a bad girl?"

Brett looked back at me and I swear his eyes turned black. My lower stomach pulled with desire as my grin faded. I hadn't intended on making that sound flirty, but it totally did.

The booth in the very back corner was empty so Brett motioned for me to slide in. A part of me wanted him to slip right on in next to me.

Ugh. I needed to stop thinking the way I was. What I needed to do was refocus on the interview.

"So, who was the blonde you were talking to earlier? She seemed to upset you."

Brett's menu dropped. The muscles in his neck flexed while he clenched his jaw.

Okay. So now my interest in the mysterious blonde was at a higher level. Ryan was right, something about the girl upset Brett.

"I don't want to talk about Emily."

Now that she had a name, she became more real, and so did the pangs of jealousy that rippled across my body. I wasn't about to let it drop though.

"Old girlfriend?"

His eyes snapped up to mine before they dropped back to the menu. "Hardly."

Damn. He wasn't going to offer up any information, that was for sure. Glancing over the menu, I decided on a bagel and butter. I wasn't one for eating late at night, not even on a drunk run in college did I ever really eat anything. While my friends used the excuse of buzzing for stuffing six tacos in their mouths, I downed water to keep from having a hangover the next day.

After placing our order, I watched as Brett looked around the restaurant.

"Do you always get recognized when you go out?" I questioned. Maybe if I start with the easy stuff, he'll open up a bit more.

He shook his head. "No. Not very often."

"Do you not like it?"

Pulling his head back in surprise, a slow grin moved across his face. Good Lord, this man is handsome as hell. My body reacted to every single thing he did and it was getting harder to ignore the urge to touch him.

"I don't mind it at all."

My head tilted to the side as I shot him a questioning look. "Then why the corner booth?"

He didn't miss a beat with his answer. "Because there is a large group of college kids in here, and once they start to figure out who I am, they'll all want their picture with me. If I was alone, I'd go ahead and stay where I was."

With a grin, I replied, "But you're not alone."

"No, I am most certainly not alone. I figured you're tired, ready to get out of that dress, and the faster we appease my pancake craving, the faster you get home and crawl into your Victoria's Secret cotton pjs."

I swallowed hard. "How did you know that was what I wore to bed?"

Brett laughed. "Lucky guess."

The waitress came back with my bagel and Brett's pancakes. I had to admit, they looked damn good.

After he buttered them up and poured half the container of syrup on them, he took a bite and I hit him with another question.

"So, are you going to tell me the story with the blonde or are you going to make me track her down and ask her myself?"

Chapter Nine

Brett

I BARELY HAD two seconds to enjoy the succulent taste of my pancakes before Aubrey brought Emily up again.

"You can't let me enjoy my pancakes?"

Her head shook and she gave me the cutest fucking smile. The last person I should be talking about Emily to was a damn reporter. But Aubrey was also the only person I trusted telling, quite honestly.

Taking another bite, I pushed the plate away and gave her exactly what she wanted.

The story.

"Emily was not invited to the event tonight. Her being there caught me off guard."

Her eyebrows rose. "I'd say it did. Why was she there?"

Thrusting my hand through my hair, I inhaled a deep breath before slowly letting it out. "It's kind of a long story."

"Start at the beginning then, Brett. It can't be all that bad."

I let out a gruff laugh. "First, is this all off the record?"

"Does it need to be?"

"Yes."

She gave me a weak smile. "Then it's off the record."

Well, here goes nothing.

"About four months ago I went to a dinner party for an old college friend of mine. He asked me to be the keynote speaker." Letting out a chuckle at the memory, I shook my head. "Your buddy Ryan Dryer was there. And he was pissed he wasn't the keynote speaker."

Aubrey rolled her eyes at me. "Why are you hateful towards him? He's a nice guy and I thought at one time your friend."

Anger swept over my body at Aubrey's defense of that asshole. "You feel whatever you want for him, Aubrey. The point is, he acted like a dick to me that night, which really isn't all that out of the normal. We had our routine exchange where he insults me and I tell him to fuck off. About an hour or so after that, Emily came up to me at the bar. Her date had left her stranded and she was about to call a cab."

"Let me guess, you offered to take her home."

I could hear the edge in her voice and I wondered if she was a bit jealous. It didn't matter, though; nothing could ever come of the two of us. But I had to admit, I kind of liked the idea of her being slightly bothered.

"No, I offered to take her back to my place and fuck her. *Then* take her home."

Aubrey dropped her hands to the table. "Ugh. Why is it every time you talk like that it catches me off guard even though I have a feeling it's coming?"

"Trust me when I say you would totally know when it was coming."

Snarling her lip, she pointed to me. "See! Like that. The shock factor is there, but deep down, I knew you would say something like that."

"Anyway," I said, trying to get back to the dreaded story. "Emily came back to my place and we had a good time. Normally, I bring the girl home and that's the end of it. I never see them again."

The look of disgust on Aubrey's face bothered me more than I wanted to admit.

"I feel like there is a 'but' in there somewhere."

"Yeah, a big one. I ran into her the next weekend and ended up fucking her in the bathroom of the bar I was at."

"Please tell me you practice safe sex, Brett, because honestly you are the biggest manwhore I've ever met."

"Yes I practice safe sex, and I get tested regularly."

"Do you expect points for that?" She asked, tilting her head.

Fuck this. I didn't need Aubrey to sit there and judge me or my lifestyle. "Never mind, it's my problem and I'll figure it out on my own. I don't need you sitting here lecturing me after you were all up on the senator."

Standing, I took my wallet out and threw money on the table and headed out of the restaurant.

Before I got to the car, Aubrey grabbed my arm and pulled me to a stop. "Wait! Brett, please wait one second. I'm sorry, I was only teasing you."

"I'm tired, and ready to get home."

Her face fell. "Please let me help you. You said you could figure it out on your own. Figure what out?"

I looked around, still trying to process the information myself. "Emily showed up tonight to tell me she's pregnant and she claims the baby is mine."

Aubrey's eyes widened in shock as her mouth slowly dropped open. "Wh-what? She's ... pregnant ... but ... you said... you said you always use protection?"

Watching her try to piece it all together in her head was almost amusing. I wondered if I looked as shell-shocked when Emily dropped the news on me.

"That's not the worst of it."

She shook her head. "What in the hell could be worse than that?"

"Emily is a student at the University of Austin."

Her hands came up to her mouth as she stood there in a stunned state.

Taking her arm, I pulled her to the car as the driver jumped out and opened the back door.

"Sir, will you be heading home now or somewhere else?"

"Home, please," I said as I slid in after Aubrey.

The door wasn't even shut when she punched me in the arm. "How could you be so stupid? Are you insane?"

"Ouch!" I cried out, rubbing my arm. "Had I known, I would've never have slept with her. Damn it!" I shouted as I hit the seat between the two of us. There was no way Emily was pregnant with my kid. I was careful.

"Did you use a condom?" Aubrey probed in a hushed voice.

Glancing up at the driver, I sighed. "Can we talk about this once we get back to the condo?"

She leaned back and looked forward. "Of course. I'm sorry."

The rest of the drive was a welcomed silence. Riding up in the elevator, we stopped at Aubrey's floor. "Do you want to go up and change and come back down to talk?" she proposed.

My heart raced at the idea of being alone with her in her condo. I needed to keep my shit together, the last thing I needed was more drama.

"We can talk in the morning," I said with a slight grin.

Aubrey's hands immediately went to her hips. "Oh, hell no. I'm not letting you walk away when you're in such a chatty mood. Come on, let me get out of this dress and into something more comfortable, and then we can talk."

The thought of slowly unzipping her dress and letting it pool at her feet had my dick jumping. Aubrey walked to her condo and quickly opened the door for us to go in. I was positive she was worried about someone seeing me enter her place in the middle of the night. I knew no one could get in, though; the security in this building was top notch and one of the reasons I lived there.

Ten minutes later, I was sitting on the sofa with Aubrey positioned directly across from me dressed in a T-shirt and sweatpants. She looked so damn cute. I wanted to pull her onto my lap and bury my face in her hair. I wouldn't even care if it didn't lead anywhere. Just to have her up against me was all I wanted.

I shook my head to get rid of my wondering thoughts.

"Okay, so Emily is a student. When did you find out?"

Exhaling, I answered, "Tonight."

Her head drew back. "Tonight? Why in the world would she go to all that trouble to tell you tonight?"

"Well, fuck, Aubrey, if I knew that, I'd be one step closer to figuring this shit all out." My voice was tight and I knew I was being a dick toward her and she didn't deserve that. "I'm sorry. This is fucked up. I could very well lose my job over this."

She leaned over and put her forearms on her legs. "You're not going to lose your job because something doesn't smell right here."

"Ya think?" I replied with a gruff laugh.

Her head tilted in the most adorable way while a frustrated look appeared on her face.

"So a college girl goes out and gets a formal gown, buys a ticket into a pricey benefit dinner, and it's all to tell you that you're going to be a dad? Why not just show up at your place or at work? No, she wanted to make sure your evening was ruined with this news."

Dropping back against the sofa, I laughed. "Well, she succeeded. I don't even think I heard anything that was said after I told her to leave."

She stood and paced. "I'm going to have to start digging up some information on this girl."

Lifting my head, I stared at her like she was crazy. "What? Aubrey, I appreciate you wanting to figure this whole mess out, but this is my problem. Not yours."

She spun around and inspected me for a moment. "It is my problem because I really don't want my piece on you spoiled by some girl who is clearly looking for money."

"Money?" I asked, lifting my brows.

Aubrey shook her head and sat next to me. "Brett, it wasn't hard to find information out about you. Before I got here, I started to research you. There are some things buried deep, like why you left the NFL, which by the way I fully intend on getting out of you."

With a sigh, I stood and walked toward the window while she continued talking.

"But what I did find out was you come from a rather wealthy family. Your father owns cattle ranches not only here in Texas, but up in Wyoming as well. My guess is this girl looked you up and saw a chance to get money out of you."

Pushing out a deep breath, I turned back to her. "She didn't mention anything about money."

"Tell me exactly what she said."

With a shrug, I closed my eyes and thought back to the short conversation I had with Emily. "She said she came to tell me she found out she was pregnant and she was keeping the baby."

"Then?"

With a grunt, I asked, "Then what?"

"What was your response to that?"

"I told her there was no way the kid was mine."

Aubrey waited for me to go on.

Kicking at nothing on the floor, I kept talking. "She said she hadn't been with anyone other than me, and that she wanted to meet with me tomorrow to talk things over."

With a quick nod of her head, she jumped up and grabbed a notebook. "I'm going to need everything on this girl. Her name, full name if you can get it, her age, where she is from, and when she started at the University of Austin."

"I could probably look her up in the system," I said. "I don't even know her last name, though."

Aubrey lifted her gaze to mine. They were filled with disappointment and it about killed me.

Her attention fell back onto the paper. "I think what you need to do tomorrow is the exact opposite of what she thinks you're going to do."

"And that is?" I inquired as I sat back on the sofa. "Because what I really want to do is get drunk and forget this night ever happened."

She jotted some notes as she spoke. "Well, by your behavior toward her this evening, she thinks you're going to freak out on her, probably tell her to get rid of the baby."

"I would never do that."

Her eyes quickly looked up to mine and she smiled. "I know you wouldn't, but she doesn't know that."

My chest tightened knowing Aubrey saw more of me than most people.

"You're going to tell her you will stand by her and support her through this. But that the moment the baby is born, a DNA test needs to be done. Tell her she can move into your condo, and you'll make sure she is completely taken care of during the pregnancy."

I was sure my jaw was on the ground. "Are you fucking kidding me?"

Without so much as looking at me, Aubrey opened her laptop and started typing. "Nope. I'm not kidding at all."

"I don't want her living in my condo! I mean, if the kid truly turns out to be mine, I'll step up to the plate. But I know it's not mine. What if she agrees to it?"

Lifting her eyes, she winked. "Then you'll have yourself a new roommate."

"Bullshit. No one is moving in with me. Hell no."

"Fine. Then tell her you'll lease out a condo unit in the building. You want her close by. After all, she's having your baby."

Balling my fists, I went to talk when Aubrey shook her head and stood up in front of me. "Wait. Before you get angry, I'm kidding. She's not pregnant with your baby. Matter of fact, I'd bet my salary she isn't even pregnant."

With a long drawn out moan, I stood. "I'm going home."

"Don't forget to get all the information on her," Aubrey called out.

Before I got to the door, I glanced back at Aubrey. "How can you be so sure she isn't pregnant?"

Standing, she crossed her arms over her chest and smirked. "Because I have a hunch."

My heart jumped to my throat. "You have a hunch?"

With a nod, she answered, "Yep."

"Oh, for fuck's sake."

Chapter Ten

Aubrey

MY PEN TAPPED against the notebook as I waited to hear from Brett. I wasn't sure why or how, but I knew this girl was a fraud. MaryJo Longing did an article a few years back about women who tried to scam teachers and coaches out of thousands of dollars by making similar claims. My gut was telling me this was the same thing.

The light knock on the door caused my stomach to plunge. "Come in," I said calmly, even though my heart was racing.

Pat walked in and flashed me a big ol' smile. "So how's it going, Aubrey? Owens behaving for you?"

Plastering on a fake smile, I nodded my head. "He has been very helpful I must say. I haven't had to hog tie him to a chair and force him to talk to me … yet."

He tossed his head back and let out a roar of laughter. I couldn't help but chuckle as well.

"Well, I have hit somewhat of a wall in one respect to Brett's NFL career."

Pat's face fell and he moved about in his seat.

Oh, oh he knew something. Reaching over, I grabbed my small digital recorder and hit the red button. "What made you hire, Brett Owens?"

"This is an official question I'm assuming?"

With a grin, I replied. "Yes."

"He knows football. He excelled here when he was a player, and I knew bringing him in as the head football coach would only improve our program."

"And it did."

With a huge smile, he agreed. "It sure did."

"But why the secrecy in the reason Brett left the NFL. He got hurt, but from what I've read, it wasn't a career-ending injury."

Pat nodded his head and looked at the recorder. "May we go off the record here, Aubrey?"

Reaching for the device, I stopped recording. "I'd never betray your trust, that I can promise you."

He smiled. "Aubrey something very deeply personal happened to Brett during that time. So much so, he chose to walk away from a very promising career in the NFL."

"What? What happened?" I asked with baited breath.

Pat held up his hands. "That you're going to have to get out of Brett. I won't betray his trust on it. Brett is more than the head football coach here. He's like a son to me. There isn't anything I wouldn't do for him."

I let out a frustrated sigh, even though I respected him for not going behind Brett's back. A thought occurred to me. If this pregnancy thing turned out to be true, would Pat hide it to keep Brett's job safe? Chewing on my lip, I focused back on the conversation.

"Is it something he'll tell me?"

His face looked so sad. Whatever it was, it not only hurt Brett, but it hurt Pat in some way as well. "I hope he does because I think it would be good for him to talk about it."

My cell phone rang with an unknown number. Quickly standing, Pat excused himself and headed out of my office. I guess that was his escape from any more questions.

"Saved by the phone!" I called as he chuckled and waved good-bye. "We need to set up a time for your interview!"

Pat lifted his hand and waved as he stepped out of my office.

"This is Aubrey Cain."

"Ms. Cain, how are you this afternoon?"

Ryan Dryer. What in the world is he doing calling me?

Spinning around in my chair, I looked out the giant window to the clear blue sky.

"Mr. Dryer, I'm doing fine. You?"

He chortled and replied, "How did you know it was me?"

With a grin, I answered, "That smooth southern drawl of yours is hard to miss."

"I like a woman who is not only beautiful, but clearly smart, and pays attention to the details."

Digging deep down, I tried my best to pull off a Scarlet O'Hara accent. "I do declare, Mr. Dryer, are you trying to woo me with your sweet talk?"

"That all depends. Is it working?" I could hear the smile in his voice, and I had to admit the silly flirting felt good.

"It might be working, but then again, that depends on why you called me."

"Dinner this evening."

Chewing on my lip, I thought about it. What harm would come from an innocent dinner? If my mother knew Senator Ryan Dryer was asking me to dinner she would tell me to go if anything for her sake. Plus, a night out would be nice.

Brett popped into my mind. It was clear he did not get along with, nor even like, Ryan. I had no idea why since Ryan said they were good friends before. I made a note to press both of them for more information.

"I probably need to make sure I don't need to be anywhere tonight with Brett."

Ryan let out a rough sounding laugh. "Owens wouldn't mind a night off from you constantly following him around, although, I'm sure he likes the attention."

Ouch. That was a jab. "Brett doesn't strike me as an attention-seeker."

I was slightly put off by Ryan insulting Brett. The few weeks I'd been here and got to know Brett better, he was actually a very sincere and humble person. "How about an early dinner? I have plans tomorrow morning and don't want to be out to late."

"With Brett?"

Narrowing my brows, I shook my head. Well now, this is getting interesting. "It's my birthday tomorrow and I have plans."

"Fair enough. Then I'm taking you out for an early birthday dinner."

Smiling, I stood and walked to the window. "Sounds like a plan. Should I meet you somewhere?"

"No, I'll have my car pick you up at say, six?"

"Six sounds great. Looking forward to it, Ryan."

"So am I, Aubrey. So am I."

The way he said my name caused a chill to rush over my body. My instincts told me I needed to be guarded around him.

Pulling the phone back from my ear, I hit "End".

Spinning on my heels, I let out a scream when I saw Brett standing there.

"Jesus!" My hands came up to my chest as I tried to settle my racing heart. "You scared me, Brett."

He didn't say a word at first, he just stood there staring at me.

Clearing my throat, I asked, "How did everything go? What did Emily say?"

Nothing. He simply stood there looking at me. There was something in his eyes, but I couldn't pinpoint it.

"Brett? Is everything okay?"

Shaking his head, he seemed to snap out of it. "Um ... yeah."

"What happened with Emily?"

He rubbed his hand over the scruff on his face and my lower stomach tightened with desire. *God, I love it when he does that.*

"She seemed to get a little flustered when I mentioned her moving into the building here and me taking care of her until the baby was born. I also told her I'd be getting a DNA test done."

I lifted my brows in a questioning look. "Flustered? Like how?"

Brett looked away from me as he continued to talk. "I don't know. She stumbled on her words. Then she said she didn't want me to be in the baby's life, and that if I wanted this to go away without the school finding out, I could give her two hundred thousand dollars and she'd leave. I told her I wanted to go to a doctor first to make sure she was really pregnant."

I knew it. I knew something about this whole situation didn't smell right.

"Let me guess, she said no."

"She handed me a positive pregnancy test and said that should be good enough."

I sat at my desk and laughed. "Does she think you're stupid?"

Brett's face was white as a ghost. "I told her it wasn't good enough so she excused herself to make a phone call. When she came back, she told me she had a doctor's appointment in thirty minutes so we jumped in a cab and headed there."

"And?" I questioned, sitting on the edge of my seat.

"She is for sure pregnant. I watched them do the sonogram."

My jaw fell open. "How... how far along is she?"

Brett looked like he was about to get sick. "The doctor said four months."

Standing, I covered my mouth. Brett was going to have a baby with this girl Emily and it actually turned my stomach. For some reason, I was more upset than I should have been.

"Excuse me," I mumbled as I rushed past him and ran to the restroom.

I barely had time to make it to the toilet before I threw up.

What in the hell is wrong with me? Why did that news hit me like that?

A light tap on my shoulder caused me to look up. Brett stood there with a wet towel. Reaching for it, I wiped my mouth and walked out of the stall and to the sink.

"Thank you," I mumbled. "I'm not sure what happened? I must have eaten something bad."

Brett barely grinned. "You did the same thing I did. I practically ran over pregnant women to get out of the office to get sick."

Brett leaned against the sink. "I know the baby isn't mine, Aubrey. I had a condom on and it didn't break."

"How can you be sure?"

"Because I know. Fuck. I'm going to lose my job over this. She's talking about going to the media."

Turning to face him, I took his hand in mine. The instant rush I felt from his touch caused me to take a few extra seconds to focus on what I was going to say.

"You won't lose your job because we're going to find out if this girl was with another guy. Did you get her last name?"

He nodded. "Yeah, I've already looked it up. Looks like she registered last fall. She is only taking one class."

Pinching my eyebrows together, I asked, "Which class?"

"A history class. It says she's pre-law."

The door to the bathroom opened and a lady walked in but quickly came to a stop when she saw Brett.

"So sorry," Brett said as he rushed out of the bathroom. The lady grinned at me as I returned the gesture.

"I got sick and he came in to make sure I was okay."

She smiled big. "Sounds like Brett Owens. He is so good to everyone around here. Such a nice guy. Cute too!"

I nodded my head and gave her a polite chuckle. I'd been interviewing a lot of the staff that worked for Brett and Pat. Everyone said the same thing when it came to Brett. He was a nice guy and would do anything for anyone.

My heart ached in my chest for Brett. I may be struggling with my feelings for him, but I knew he didn't deserve this hand that was being dealt to him.

I was going to find out what in the hell was going on. Even if that meant Joe finding out I was digging into something I shouldn't have been.

Chapter Eleven

Brett

MY THOUGHTS WERE scattered while I tried to pay attention to the video of last year's opening game.

Tossing the remote on the coffee table, I scrubbed my hands down my face and stood. "Fucking hell, just go out, Owens," I mumbled to myself.

I made my way to the kitchen and grabbed the third beer I'd had since getting home. Between the bullshit accusations from Emily and Aubrey out with dickhead Ryan, I didn't know whether I was coming or going. I hadn't dealt with these feelings in a while, and I wasn't so sure about anything anymore.

The cell phone on the counter caught my eye. Picking it up, I hit the number to the one person I know would understand. He was also the one who could change my entire life with what I was about to tell him.

The cab pulled up to The Backspace and parked out front. Handing over a few twenty dollar bills, I said, "Keep the change, buddy."

"Thanks, dude!" the driver called out with a huge grin.

It didn't take long to locate Pat and his wife, Sharron. With a nod directed to both of them, I headed to the table.

Pat stood and shook my hand. Leaning over, I kissed Sharron on the cheek. "You look beautiful as always, Sharron."

"Charmer," she replied with a warm smile.

I took a seat and ordered a beer. Pat lifted an eyebrow, but I choose to ignore it.

"Looks like you have something heavy on your mind, son."

Pat was like a second father to me when I played football at the University of Austin. Anytime we were away from work, he treated me like a son instead of acting like my boss.

With a curt laugh, I replied, "You could say that."

Leaning back in his chair, Pat cleared his throat. "Aubrey was asking about your NFL career."

My head pulled back some, as if I should really be surprised by that. I'd been redirecting her questions anytime she asked me about my few years of pro football.

With a hard look, I asked, "What did you tell her?"

"That it was your story to tell … not mine."

The waitress set the beer down and I ignored her fuck-me eyes she was flashing at me. "Thanks," I mumbled.

"Would you like something to eat?" she inquired while batting her long eyelashes at me. Any other time, I'd probably flirt with her. I wasn't in the mood, and I sure as hell wasn't doing it in front of Pat and Sharron.

"No thank you."

Glancing back up, I observed Pat and Sharron holding hands. I couldn't help but grin. They reminded me of my own parents who were still madly in love after thirty-five years of marriage. If I could ever find a love like that I vowed I would never let it go. It didn't look like it was in the game plan for me though.

"I appreciate that. I'm sure the best thing to do would be to tell her. I've come to know Aubrey, and there is no way she would print it."

Pat nodded in agreement. "She's a sweet girl. Smart too."

My brows lifted and a crooked smile grew over my face. "You're surely not suggesting anything there are you, Pat? You of all people."

He held up his hands and chuckled. "I wouldn't think of it. But since we aren't wearing I'm-your-boss-and-you-work-for-me hats, let me ask you something."

"Ask away."

"You're not the least bit interested in her?"

With a fixed looked at Pat, I answered. "I wouldn't put her job on the line."

"There isn't anything that says you can't date an ESPN reporter."

I let out a gruff laugh. "Even one doing a full spread on me and the university I work for? That might make her a little biased don't you think?"

"Not if she is good at what she does and she writes a fair and truthful article," Sharron said. "Your eyes light up when she's mentioned, Brett."

Grabbing my beer, I took a long drink and shook my head. "I've got bigger problems than my so-called feelings for Aubrey Cain."

"How big?" Pat questioned with a trouble looked on his face.

Glancing down at the table, I inhaled a deep breath and held it in for a few moments before slowly letting it out before speaking.

"I met a girl about four months ago at a dinner I was speaking at. We hooked up twice, and now she says she's pregnant and the baby is mine."

Sharron's expression turned grim. "Oh, Brett."

The disappointment in her voice was almost more than I could take. It was a prequel to what my own mother would say.

Pat cleared his throat. "Okay, I'm sure you'll do the right thing here, Brett."

I laughed. "I don't think the baby is mine. I always use protection and nothing was wrong with the condom both times." Turning to Sharron, I mumbled, "Sorry, Sharron."

She held up her hands as if to say she wasn't bothered by my words.

"That's not the worse of it, Pat."

Closing his eyes, he blew out a deep breath. "Please tell me she's not a student."

My throat felt as if it was closing in on me as I fought for air. "Looks like she just transferred here and is only signed up for a history class."

"Damn it, Brett!" Pat grumbled.

"In my defense, there is no way a student would have been at that dinner. None. I swear I would never put my job or the university at risk if I had any indication she was a student."

"What's her name? I'll look into her records."

"I've already given it to Aubrey. She said the office can't find her transcripts. They haven't even been scanned into the system."

Sharron leaned forward with a confused look. "Well they must have had them for her to register for classes. How would she be able to do that with no transcripts?"

I pointed toward her. "That's the million-dollar question. Aubrey said she would dig a little more tomorrow, but so far she can't find anything on Emily Claire.

"How did Aubrey get dragged into this?"

I glared at Pat. "Well, considering the woman is with me practically twenty-four-seven."

"Speaking of, where is she?" Sharron probed.

Bile moved up to my throat. Taking another drink of my beer, I replied, "She's out on a date."

Pat's brow furrowed. "A date? With who?"

Just the idea of Aubrey with Ryan boiled my blood. With a scowl, I answered. "Ryan Dryer."

"Oh, hell," Pat whispered while running his hand across his chin. "Did you warn her about him?"

With a shrug, I shook my head. "She wouldn't believe anything I said even if I tried. In her eyes, he is a great guy even though she's only been around him for two minutes. I think because he's a senator, and her mom feels like she can trust the guy. Little does she know what a downright dirty rotten rat he is."

"Jealousy does not become you, Brett Owens," Sharron said with a chuckle.

Letting out a frustrated grunt, I shook my head.

Pat folded his arms on the table. "I want you to take some time off."

With a huff, I asked, "What? Time off? I can't take time off. I've got commitments and bullshit speeches to make. Off is not an option, and you know that, Pat. Besides, we're still in spring training. Plus, I need to make sure we get the kid from Marfa to commit."

"Exactly. This kid should be in the bag with him attending your high school alma mater. Head there, show him how bad we want him, and visit your parents. It gets you away from this girl and gives me time to look into a few things."

I sighed. "What about Aubrey?"

I'd never seen Pat with an evil smile like the one he was wearing now. "There are plenty of rooms at your folk's ranch. Take her with you so she can see the other side of Brett Owens."

My jaw dropped. "You cannot be serious."

Glancing at Sharron and then back to me, he replied, "Oh, I've never been more serious."

Chapter Twelve

Aubrey

THE MOMENT WE pulled up to the restaurant, I knew this was going to be an interesting dinner. Stepping out of the limo, my eyes glanced up at the historical building.

Ryan walked up and placed his mouth close to my ear. "The Austin Club. They have amazing food."

I nodded my head. "Why do I have a feeling I'm underdressed?"

He laughed. "Nonsense. No one will be able to look past your beauty to even notice how you're dressed."

I felt my cheeks heat up as I quickly glanced away from Ryan. Any decent man would tell me I looked good.

With a slight sigh, I said, "I'm really a simple girl, Ryan. I don't need to be impressed with fancy restaurants."

When he slipped his arm around my waist, I waited for it to make me feel something. Anything. It didn't. His smile though, I had to admit there was something about it. I'd give him one thing; he could probably charm the panties off any girl if he wanted to. Just not this girl.

The second we entered, everyone jumped into action. I'd never seen so many people fall over one man in my entire life. Jesus, you'd think the president had walked in. I wasn't used to this kind of behavior, not even with my own mother, who was also a senator.

"Mr. Dryer, good evening, sir. Would you like to dine privately this evening?"

With a wink to the young blonde, he answered her. "No. I want to show off the beautiful woman on my arm."

My face screwed up at his comment. "I'm not an ornament, senator," I softly stated. He tossed his head back like I had told him a joke.

"No, that you are not, Ms. Cain, and forgive me for trying to pay you a compliment. It was in rather poor taste. I'm not really used to taking women out on dates."

My brows lifted. "Really? I find that hard to believe."

His hand moved to the small of my back. It felt nothing like when Brett touched me. He brought my body to life and made me feel things I'd never felt before.

Lust. That was all that was with Brett.

"Why do you find it hard to believe I don't date? Unlike Mr. Owens, I don't sleep with every woman I talk to."

I underestimated his dislike of Brett. "Have you looked at yourself in the mirror lately, senator? I'm sure you have women falling at your feet."

"Call me Ryan, please."

With a nod, I replied, "Ryan it is."

We climbed a set of stairs and made our way to a large room. I gasped when I took it all in. It was beautiful with all of the old ornate décor. The building itself was breathtaking. I could only imagine the weddings that had been held here in this room.

"It's so beautiful," I whispered.

A single rose appeared before me. Smiling, I looked at Ryan. "For you. An early birthday present."

I took the flower and thanked him. It was clear he was trying to impress me. I'll admit it was a sweet gesture.

As we walked up to the table, my eyes widened in surprise.

Ryan took the rose from me and pushed it into the huge bouquet of roses. "The rest of your flowers."

Swallowing, I glanced around. What did these people think? The stares from everyone in the room made me uncomfortable. Not to mention the guy standing in the corner with a camera in his hand. "Um... how many flowers are in that thing?" I asked.

"Three dozen," Ryan replied with a proud look on his face.

The gesture might have seemed romantic for most women, but the cocky look on his face and the way he peered around the room had the complete opposite effect on me.

"Goodness," I barely said as I sank into the chair Ryan was holding out for me.

"I hope you like roses."

Trying to be polite, I forced a smile. "I do, they're not my favorite flower though. Tulips are."

Ryan frowned. "Tulips? Huh. What a strange flower to like."

A weak grin played across my lips as I tried not to let his words bother me.

Half of the dinner Ryan talked about everything him or the great state of Texas. At one point, I swore my head dropped as I fought to keep from falling asleep.

With a laugh, Ryan shook his head. "I'm boring you. I told you I wasn't good at this dating thing."

I brushed off his comment with a wave of my hand. "No, you're fine. I have to admit, I hear all of this with my mother as well, so it tends to be tedious."

He smiled but something moved across his face. I couldn't really figure Ryan out. He seemed genuine and nice at the gala. Now, I got a totally different vibe from him. One I didn't like at all.

"So, how are things going with the piece you're writing on Mr. Owens?"

With a nod, I replied, "Good. But I'm not just writing about him. The article itself focuses on college football, the University of Austin, and Brett."

He lifted his brows. "Just good? Is he being a jerk to you? He's known for being a bit of an asshole. I should know." Grabbing his drink, he took a shallow sip.

His voice turned tight when he started talking about Brett, and I was caught off guard by the total turnaround of his tune. He had been proper the entire evening, not uttering a single curse word.

"I haven't experienced that side of Brett. He can be a bit out-spoken on things, but he has never been rude to me. He's actually been very accommodating, if I do say so."

Ryan downed the rest of the alcohol and motioned for another. The muscles in his neck seemed to tighten, but that could have been my imagination. "Well, I knew a different side of Brett at one time, so please forgive me for my short outburst. I mean, he was my best friend once."

I nodded. The rest of dinner was spent almost in silence. Something happened between Ryan and Brett and I was bound and determined to find out what. First I had to help Brett with this Emily problem.

"You suddenly seem like you're miles away, Aubrey."

I grinned. "Sorry. My mind was drifting to a problem I'm helping Brett with."

Ryan leaned forward. "Really? Is everything okay? I may have my differences with Brett, but like I said, we were like brothers at one time."

The moment the words were out of my mouth I wanted to hit myself. Why I had blurted that out I had no idea. Ryan had caught me off guard when I was in the middle of thinking about Emily. Trying to cover for the stupid slip on my part, I grinned and answered him. "It's really nothing big, a hiccup I'm trying to help him with."

Reaching across the table, Ryan took my hand in his. "Is there anything I can do to help?"

I looked deep into his eyes. He was being sincere. "Thank you, but really, it's nothing."

He squeezed my hand. "Of course. But please know if you need any help with anything, I have connections and resources I'm sure you don't have."

Wanting to change the subject, I nodded. "Thank you, Ryan. I appreciate the offer."

He dropped my hand and took another sip of his wine. "Anything to help a beautiful woman."

The rest of the evening seemed to flow a bit better. Ryan relaxed a bit more. It was almost as if he was suddenly in the best mood ever. He cracked a few jokes, we laughed, drank probably a little too much, danced a few times, and finally called it a night when I saw it was so late.

When the limo pulled up to my building, I sighed and looked at him. "I had fun tonight. Ryan. Thank you. It was a rare occasion to get out. I needed it more than I thought."

"Let me walk you up to your place."

Pressing my lips together, I scrunched up my nose. "That probably wouldn't look good for you or me. Rumors could start, ya know." I chuckled.

He reached over and pushed a piece of my hair behind my ear. I found myself pulling away from him. I wasn't the least bit interested in Ryan Dryer and tonight was simply a dinner, nothing more. At least it was for me. What Ryan thought it was was entirely different. "I don't care about rumors, Aubrey."

Oh shit. He thinks this is going further. I may have enjoyed my evening, but I didn't see anything moving on with Ryan at all.

"Well, I do. I've worked hard to get where I am, and the last thing I need is rumors that I'm dating a senator from Texas. Thank you for the evening, Ryan. I had a lovely time, but I think it's time to call it a night."

Ryan tilted his head and flashed me what I assumed was the smile he used to seduce women. Almost as if he thought it would change my mind. I reached for the car door and opened it. Al, the doorman, was there to help me out of the limo. Not two seconds later, Al's hand was replaced by Ryan's.

"At least let me walk you inside the building."

An uneasy feeling washed over my body, and I finally figured out what it was about Ryan that made me uneasy.

I didn't trust him.

Ryan placed his hand on my lower back and led me into the lobby of the building. I stopped short of the elevator to say my goodbye. When he wrapped me in his arms and pulled me up against him, I was momentarily stunned. I quickly snapped out of it when his lips pressed against mine.

Pushing him away from me, I glared at him. "What in the hell was that all about?"

"I don't even get a goodnight kiss? How about a happy birthday kiss?"

The driver came walking in with the roses. My eyes widened as I glanced between the flowers and Ryan. "You brought the roses?" I asked.

"Of course. They're yours."

I quickly shook my head and put my fingers to my temple. "Ryan, I really enjoyed this evening, but honestly I don't see this going anywhere else. I'm sorry if I gave you the impression that I wanted something more."

He stood there staring at me, as if waiting for me to come to my senses and kiss him.

"Ryan, anyone could take a picture of you kissing me and blow it out of context. I don't need that in my life right now."

"It's one in the morning, Aubrey. There is no one following you or me around. It was an innocent kiss."

Anger washed over me and I felt my face heat up. "No, it was an unwarranted kiss. There is a very big difference."

He winked. "You're right. I've had too much to drink, and I let my manners slide out the door. Will you forgive me?"

A look moved across his face and I couldn't really tell if he was pissed or not.

"Of course. Thank you for the dinner and the lovely evening. Now if you'll excuse me. I've really stayed out much later than I wanted to."

"Of course and it was my pleasure. I hope you have a wonderful birthday. I'd offer to take you to lunch or dinner, but I'm afraid I'll be in meetings all day and I have an engagement tomorrow evening."

The last thing I wanted to do was lead him on by going out with him again.

"No don't even worry about it. Thank you for the um ... for the flowers."

Ryan turned to Al. "You'll help Ms. Owens with the flowers?"

Al nodded. "Yes sir. Yes, Mr. Dryer. Sir."

Ryan barely acknowledged Al. "Thanks." Turning back to me, he kissed me on the cheek and whispered, "I hope you dream of me tonight."

What? What part of I'm not interested did he miss?

Forcing a smile, all I could do was nod.

"It was good seeing you again, Senator Dryer, sir."

Ryan acted as if he hadn't heard Al while he walked out of the building and slipped back into the limo.

Al shook his head and mumbled, "Asshole."

Laughing, I looked at the flowers. "Is there anywhere we can take those? Maybe a few residents that might like a little pick me up?"

We both stared at the flowers. "I say toss them in the trash."

Covering my mouth, I giggled. "That's so bad, Al."

"That man is not what you think, Ms. Cain. Please be careful with him."

With a furrowed brow, I wanted to ask him what he meant by that, but the phone at his desk rang. Taking one last look at the roses, I decided to leave them. I appreciated the gesture from Ryan, but it hadn't felt sincere. I wondered if we hadn't been in a room full of people would Ryan have given me the flowers. I doubted it.

I didn't like the smell of roses anyway.

Standing outside the door to my condo, I fumbled with the latch on my small clutch purse.

"Need help?"

His voice had been so low I hardly heard it. Glancing up, I tried to act normal when everything inside of me was screaming holy shit.

Standing before me was Brett. And Lord have mercy if he didn't look hot as hell.

"Brett, um … hey … ah … what are you doing up so late?" I questioned with a nervous chuckle.

He took a step toward me. His blue eyes felt like they were pinning me in the very spot I stood. "I couldn't sleep, so I went for a run."

My gaze drifted over his body. Shorts. Tight T-shirt soaking wet with sweat. Yep. My ovaries combusted at the sight of him. I couldn't help it … I licked my lips at the thought of lifting that shirt up and seeing his body under it.

I looked away.

Oh. My. God. What is wrong with me?

Brett took another few steps closer to me until he was right in front of me. "Did you enjoy your evening?"

Lifting my head, I was captivated by the way he was looking at me. "It was okay. I enjoyed it ... I guess."

A single eyebrow lifted as Brett continued to stare at me. "Did you enjoy it when he kissed you?"

I swallowed hard. "Wh-what?"

My head was spinning. Had Brett been in the lobby? No. I would have seen him. He said he was out running, he must have come back when we were in the lobby and seen Ryan kiss me.

Trying to get my thoughts together, I wasn't about to let Brett play his head games with me. "Why do you care if I liked it or not?"

Surely he had to have seen me push Ryan away and heard the exchange if he had witnessed the kiss.

He took another step closer, causing me to back up against my door.

The way he searched my face had me fighting to hold back the urge to reach out for him. My fingers itched to reach up and touch his soaked T-shirt.

His hands came up and slid into my hair, gripping it hard as he pulled my head back, lifting my lips to his.

I fought to keep my breathing under control.

Focus. I need to focus.

"When you lay in bed tonight and your hand slips inside your panties, I don't want you thinking about his kiss."

What kiss?

Between my legs throbbed as I watched Brett's soft lips move with each word. Pulling my hair tighter, I let out a soft groan from the back of my throat. "I want you thinking about mine."

His lips pressed to mine while he pulled my head back more, causing me to open to him and gasp at the slight pain I felt. Our tongues danced in perfect unison. I was quickly taken to a state of euphoria I've only ever experienced when this man kissed me. We both moaned into one another's mouths as my hands clutched onto his forearms. Holding on for dear life as he kissed me like I'd never been kissed before.

I wasn't sure how long the kiss lasted, all I knew was I was breathless when it ended. With a wink, he whispered, "Get some sleep. We have a long day tomorrow." He went to turn but stopped. With a smile that had my heart melting and panties instantly wet, he whispered, "Happy birthday, Aubrey."

And like that, he turned and walked toward the elevators while my entire body quivered. I couldn't even think straight. My mouth opened to call out his name, but I knew even if I did ask him to come in, he wouldn't.

Looking over his shoulder, he winked before stepping into the elevator. My heart raced and my stomach fluttered as I watched the doors close, taking his smile with it.

After a few minutes of standing in the hallway like an idiot, I finally opened the door to the condo. I instantly knew the smell and grinned from ear to ear. Flipping on the lights, my heart dropped at the simple display of flowers on the bar.

Tulips. My favorite.

Kicking off my shoes, I dropped my keys and purse on the small table and headed over to the bright yellow flowers while I ran my fingers along my kiss-swollen lips. I would call my parents first thing in the morning and thank them for the flowers.

Lifting the card out, I opened it. With a stunned expression, I read the words.

The smile that spread across my face almost hurt my cheeks. I didn't know what made me happier. The fact that Brett actually was listening the day I mentioned tulips were my favorite flower. Or that he called me Bree.

My hand went to my stomach. I swore it felt like a swarm of butterflies were dancing around in there.

Every nerve ending in my body tingled. All those nights with my girlfriends talking about how a man should make a woman feel. This was the way I imagined it. The warmth that spread over my body was hard to ignore. It was too bad the man who made me feel this way was the man I was supposed to be focusing work on. Not falling in love with.

Chapter Thirteen

Brett

LIFTING MY COFFEE to my lips, I took a drink as I knocked on her door.

For some reason, my heart was pounding in my chest. The flowers weren't a last minute thought. I had ordered them right after I found out it was her birthday. I wasn't going to lie and say it didn't please me she left Dryer's flowers in the damn lobby. I chuckled at the thought.

The door opened and I was greeted by a beautiful smile and bright light brown eyes. Her hair was piled up on top of her head.

"Brett. The flowers!"

I couldn't hide my happiness. Of course, I was hoping she would say something like she dreamed about me all night after that kiss, but I'll take her smile any day.

"You like them?"

"I love them! That was very sweet of you. I thought at first they were from my parents."

Ouch. Well at least she didn't think they were from another man.

Aubrey held the door open, allowing me to walk into her condo.

"So, I've been thinking about this Emily girl. Something about all of this doesn't sit right with me. Why all of sudden is she showing up? If she's four months pregnant, why not show up the second she found out she was pregnant? Wouldn't you think that would be the normal reaction?"

Swallowing my coffee, I shrugged. "I don't know."

"And they all of sudden can't find her transcripts or anything on her? No. This feels crooked. Have you talked to her today?"

With a nod, I sat on her sofa. "Yep. Told her I was having to leave town for a bit and when I got back, we'd talk more."

Her face dropped. "You're going out of town?"

"Emily wasn't so thrilled about it and said if I was planning on skipping out, she'd go to the news with her pregnancy."

"That's a rash reaction from her just because you simply told her you were going out of town."

I lifted a brow. "Is it? You reacted."

Her arms crossed her chest, lifting her breasts enough to make my dick jump. "I was surprised. That's all."

Well, here goes nothing. Aubrey was either going to go along with this, or tell me to fuck off. "You should probably pack a bag."

"For?" she asked with a cautious look on her face.

"You're coming with me."

She let out a little laugh. "You can't be serious? You want me to just up and go off with you?"

"I'm trying to bring a kid in to play for the university. The deal is pretty much sealed, but I need to go in. He lives in my home town."

"That's like … five hours away."

"Five hours and fifty-two minutes, to be exact."

With a frown, she shook her head. "You have it down to the exact minutes?"

"Yep."

"Why?"

Standing, I finished my coffee and walked up to her. "Because my parents' ranch is right outside of there. After I get this kid to sign, I'm heading home for a bit. Pat thinks you need to see the other side of me. Whatever the fuck that means."

Her eyes lit up and although she was trying to hide her excitement, it was coming through in the barely-there grin on her face.

"Really? This might be a good thing. I've pretty much got everything I need on you for the coach bit, now I need the *real* you."

Laughing, I slipped my hand around her waist and pulled her closer to me. "Are you sure you want to know the *real* me, Bree?"

Her mouth parted and she absentmindedly rolled her tongue along her lips. "If I gave you the real me, my cock would be pounding in and out of you right now and the last thing you'd be worried about is the article as you screamed for more."

Passion burned in her eyes before she placed her hands on my chest and pushed me away. "Ugh. Must you talk like that? Do you really think women like that?"

With a shrug, I grinned. "Let me check between your legs and I'll answer that for you."

She let out a frustrated sigh and turned to walk away from me. With a smirk, I knew she was turned on. I saw it in her eyes.

"And you think I'm going to spend hours in a car with you while you talk to me like that?"

I threw my head back and laughed. "You're right. I'll keep my thoughts to myself, after all, this is business only."

It seemed like Aubrey wanted to argue with me on keeping my thoughts to myself, but she simply rolled her eyes.

"How long would we be gone for?"

I wanted like hell to tell her two weeks. What I wouldn't give to spend time with her. Getting to know her better, memorizing her body. What types of things she liked to do. What movies she liked. For the first time in my life, I found myself longing for something deeper with a woman.

She stood there waiting for my answer as my thoughts took a

sudden turn. How many times could I make Aubrey come around my cock as I fucked her fast and hard?

My dick was throbbing as it pushed against my pants.

"Brett? Hello? What are you thinking about?"

Shit. I wasn't going to make it ten miles in the car with her if I kept thinking like that.

"A week?" I needed to call Pat and let him know we were staying a week. He said take a few days, there was no way I was going to pass up time with Aubrey. Especially with her on my turf.

"That would mean when we get back to Austin, I'd be leaving a few days after that." The thought made my stomach drop. She looked up in thought. "Being in the country with no distractions could be just what I need to get started writing. I've already interviewed the president of the university so I have everything I need for that."

My heart leapt to my throat at the thought of Aubrey being at the ranch. I'd never brought anyone there … not even Nicole, my ex. She never had the desire to see where I grew up or where my parents lived. I never had the desire to bring her home to meet my parents so it all worked out.

A smile grew across Aubrey's face. "Do I need to pack anything special?"

"Jeans, if you want to ride."

With a little jump and a clap of her hands she took off toward her bedroom. Okay, so she likes riding. Closing my eyes, I pictured Aubrey on top of me. Slowly moving up and down as she grasped onto her tits.

"Fuck," I mumbled, shaking my head to clear the thoughts as I adjusted my dick.

Aubrey called out from her room, "What did you say?"

"Be sure you have your chargers. The nearest store is over an hour away from my folks' place."

"Wow! Okay!" she yelled out.

Running back into the living room, she held up a pair of cowboy boots. "Thank God Michelle talked me into boots!"

I couldn't help but laugh. To see how excited she was made me happy. A happy I hadn't felt in a long time.

The happiness was soon to fade when my phone went off.

Emily: Will I get to see you before you leave?

Dragging in a deep breath, I slowly blew it out. Aubrey was going on and on about how excited she was to see a ranch. Hitting reply, I typed out my response.

Me: Why? Is something wrong?
Emily: No. I can come to your office if that's easier.

I had to run to my office to pick up a few files and tapes I wanted to review anyway, so I didn't see the problem with meeting Emily there.

"Hey, are we stopping by the office? I actually left my notes there and I need them."

Glancing up, I answered her. "Yeah, I need to stop by there as well, but Emily wants to meet me there. She said she wanted to talk to me."

A concerning look moved across Aubrey's face. "At the office? I hope you told her no."

With a shrug, I replied, "I was about to say yes. Since I'm heading that way."

"Are you crazy, Brett? The last thing you want is for this girl to be seen walking in and out of your office."

Her phone buzzed and she grabbed it. Reading a text message, she chewed on her fingernail.

"What's wrong?" I probed.

Her gaze lifted and met mine. "Ryan was asking how my day is going."

"You didn't tell him about Emily did you?"

She shook her head. "Of course not, but I'm wondering if he might be able to help."

I lifted my brow. "Did you say anything?"

Chewing on her bottom lip, she said, "Just that I was helping you with a problem."

My eyes closed and I shook my head. "Son-of-a-bitch."

We stepped into the elevator and I turned to Aubrey. "I still can't believe you told that mother fucker what was happening."

"I didn't tell him what was going on. It was a slip on my part and not even a big one."

"You shouldn't have told him a fucking thing."

Turning to face me, her hands went to her hips. "What is it with you hating him so much?"

My blood boiled. I couldn't stand the thought of Dryer in my business.

"You wouldn't understand."

"Maybe you should trust me a bit more."

Moving closer to her, my body burned with anger. Aubrey took a few steps back and hit the elevator wall. "Trust you? I do trust you. I told you about Emily, and what did you do? Turn around and told the one person I hate more than the air I breathe."

Her eyes widened in shock. "Hate is a strong word, Brett. And I didn't tell him everything. Hardly anything really and he obviously doesn't have the same feelings for you if he offered to help out."

"Yeah well, I didn't fuck his wife."

The doors opened and I left Aubrey standing in the elevator with a stunned expression on her face.

My hand combed through my hair as I silently cursed. Slamming my office door shut, I sent Emily another text.

Me: Coffee shop in twenty still?
Emily: Looking forward to it, Coach Owens

Jerking my head back in shock, I stared at the text. "Why in the hell is she calling me Coach Owens?"

"Because she is setting up the teacher/student role."

My head snapped up to see Pat standing there.

"What?"

"I just got back from HR. Seems like last year one of the professors found themselves in a similar situation as you. A woman who claimed to be a student, and pregnant."

My mouth went dry. "You didn't tell them about me did you?"

He held up his hands and shook his head. "No, of course not. I told them you had a family situation you needed to attend to and would be gone for two weeks."

"Two weeks?"

He sat and let out a long sigh. "Take whatever you want, but know you have two weeks to get this figured out. Find out who this girl is and what she wants from you. But most of all, keep her mouth shut."

"She threatened to go to the media when I told her I was leaving town. I told her I was going to tell my parents about the baby, and that I had a high school kid I was trying to sign on."

"I take it she bought it."

"Hook, line, and sinker. But she wants to meet before I leave."

"Whatever you do, don't have her come here, and be mindful this might be only a girl you got pregnant, or it could all be a scam for money or to bring you down."

"Bring me down? From what?"

"Coaching the number one ranked college football team in the nation."

I swallowed hard and whispered, "Fuck."

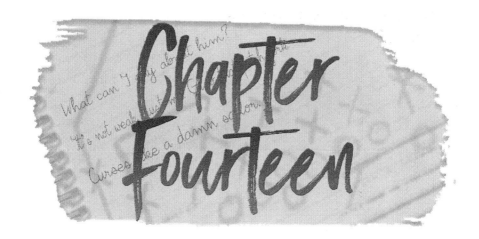

Chapter Fourteen

Aubrey

BRETT WAS IN a terrible mood. Ever since he came back from meeting Emily, he seemed distracted. I was torn inside on what to do. I wanted to ask what happened, but I was still trying to wrap my head around the comment he made in the elevator.

Had Ryan been married? Had Brett been married? No. I researched the shit out of him and there was never any mention of a wife. There had been a college girlfriend named Nicole. That was the only serious relationship I ever read about.

Peeking over, I watched as Brett gripped the steering wheel and clenched his jaw together.

Yikes. He looks pissed. I think I'll wait to question him later.

Hitting play on my iTunes app, I quickly got lost in my music. Before I knew it, I was jamming out to Brittney's "Baby One More Time."

Brett touched my arm and I jumped. The energy that raced through my body any time he touched me still caught me off guard. He said something to me, but the music was too loud. Pulling the earbuds out, I asked, "What?"

"What in the fuck are you listening to?"

"Brittney Spears."

He took a quick look at me and frowned before peering back out at the road. "I figured with the way you're belting out the words. Why are you listening to Brittney Spears?"

"I like her. Why else would I be listening to her?"

"That song is so … old."

"You have something against good music?"

He shrugged. "It's just so … old."

Rolling my eyes, I looked over at his gas gage. "Don't you need gas?"

Brett looked down and shook his head. "No."

"You're under a half a tank of gas. You should really get some."

"I think I know when I need gas."

With a shrug of my shoulders, I smirked. "When you get gas, I can add my phone to your Bluetooth and school you in good music."

"School me in good music? Please, I don't think so."

Ten minutes later, Brett pulled into a gas station and I was connecting my phone to his car. I loved his muscle car, but for some reason, I pictured him driving a big truck. But I had to admit, the Hell Cat was sexy as hell.

"You better use the restroom now. It's a long ass drive from this point on with no stops but the side of the road."

I waved him off, too excited to share my awesome traveling playlist. "Nah, I'm good. Do we have enough gas, though?"

He looked at me like my mother did when I was five. "Are you sure you don't have to go potty?"

Snarling my lip, I replied, "Yes, *Mommy*, I'm sure."

Brett huffed and drove out of the gas station and back onto the highway.

"Are you ready?" I asked rubbing my hands together.

"For?"

"My travel playlist!"

Brett groaned. "What's wrong with listening to CNN?"

"I'm sick of hearing about politics."

He laughed. "You're not! You had your headphones in. I was listening to politics."

"Too bad. You're listening to my playlist. And first we start with one of the best songs in history."

"This should be good," he mumbled.

I hit play and grinned from ear to ear as Belinda Carlisle's "Heaven Is a Place On Earth" began playing.

Brett snapped his head over and looked at me with his mouth agape. "You've got to be shitting me? Please tell me this is not loaded down with eighties music, Bree."

My stomach fluttered when he called me Bree. I prayed like hell he hadn't seen my reaction. Something was changing between the two of us, and I wasn't sure if that was a good or bad thing.

Laughing, I threw my head back and started singing to the top of my lungs along with Belinda. It didn't take long for Brett to join in when INXS's "Need You Tonight" started playing.

Pointing to him, I shouted over the song, "I knew it! You are a closet eighties music lover!"

Brett laughed and turned up the music. I'd never laughed and had so much fun in one road trip as I did with him. We listened to music, talked about sports, and debated on who was going to the Super Bowl next year. Eventually, he admitted he agreed with me. His foul mood was completely gone.

When our conversation seemed to fall into a comfortable silence, I stared out the window at the rugged landscape. The mountains in the distance were beautiful. "It's so different from Austin," I mumbled.

"Yep. It's like another world."

I chuckled. "Why did your parents settle way out here then?"

"My great-grandfather started a cattle ranch here and another in Wyoming. I'm guessing he was motivated by the cheaper land."

"How much land do your parents own?"

"Twenty-five sections here in Texas and nineteen in Wyoming."

I had no clue what that meant, but I was assuming it was a lot of land.

"One section is six hundred and forty acres," Brett explained. It was almost like he read my mind.

"Wow. That's a lot of land. Do they have people helping them?"

He nodded. His hand came up and rubbed the side of his face. I could tell he was bothered by something. My stomach tugged as I watched him struggle with an internal thought. Even now he looked so handsome. He had no idea I was sitting next to him completely and utterly turned on by the mere sight of him. No man had ever made me feel the way Brett did.

"Brett? Is everything okay?"

He glanced at me and gave me a weak grin. "Yeah. I've got a lot on my mind, I guess."

"Want to talk about it?"

"Is this off the record?"

I nodded and replied, "Of course."

With a deep sigh, he cleared his throat. "My father had cancer a few years back. We didn't think he would make it, but he did. I didn't get to spend very much time with him when he went through his treatment and it still bothers me. My mother had to do it all on her own, and I'll never forgive myself for putting my job first. I vowed I'd never do it again. There's been some talk about selling the ranch in Wyoming. My father loves that place as much as he loves the place here in Texas."

"Why do your parents want to sell the ranch in Wyoming?"

Brett shrugged. "I'm not sure."

"I'm so sorry about your father, but he's cancer free now, right?"

"Yeah. But I have a feeling my parents are keeping something from me. In a way, I'm kind of glad Emily showed up with all this bullshit. Gives me a good reason to go home."

I looked at my hands. I was conflicted with my own thoughts on Emily. A part of me wanted like hell to believe she was a scam. The other part was scared to death that she was really pregnant with Brett's child. That thought bothered me more than I wanted to admit.

"Tell me what you're thinking about, Bree."

Smiling, I looked up at the long road ahead of us. "I like that you call me, Bree. My parents and sisters call me that." It was in that moment I realized I hadn't really talked to my parents or my sisters since coming to Texas. I made a mental note to call them that evening.

"That couldn't have been what you were thinking about," he replied, giving my leg a push. If I didn't have jeans on, I'd have sworn his touch burned my skin.

A nervous chuckle slipped from my lips. "You got me on that one. I was thinking about Emily and the meeting you had with her before we left. You seemed rather upset afterwards."

He gripped the steering wheel harder. "She wanted money."

It felt like someone sat on my chest. "What? Money? Why?"

"She didn't believe my reasons for going out of town, and she wanted to make sure I would be back. I guess giving her ten thousand dollars would make her feel better."

Anger raced through my veins. "She asked you for ten thousand dollars? I hope you told her no."

He laughed. "Fuck yes I told her no. The funny thing was, it was almost as if she threw it out there to see if I'd bite or not. I don't think that was her original plan when she asked me to meet her."

"To ask you for money?"

Brett shook his head. "Yeah. It almost seemed like she came up with it off the top of her head. She seemed nervous. Really nervous. She kept looking out the window and acted like she wanted to tell me something. It was weird."

Pinching my brows, I chewed on my lip. "This whole thing feels so wrong."

"It is wrong, because she's wrong. That baby is not mine. There is no way it could be."

I prayed he was right.

Clearing my throat, I decided now was the time to keep hitting him with stuff. He seemed pretty chatty right now.

"May I ask you something, Brett?"

He chuckled. "It depends. Are we on the record or off?"

I couldn't blame him for asking. I'd ask to if I were him. "Off. Let's make this a rule. Anything said in the car is off the record."

"I like that rule. Does that mean I can pull over have my wicked way with you? I've always wanted to fuck in the Hell Cat."

My heart raced and I was more excited than I should be knowing he'd never had sex in his car. I was two seconds away from saying yes, when he continued talking. "I'm kidding. I made a promise to you, Bree, and I won't break it."

Shoot me. Someone just shoot me right now because I want this man. Every time I thought of Brett's kiss last night my body caught fire. This man knew how to drive me wild.

I turned and looked out the window again. *Did I really want to be a reporter for ESPN?*

With a frustrated sigh, I pushed the silly thoughts away. Brett and I could be friends, but that was as far as it could go. If Joe ever found out something sexual happened between us, he would surely use it against me. That I had no doubt about. I was positive he was banking on something happening. I wouldn't give him the satisfaction.

"What else did you want to ask me?"

His voice drew me from my thoughts. "Earlier, in the elevator. What did you mean when you said you never slept with Ryan's wife?"

The air in the car instantly changed and I regretted the question almost as soon as I asked it. Especially when Brett pulled over on the side of the road and got out of the car.

Watching him round the car, I whispered, "Oh shit." I watched while he walked away from the car and into the thick brush.

"Oh shit. This can't be good," I whispered.

Chapter Fifteen

Brett

I HEARD THE car door slam behind me and knew Aubrey was following me. Knowing she would walk right up on me, I turned my body, giving her a clear view.

"Brett! Brett, wait I wasn't—"

She came to an abrupt halt. "Oh my god! Your dick is out!"

Glancing down, I nodded. "Yep. That's what usually happens when you take a piss."

It was then she crossed her legs and jumped all around. After I finished pissing, I zipped up my pants and walked over to her. "What in the hell is wrong with you?"

"Pee. Oh my gosh, I have to pee so bad!"

With a laugh, I shook my head. "Then pee."

She pressed her lips together and moaned. "Oh! I can't. I have to go so badly, I'm going to pee my pants!"

"It hit you that fast?"

She nodded.

"That bad?"

Another nod.

"Oh god! Unbutton my jeans! Quick!"

I took a step back. "Me? Why do I have to unbutton your jeans? You do it!"

"No! If I make the motion like I'm doing it, I'll pee. I know my body!"

She had her legs crossed and I swore she looked like she was holding her breath.

I had half a mind to let her piss her pants for saying something to Ryan about me.

With a frustrated grunt, I unbuttoned her jeans and unzipped her pants. My body trembled when I saw the lace of her panties. What I wouldn't do to rip her jeans off and fuck the hell out of her.

"Okay, I've got this!"

I took a step back and was about to head back to the car when she quickly dropped both her jeans and panties and squatted.

"Sweet baby Jesus! Relief!"

Standing there stunned, I watched her while she took a piss in the woods. Any other girl I'd have been grossed out, but with Aubrey, I was worried about the poison ivy her ass was about to touch.

"Lord, that feels good," she mumbled. Totally oblivious to both me and the ivy. "I should have gone at the gas station."

"Um … Aubrey?"

She waved me off. "Turn around, Owens! Would it be too much to give me some privacy?"

"Hey, you pulled your pants down in front of me, remember?"

Finally, she finished peeing.

"Watch out for the poison ivy."

She jumped up. "What? Where?"

I had to catch her before her feet got all tangled up and she landed on the ground.

"Whoa! I got you," I said as my hands touched her soft skin. Pulling her up against me, I realized she was pretty much naked from the waist down.

Her mouth parted to say something, but quickly snapped back shut. My hand shook as I fought to keep it from slipping between her legs. I'd never in my life wanted to touch someone as bad I wanted to touch her. But I already decided if anything was going to happen between us, she needed to make the move first.

Letting go of her, I turned and called out, "I'll wait in the car."

"Wait!" Aubrey called out. "Did I touch the poison ivy? I feel itchy!"

Rolling my eyes, I sighed. "You didn't touch it."

She came running up next to me flailing her arms all over herself. "I've never had poison ivy! What if it's on my ass?"

Well, if I had to get her to forget about the question she asked me a few minutes ago, this would do the trick.

"It will itch."

She rubbed her ass as I walked up and opened the car door for her to get in. Aubrey stopped and stared up into my eyes. "Brett, what if I … my ass … I can't meet your parents' with an itchy ass!" I loved that she was worried about her impression on my parents. They would love her, itching ass or not.

Narrowing my brows, I tilted my head and took in those beautiful brown eyes. "I can honestly say I never thought I'd hear a woman say those words to me."

With a frustrated moan, Aubrey pushed me out of the way and got into the car, slamming the door in the process.

I couldn't help but laugh as she rubbed her ass around on the seat.

Aubrey had squirmed around in her seat for almost an hour before she decided she didn't have poison ivy after all. I even offered to pull over and inspect her ass, to which she politely declined.

She had dozed off about thirty minutes ago and I hated waking her up, but I couldn't very well leave her in the car.

Reaching over, I touched her leg lightly. "Bree? Hey, we're here."

Mumbling something, she turned her head my way and opened her eyes. "Your parents'?"

With a grin, I replied, "Nope. Dave Richardson's house."

Frowning, she questioned, "Who is that?"

"The kid who I'm getting to sign the letter of intent to play with the University of Austin next year."

The next thing I knew, Aubrey flew up, had the mirror down and was fixing her hair and make-up. "Why didn't you wake me up before we got here?" she asked with a sharp voice.

Hiding my smile, I shrugged. "You didn't tell me to."

"I didn't know we were stopping here first!"

"Did I not tell you, princess?"

Her mouth parted open before she shut it and snarled her lip at me. "You anger me so much."

"Then my work here is done." With a wink, I opened the door and got out of my car. Reaching into the back seat, I grabbed the folder and headed to the front door with Aubrey hot on my heels.

"Can I put this in the article?"

"If his parents are okay with it, I don't care."

With a fist pump, she whispered, "Yes!"

Not long after we arrived, Dave was signing his letter of intent and Aubrey was taking pictures. She had to run back out to the car to grab her camera.

"Thank you so much Mr. and Mrs. Richardson for letting me capture this moment not only for you, but for the article."

Smiling, Mrs. Richardson said, "Thank you for offering to send the pictures. That's very sweet of you."

"Well, I'm sure his high school will have another mockup of the signing, but since this is the official one I'm sure you would like that memory captured."

I wasn't surprised everyone feel immediately in love with Aubrey. Dave's parents, his grandparents, and most of all, his seven-year-old sister. Aubrey had made sure to pay special attention to little Rose as she watched her big brother get all the attention.

Slipping into the car, I looked at Aubrey. "Have you always had such a knack with people?"

She shrugged. "I like seeing people happy. You could tell his parents are so proud and wanted this opportunity for him. It was easy talking to them about it."

I started the car and lifted my hand in a wave to Dave as he watched us pull off and drive down their long driveway. "He will for sure have opportunities. Every college recruiter under the sun was after this kid."

"How did you get him? What did you say to him on that walk?" she inquired.

Dave and I had gone for a walk alone together shortly after we arrived. He was still on the fence about what college he wanted, until I was done talking to him.

"I told him my story. How I grew up here in this same town, what I had wanted in life, what the University of Austin could do for him. Straight up, no promises. Just a chance to play ball for a top-rated team."

The heat from her stare was almost more than I could stand. I glanced over quickly to see her smiling at me.

"What?" I asked.

"Nothing," she murmured as she turned and looked out the window. "How much longer to your parents'?"

"A little over an hour. I called them to let them know we would be there soon."

"You're sure they won't mind me being with you?"

Letting out a laugh, I shook my head. "Are you kidding? My mother is giddy as hell at the idea I'm bringing a girl home. Never mind the fact I've tried explaining to her why you're with me."

"And that is?"

Turning to her, I answered her. "Business. You're interviewing me and you work for ESPN."

Her face dropped and she quickly looked away. I wasn't sure if she meant to speak out loud because I barely heard her next words.

"Yep. Business."

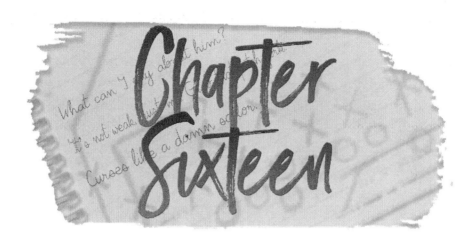

Chapter Sixteen

What can I say about him?
It's not weak, but —
Curses like a damn sailor.

Aubrey

WHEN BRETT ANNOUNCED we were at his parents' place, I tried to push away the nerves. Of course, that was damn near five minutes ago.

"Holy hell, how long is this driveway?"

"Well, twenty-five sections is a lot of land," Brett replied.

Finally, there was a house I could barely see through the trees. I could tell we were getting closer as more and more oak trees lined the gravel driveway.

The large white house came into view as Brett turned slightly right, following a circular driveway.

"Oh. My. Lord."

The two-story house was breathtaking. *Wait. Is that a third floor?*

Brett pulled up as I continued to stare at the house. The porch appeared to wrap completely around the large home.

"You grew up here?" I gasped.

"Yep," was his only response.

"Just you and your folks?"

With a slight laugh, he replied, "Just us three. And Julia."

"Who's that?"

"Technically, she was the nanny, but she was more part of the family than anything."

I slowly shook my head as I peered back at the house. "I'd never leave if this was my home."

"I would imagine with two lawyers for parents you grew up in a nice home."

With a nod, I glanced back to the house. "I did. It was modest, my parents believed in keeping things simple. But this is beyond amazing. I could sit on this front porch and never leave and be perfectly happy."

Peeking back to Brett, he was staring at me with a strange look on his face. Almost like he was in shock I would say such a thing. Or maybe he was thinking the same exact thing I was.

He smiled and my heart skipped a beat. "Yeah, me too."

And like that, he was out of the car and walking around to my side. I could get used to Brett's chivalry. The man may have a dirty-talking mouth, but my-oh-my, his southern charm and manners were out of this world.

Opening the door, he reached for my hand. "Don't get overwhelmed with my mother."

With a nervous chuckle, I replied, "Okay."

"And don't believe anything my parents say."

Looking into his blues eyes, I was taken by how full of life they were. Brett was happy to be home. He may have acted like he wasn't, but I could tell from the way his eyes sparkled and came to life, he was thrilled to be here.

"Brett Joseph Owens!"

Glancing over Brett's shoulder, I saw a woman with light brown hair coming our way.

With a chuckle, Brett leaned in closer and whispered in my ear, "It took everything I had to keep my hands off you, Bree. How easy it would have been to make you come all over my leather seats."

The sharp intake of air was the clear indication of how his words affected me. I was momentarily stunned as he turned around and walked to his mother, wrapping her up in his arms and spinning her around.

Between my legs pulsed as his words replayed in my mind. I needed to get my thoughts together and calm my libido down before I made a fool out of myself. Or worse yet, let him know he rocked my world just now.

I shot daggers at him as he kissed his mother on the cheek. My heart quickly melted though. It was so sweet to see how much he loved her.

Damn you, Brett Owens.

Before I had a chance to even move, his mother was in my face. "Mom, this is Aubrey Cain, the reporter from ESPN I told you about."

My hand reached out to shake hers, but I was soon wrapped up in her arms. "Lord almighty, the boy has never brought a girl home. Not even ..."

Brett cleared his throat and his mother instantly stopped talking.

Not even who? Who was she going to say?

Pushing me back to arm's length, she quickly scanned me over. It gave me a moment to take her in as well. She didn't look a day over forty. Her light brown hair was pulled half up, with the other half falling to below her shoulders. I could see where Brett got his good looks from. His mother looked like she was a model she was so gorgeous.

I finally snapped out of my daze and spoke. "Oh, Brett and I are friends. I mean, business friends. And all of that. Nothing more." The nervous laugh that escaped my lips were betraying the words I had just spoken. Little did she know her son turned me on every moment I was near him. How his dirty talking mouth was something I longed to hear every day. No one was more surprised by that than me.

My face blushed at the memory of what he had said to me only a few moments ago.

She lifted a brow. "Uh huh. Well, welcome to our home."

With a smile, I looked into her sky blue eyes. "Thank you for having me, Mrs. Owens."

Her hand came up and rested on the side of my face. "There will be none of that here. Call me Birdy."

There had to be a story behind that name. I made a mental note to ask Brett about it and to question him again about his comment about Ryan and a wife and the girl he never brought home.

"Birdy it is," I replied as I glanced up. My eyes about popped out of my head at the sight before me.

Brett's mom bumped me on the shoulder and chuckled. "Now you see where my son gets his good looks."

All I could do was nod. The older version of Brett stood before me with a huge grin on his face while he talked to his son. You could tell he wasn't the type of man who ordered other people to work while he stood by and watched. He was the type of man who worked right alongside of them. His dark tan and built body was evidence of that.

The two men looked almost identical. If they hadn't been separated by age, you'd think they were twins. When Brett's dad turned to look at me, I was stunned by how blue his eyes were.

Birdy laughed. "The man has been known to sweep a few girls off their feet."

Throwing his head back with a roar of laughter, he walked up to Birdy and picked her up, kissing her smack dab on the lips. "Ah, but you're the one who fell for my sweet-talking ways."

Birdy slapped her husband on his broad muscular chest. "Stop it, you big goofball. Say hello to Brett's *friend*, Aubrey."

The way she stressed friend had me instantly wanting to explain our relationship all over again.

Brett wasn't helping any when he walked up to me and pressed his lips to my ear. "You keep looking at my dad like that and I'm going to get jealous."

Snapping my head over to him, I shot him a dirty look. The way he was fervently staring at me had me struggling to swallow. Not taking his gaze off of me, Brett spoke. "Dad, this is Aubrey." There was something different in his voice. For one brief moment I wished he was introducing me as someone more than just the reporter writing about him for ESPN.

I had to force myself to look away from his glowing blue eyes. With a smile, I extended my hand. "Mr. Owens, such a pleasure to meet you."

The man had a smile like his son. "Call me Joseph, and the pleasure is ours. As long as you write good things about my boy here and you tell me you can ride a horse, you and I will get along great."

With a chuckle, I nodded my head and looked between the two men. "Well, he hasn't given me anything bad to write about so far."

Brett seemed so different here. He was relaxed like I'd never seen him before. Lifting his brow in question, he asked. "And riding?"

Turning back to Joseph, I grinned. "My father had all his girls in riding classes by the age of six."

He nodded and wrapped his arm around Birdy's waist. "Good. But none of that English riding bullshit allowed here on my ranch."

Thank goodness I took western and English riding. "Well, actually I'm versed in both."

Brett laughed. "We'll see."

Placing my hands on my hips, I asked, "Is that a challenge?"

His eyes turned dark. "Do you want it to be?"

I knew exactly how I was going to get my answer about that statement from Brett. "Yes. I do."

Joseph let out a roar of laughter. "I'll have some horses saddled up. Why don't you two go get settled into your rooms?"

Brett grabbed our bags and motioned for me to follow his parents up the stairs. The moment I stepped into the house I fell in love.

"Oh my word," I whispered. The entry was formal, yet comfortable. Like you could imagine kids running around the circular table that was placed in the center of the foyer. To the right off the entry was the formal living room.

"Brett, you take Aubrey's stuff up to her room, and I'll give her a quick tour so she feels at home," Birdy instructed.

Kissing his mother on the cheek, he replied, "Sounds good." And like that, he bounded up the grand staircase carrying my two bags and his two bags like it was nothing. I watched him until he was out of sight. When I finally turned back, Birdy was smiling at me like she knew something I didn't.

"Shall we?" she asked.

"Yes! Your home is so beautiful," I gasped as we entered the formal living room. The furniture was very traditional, yet I caught a glimpse of some antique pieces as well. It was so warm and welcoming. The light yellow walls were calming. I could imagine a fire going in the fireplace with me snuggled up reading a book or working.

"The house has seven fireplaces," Birdy stated walking through the living room.

My mouth dropped. "Wow," was all I could get out.

We made our way into the kitchen, passing the butler's pantry on our way. The dark mahogany cabinets were beautiful. I was instantly transported to my childhood. The kitchen was large, yet so simple. It reminded me of my parents' kitchen.

My body shivered as I ran my fingers along the cold granite. "I love this kitchen!"

Birdy beamed with pride. "Do you like to cook?"

My eyes wandered everywhere. "I do. My sisters and I used to spend Sundays with my mother and grandmother baking up a storm. My grandmother was an amazing cook. When my mother turned to politics, there never seemed to be time to do it. Then my grandmother passed away." My eyes filled with tears. I hadn't realized how much I missed those moments.

Birdy walked up and took my hands in hers. Giving them a squeeze, she nodded her head. "Let's keep moving along."

Forcing a grin, I softly spoke, "I'm so sorry. I'm not normally so emotional like that." With a short laugh, I shook my head. "I don't know what came over me."

"I do. You were hit with a memory and that caused you to miss your family. I'd imagine in your job you have to travel a lot like Brett does."

My chest constricted. Traveling before never bothered me the least bit. "Well, truth be told, I have grown to hate the traveling. But I love my job."

Wrapping her arm around mine, we continued on. The breakfast room had an incredible view of a lake and the Davis Mountains that were behind the house.

"How pretty," I said as I peered out the window.

We then made our way into the formal dining room that housed one of the seven fireplaces. The family room was right off the kitchen and you could tell this was where they spent much of their time. I walked along the fireplace and smiled at the pictures of Brett. From the time he was a baby up until what looked like last Christmas, maybe.

"He's handsome, isn't he?"

My fingers moved lazily over one of the pictures of Brett. He was standing on the sidelines of a football field with a serious look on his face as he watched a play.

"That was his first pro game. A reporter shot that photo and sent it to me."

Spinning around, I looked at Birdy. "Has football always been something he loved?"

With a huge grin, she nodded. "Yes. Since he was probably four, the boy has done nothing but eat, sleep, drink, and live for football."

I chortled and followed her out of the room. Birdy showed me a library that I already knew I'd be in most of the time I was there. If not reading, working. Then it was on to Joseph's office, which was equally amazing.

"I'll let Brett show you the media room and the theater room."

The idea of Brett showing me the theater room had my mind venturing totally where it shouldn't. I said a quick prayer I hadn't made a mistake by joining him here. There was something about being in his family home, meeting his parents, and seeing a part of his life that he kept so private. I wasn't sure how much longer I could deny my feelings.

"Mom? Bree?"

The left side of Birdy's mouth rose in a grin. "You ready to see the ranch?"

Excitement bubbled up in my chest. "Yes!"

Brett walked in and I had to grab onto a chair.

Holy mother of God.

My blood rushed through my veins, leaving me feeling weak.

Birdy walked up to Brett. "Don't you fall right back into the role of cowboy so well?"

Brett tipped his cowboy hat and winked at his mother while my eyes slowly moved to see him dressed in tight jeans and cowboy boots.

Stay. Strong. Aubrey. You do not have a thing for cowboys.

Lies. I did have a thing for cowboys. And football coaches, dressed like cowboys.

I am so screwed.

Chapter Seventeen

Brett

AUBREY LOOKED AS if she was about to pass out when I walked into the room.

"Bree, you okay?"

She widened her eyes and shook her head. "Um." Her hand came up to her neck and she looked away. "I think I'm thirsty. I just got really thirsty."

My mother chuckled. "Brett, take Aubrey to her room so she can freshen up." She turned to look at her. "And if you don't want to go riding now, you don't have to."

Aubrey shook her head. "No, honestly, I'm fine."

I motioned for her to follow me. When she passed my mother, she stopped. "Thank you for the tour, Birdy. You really do have an amazing home."

Mom smiled and kissed Aubrey on the cheek. "You make yourself at home while you're here, you understand?"

"Yes ma'am," she replied before turning and walking along side of me.

We climbed the back stairs in silence before Aubrey stopped. "Wait. There are back stairs?"

With a chuckle, I kept walking. "Yep. Just explore the house and you'll find your way around quickly. Mom has you in the room next to mine in case you need anything."

She let out a nervous chuckle at the top of the stairs and then huffed. "What could I possibly need?"

I moved quickly and pinned her against the wall. I loved seeing her reaction when I was this near to her. Her breathing increased and her eyes danced with anticipation.

"My mouth on yours."

She rolled her eyes and looked down the hall. "You're not going to do this to me, Brett. That little stunt you pulled outside when your mom showed up didn't work."

Her head turned and her gaze met mine. Slowly smiling, I leaned in closer. "Tell me you don't want my mouth on yours."

Quickly replying with, "I don't," her brows shot up in defiance.

Moving in closer, my gaze fell to her lips. When her tongue glided quickly over them, I felt my cock jump. "What about my mouth buried between your legs."

Her mouth parted and I could see her pulse racing on the side of her neck.

"You talking dirty to me does nothing to me. You're wasting your time," she whispered in a faint voice.

Leaning in more, I ran my mouth lightly along her jaw and whispered into her ear, "What a shame. I really enjoy telling you how much you turn me on. And how amazing it would feel with your pussy squeezing my cock as you call out my name."

Her hands landed on my chest. The feel of her touch sent a wave of heat through my body. With a hard push, she glared at me as I took a few steps back.

"And how many girls have you said that to, Romeo?"

Laughing, I had to hand it to her. She was hard to crack. I grabbed her hand and hauled her to her room. Opening the door, I walked in. "My room is out your door and to the right. Change into some jeans and your boots and meet us back in the kitchen."

"Don't boss me around, Brett. I'm not some woman you picked up in a bar and brought home to fuck," she spat out. I could see the frustration laced in her eyes. She wanted me as much as I wanted her.

My grin faded as I took her in. I'd never want her to think I thought of her that way. My heart dropped and I slowly shook my head as I took a few steps back. "No. You must certainly are not. You're so much more."

She froze and gave me a befuddled look.

Spinning around, I headed out of her room. I needed to stop this game I was playing. I wasn't interested in starting a relationship. And for sure not one with someone who would never be around. I needed to ignore the way Aubrey made me feel.

This was business and nothing more.

Feeling the tightness around my heart grow, I let out a laugh. I was totally fooling myself. If only I didn't long for something more with Aubrey.

We'd been riding for over an hour, and I'd managed to keep my thoughts occupied on the ranch. Dad filled me in on some things that needed to be done, but he was having Mac, the foreman, take care of it. Mac had worked for my father since high school. We had been good friends and I never really understood why he choose to stay behind and live this life when he could have gone and played college football, and probably pro football.

The guilt of not being here for my father quickly overtook me. "I can do it, Dad. I mean, if I'm going to be here, I might as well work."

He grinned. "Well, you know I'll never turn down work. I'm just happy to have you here. It's rare to have you back here in the spring. What made you come for a visit now anyway?"

Glancing over his shoulder, I saw Aubrey peeking at me.

"I wanted to get the other side of Brett for the article. You know, make him feel more real to the readers."

Turning away, I focused straight ahead of me.

"So, Joseph, tell me about your ranch," Aubrey probed.

Oh, my father would love this.

"Well, what do you want to know, pretty lady?"

Aubrey chuckled. "What do you do here? Cattle? Grains? Horses?"

My father launched into the history of how the ranch started with his grandfather, my great-grandfather. It started with horses.

"My granddaddy bred the best roping horses in the country."

"Can you rope, Brett?" Aubrey asked.

My father answered before I could. "Hell yes, the boy can rope. He was damn good at it too. Has buckles in his room from all the rodeos he won."

"Ah, learned something new," Aubrey purred as I shot her a warning look. "What's wrong, Owens? Don't want me digging to deep? I'd love to see all of your buckles and trophies."

My father let out a whistle. "Lordy, there are a lot of them. Birdy had to box some up and put them in the attic."

Clearing my throat to mask the frustration of my father talking about my past, I brought the conversation full circle. "It's a cattle ranch mostly, but we produce wheat, oats, milo, and hay grazer."

Aubrey lifted a brow at me. "Wow that's kind of cool. What kind of cows?"

"We have about thirty percent, Angus/Hereford and Brangus/Hereford cross and seventy percent Hereford. They are mostly bred with Hereford, Angus, and Charolais bulls."

The grin that spread across her face before she turned to my mother to speak with her, caused my heart to drop. I seriously doubted she really wanted to know all of this, but I liked it more than I wanted to admit that she was showing an interest. Even if it was only for the damn article.

"So, are you ready for that challenge?" Aubrey asked as she brought her horse up alongside me.

"What did you have in mind?"

"Barrel racing. If I can do it faster and clean, you have to answer any question I ask. *Any* question. Nothing is off limits."

I knew what she was getting at. But there was no way in hell she could beat me. Please. The thought alone made me want to laugh. I'd practically been born on a horse.

"Bree, I grew up on a damn ranch. Just because you can ride a horse doesn't mean you can barrel race."

She shrugged. "It doesn't look that hard on TV. Are you afraid to do a sport dominated by women?"

For a quick moment, she had me riled up, but I wasn't going to let her see it. If this meant she would stop trying to figure out my slip up, I'd do it.

"Fine. We happen to have some set up for a class my mom teaches."

With a wide grin, she sat up straighter. "Then let's go for it."

"Mom, Dad, Aubrey seems to think she can barrel race."

My mother's face fell. "Oh, sweetheart, I don't want you getting hurt."

"Trust me, Birdy. I've got this."

Her confidence was sexy as hell, but if she got hurt, I'd never forgive myself.

Twenty minutes later, Dad had his stopwatch out and timed me as I raced around the barrels. I'd only done this a few times at the request of my mother. Pressing into Whiz, a six-year-old blue roan gelding, as hard as I could, we came tearing back across the line.

I shouted out. "Hell yes!" My parents cheered me on as Aubrey looked up at me and laughed.

"Impressive, cowboy. For a guy."

With a wink, I replied, "Yeah well, what can I say? I know how to ride."

Her eyes turned dark. "I bet you do. But so do I," she purred.

Mac walked up with Spike, my paint horse from high school and one of the best cutting horses we had. He happened to also be the horse my mother gave lessons on.

"Mac, what are you doing with Spike?" I questioned.

He tried not to smile, but failed miserably. "Ms. Cain wanted to see the best horse we had for the job. I had to show her Spike. She asked your daddy if she could ride him."

My head snapped up as I glared at my father. "Traitor!" I yelled out before looking back at Mac. "Well, he's my horse. Maybe Ms. Cain should have asked me."

Focusing back on Aubrey, I stated, "You can be on the best damn horse we have, but unless you know what you're doing, you won't come close to my time."

Without a word, Aubrey climbed on top of Spike. Fuck if she didn't look damn good on top of him. Lucky horse. I could tell Spike was smitten with her right away, that bastard. Aubrey rode around the arena a few times and kept leaning over and saying something to my horse.

"What are you doing?" I called out.

"Getting to know him and how he feels."

With a frustrated groan, I replied, "He feels like you shouldn't be on my damn horse!"

They rode by me and if I hadn't known better, I would say my own horse just snickered at me.

"Just fucking ride already, Aubrey."

"Brett Joseph Owens!" my mother gasped. "Do not talk to a lady that way."

"Sorry, Mom." She motioned with a look for me to apologize to Aubrey.

Forcing the words out, I shouted, "Sorry, Aubrey!"

She rode up to me and stopped on a dime. "What was that, Brett? I didn't seem to hear you."

Leaning closer, I shot her a look. "Just ride the goddamn horse, Aubrey."

Her head pulled back in surprise. "Why, Brett. You're not starting to worry, are you?"

It was in that moment I realized I had been played by her. She knew how to barrel ride. With the way she was moving on my horse, she knew exactly what she was doing.

"You lied," I gasped with my eyes widened in surprise.

"I withheld a part of the truth. Kind of like what you've been doing."

My hands balled up in fists, I glowered at her. "I haven't withheld shit from you, and you know it."

With a wink, she called over her shoulder, "Ready, Joseph?"

My father stood and held up his thumb. "Ready!" *Oh, he was enjoying this way too much.*

Before I knew it, Aubrey and Spike were racing to the first barrel. They cleared it perfectly. Then she cleared the second, then the third. The way she was racing back, I knew she beat my time.

My parents started jumping and shouting out Aubrey's time of thirteen-nine.

Stopping in front of me, she looked and winked before slowly walking out of the arena and to the stables.

Son. Of. A. Bitch.

Aubrey Cain just changed up how the game was played by taking a play right out of my own fucking book.

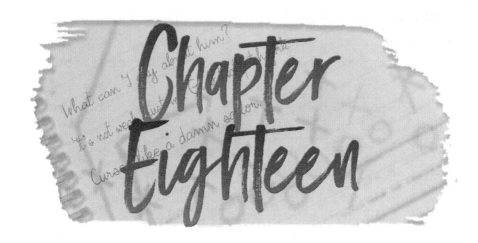

Chapter Eighteen

Aubrey

SITTING ON THE window seat in the library, I stared out at the blue sky. It reminded me of Brett's eyes. The same eyes that invaded my dreams over and over last night.

"Am I interrupting?"

His voice sent a shiver down my back.

Facing him, I smiled. "No. I was going to do some work, but this view has captivated me."

Brett walked up and stood next to me, taking in the scene outside. "I have to hand it to my parents, they picked a good spot to build a house."

I giggled. "Yes they did. What's up?"

He handed me his phone and sat next to me. Glancing at it, I saw a text message.

Emily: So you brought the reporter with you? You're having a child with me and you're sleeping with another woman? What would ESPN think about this?

My head snapped up. "Is she insane? Does she think she owns you? And is that a threat?"

Scrubbing his hands over his face, he shook his head. "She seems to like the threats lately. Pat hasn't found anything else about her transcripts, but he did find out from the professor she has only been to a few classes."

I raised an eyebrow. "You do realize she probably isn't even a student at the university. This is all a game."

"Pat agrees. And now she has dragged you into it. I'm not even sure how she found out about you. All I know is, until I can prove her to be a liar, I need to keep her happy or she'll go running her mouth."

Birdy walked into the library. "Who do you need to keep happy? Is there a problem?"

Brett jumped up. "It's nothing, Mom."

"That didn't just sound like nothing. Brett, is there something you're not telling us?"

My stomach felt sick for Brett and I knew this was tearing him apart.

"It's nothing to worry yourself with, Birdy. Just a mix up that's all."

Brett turned to me, a look of anger on his face. "I've got this, Aubrey. I don't need you coming to my defense."

It felt as if he had slapped me in the face. He wasn't the only one, now, who risked losing something. Standing, I started to head out of the room when he took me by the arm.

"Wait. Please don't leave." Looking over to his mother, he asked, "Mom, can I have a few minutes with Aubrey? Then I need to talk to you and Dad, alone."

Birdy slowly nodded. Confusion moved over her face as she looked between the two of us. "We'll be in your father's office. You can speak with us in there."

He nodded and slowly let out a frustrated sigh. Brett's gaze met mine. "I'm sorry I snapped at you. The idea of telling my parents about Emily is nerve racking."

"It's okay. I shouldn't have said anything. It's none of my business."

"I'd never purposely hurt you, I hope you know that."

I couldn't help the small gasp of air I inhaled quickly. His voice was filled with so much compassion it made my knees weak. He truly cared about my feelings and that was not something I was used to. Lifting his hand to my face, I leaned into it. Brett looked at me in a way I'd never had a man look at me before. My heart raced in my chest. Why, of all times, does the man of my dreams have to turn out to be Brett? Fate was cruel.

"Bree," he whispered. The sound of his voice covered my body like silk. How could he make me melt with a simple touch and one whispered word?

His eyes fell to my lips and I prayed like hell he would kiss me. It was so wrong, wanting him the way I did. I couldn't help myself when it came to Brett. Would it really be so bad if we had a relationship? Other ESPN reporters dated coaches, players, managers. It happened all the time.

Gently pressing his lips to mine, I wrapped my arms around his neck. We quickly got lost in the kiss. Each kiss from Brett had been powerful and full of passion. This one was so completely different. It was slow, and what flowed between our two bodies was amazing. Whatever this feeling was, I knew it was going to change everything from this point on.

Brett gently placed his hands on my hips and pulled my body flush against his. I could feel his hard-on pressed against my body as my pulse raced even faster. There was nothing rushed or frantic about this exchange between us. It was gentle, beautiful, heart stopping.

When he broke the kiss, he leaned his forehead against mine. "Why didn't we meet sooner, Bree?"

I was so taken aback by his comment, all I could do was close my eyes and whisper the only word my lips would produce. "Brett."

He quickly dropped his hands and stepped away from me. His stare met mine and I saw nothing but confusion and fear. I'd never imagined in my life I'd see that from Brett Owens.

Walking past me, he left the library without saying another word.

Two days had passed since the kiss. Each night I laid in bed and thought about it and his whispered question to me. It haunted my thoughts.

Was Brett developing feelings for me? Was that why the last two days he had done everything he could to stay away from me?

I went over and over in my head if a relationship between us could work. Michelle made it work, but her boyfriend was a doctor who never traveled. Half the year Brett and I would be in different places. He lived in Texas. I lived in Connecticut.

Sighing, I dropped my head back against the chair. Then there was the question of could Brett even be in a committed relationship. Talking to my sister, Christine, last night brought out a whole new problem for me.

Kids.

When she told me she was pregnant with her second baby, I was so thrilled for her, yet sadness crept over me like a thief in the night.

My email dinged on my computer. Opening it up, I immediately saw his name.

Ryan Dryer.

Ugh.

Clicking on the message, it opened and I began reading.

My Dearest Aubrey,

I hope this email finds you well. It's been a few days since we've talked and I'd like to extend an invitation to lunch tomorrow. I know an amazing Thai restaurant near the capitol. I'll have my car pick you up at eleven.

My best,

Ryan

Seriously? He's going to assume I'm going to lunch with him? The more I interacted with this guy, the less I liked him.

Hitting reply, I typed out my reply as I mumbled, "I don't even like Thai food!"

"Who wants Thai food?"

My eyes lifted over my lap top and I couldn't help the smile that spread over my face. The sight of Brett in jeans, boots, and a cowboy hat did funny things to me.

"No one important."

He grinned and removed his hat, causing me to attempt to find the motion to breathe. His sweat damped hair looked sexy as hell. I imagined him over me, riding me fast and hard, his cock moving in and out of my body bringing me to one orgasm after another. Our bodies covered in a sheen of sweat.

"Bree? Are you okay? Your face is turning red."

My hands slapped against my warmed cheeks. *Where in the hell did that come from?*

"I'm ah … totally fine. Got a lot done today."

He gave me a quick head pop. "That's good."

Forcing myself to act normally, I questioned him. "Where have you been, stranger?" My voice cracked and I tried like hell to push my naughty thoughts away.

The way his eyes lit up told me how much Brett had missed his family home. "Getting back to doing what I love. Helping my father run the ranch."

I loved how relaxed he had been since coming here. Brett was a whole different person. Anyone could see how much he loved this place. That was another question I had for him. What made him leave?

Wiggling his eyebrows, he asked, "Wanna go somewhere with me?"

The grin that moved across his face had me feeling giddy inside. *Good lord, girl. You're not in high school.*

At some point, I was going to have to be honest with myself and Brett. I wasn't sure I wanted to hide the way I felt about him any longer.

I glanced at the computer screen. I had started writing the article and had been on a roll, but my aching neck muscles were telling me it was time to take a break.

"Where we going?"

"Town."

Chewing on my lip, I turned back to my laptop, hit save, and shut it. "I'd love to go. I want to see where you grew up."

Brett shook his head and chuckled. "It's not much to see, but if you want to see it, we can."

"Even your high school? And were you lost your virginity for the first time?"

His head jerked back in shock. "Surely you're not putting that shit in the article?"

Walking up to him, I placed my hands on his chest and grinned. The energy rippled between us and I was positive he felt it too. "Nope, that one is off the record and only because I'm guessing it was somewhere insane."

The left side of his mouth rose into a sexy smirk. "You wanting to top it, sweetheart?"

A tinge of jealousy raced through my body at the thought of another woman with Brett. Sharing something so intimate. It was quickly replaced with butterflies in my stomach as his pet name whirled around in my head.

Sweetheart. Oh, to hear that whispered in my ear as he made love to me. If he even made love. He probably only fucked.

Stop. This. Aubrey.

Deciding to have a bit of fun, I answered, "Maybe."

I quickly headed out of the library and raced up to my room to change, leaving Brett behind to think about my little flirtatious moment. It was obvious from how giddy I was I enjoyed flirting with him.

A cold front had moved through and the temperatures were in the mid-sixties. Jeans and a long sleeve T-shirt should work nicely, plus keep me covered from wandering hands.

"One can never be too safe," I said to myself as I grabbed my bag.

I bounded down the stairs and out front where a Ford F250 was parked. Brett and Mac stood next to the truck and were in a deep conversation. I'd never seen Brett so angry looking.

"Hey," I said as I made myself known. The two of them looked like they were about to go after each other. Glancing between the two of them, I looked into Brett's eyes. "Everything okay?"

He jaw was clenched. "Yeah, let's go." Opening the door for me, I went to get in when Mac reached for my hand and helped me in. I quickly turned to look at him to thank him, but Brett placed his hand on Mac's shoulder.

In almost a growl, Brett stared at Mac and said, "She's mine to help, not yours."

Well. *That* was interesting.

Chapter Nineteen

Brett

IT TOOK EVERYTHING out of me not to punch Mac in the face when he put his hand on Aubrey. I was already about to go off on him as it was. The idea of him running the ranch in Wyoming set me off. It was bad enough he was working his way in more and more with the daily running of this ranch, the last thing I wanted was him to be up there alone and taking over completely.

I'd looked up the logs that were kept and was surprised at some of the stuff that was happening on the ranch and intended on talking to my father about it this evening.

I grabbed his shoulder and slightly tugged him back. "She's mine to help, not yours."

Mac smiled. "Sure thing, buddy. We'll talk later."

Staring at him with a hard look, I mumbled, "You can count on it."

Turning, Mac walked toward the foreman's house.

"Um, what was that exchange all about?" Aubrey asked.

"Nothing I can't handle."

I shut her door and jogged around the truck. It had been a week since we'd arrived and we hadn't left the ranch once. Aubrey didn't seem to mind at all that we had hung around the ranch, as matter of fact; she melted right into place. It warmed my heart to see how much she loved it here.

"All right, let's go check out Marfa," I said as I shifted the truck in gear.

"Whose truck is this?"

"Mine," I replied.

I could feel her stare. "You keep your truck here at the ranch? Why?"

With a laugh, I shrugged. "What am I going to do with a truck in downtown Austin? I barely have space to park my car."

"That's true. I didn't think about that."

We drove down the long driveway in silence. The moment we pulled out onto the highway, she went for the attack.

"What did you mean when you said you didn't sleep with Ryan's wife?"

Fuck. All I wanted to do was enjoy one day. Just one fucking day.

"Do we have to talk about this now, Bree?"

She turned her body more to face me. "Yes. You promised and you've been avoiding me the last few days. I figure since I have you trapped in the truck, you have to answer me."

Glancing over to her, I asked, "Is that the only reason you came? To hammer me with questions?"

Her eyes brightened. "No. I really wanted to see where you grew up and went to school."

"And where I lost my virginity?"

She giggled. "Yes, that too."

With a quick look in her direction, I gave in. "What I'm about to tell you needs to stay off the record. Not one bit of it can be printed."

She nodded her head. "You have my word. And we're in a vehicle. Remember, off the record when we're in vehicles."

I grinned and nodded my head.

All right, I might as well get this over with. "I was married before."

The quick intake of air through her mouth caused me to look at her. Aubrey wore a stunned expression.

"Wh-what? I didn't see anything anywhere about you being married."

"The marriage was annulled."

"Oh," was all she said.

"I met her when I played college football and continued to date her after I got drafted."

"Wait, I don't ever remember seeing you with the same girl. No, I take that back. Your senior year there were pictures of you with the same girl. A blonde."

"Nicole."

Her name on my lips pissed me off. It had been years since I'd even spoken her name.

"She didn't think I should have gone into the NFL."

"Why?" Aubrey probed with a confused look on her face.

All those emotions I buried came rushing to the surface.

"Who the hell knows? Worried I was going to hook up with women I guess. I asked her to marry me, hoping that would show her I was committed to her only. It was stupid. I was young, thought it would help our relationship. It didn't help at all. It only made it worse. Once I got into the NFL I was being named most eligible bachelor and all that shit. I ignored it, but Nicole couldn't. I begged her to come on the road with me. I really thought if we spent more time together we could work on the marriage. I loved her, at least I thought I did. Told myself I did."

"Did you give her reason to doubt you?"

My eyes snapped over to her. "If there is one thing about me you should know, it's that I would never cheat. If I give my heart to someone, I give it to them one hundred percent."

"How many women have you given your heart to, Brett?"

"One. And it was the biggest mistake of my life."

"How can you say that? You must have loved Nicole to marry her."

Shaking my head, I blew out a tiresome sigh. "I loved her, don't get me wrong. But looking back, we got married for all the wrong reasons. I was never in love with her if that makes sense. Hell, I never even brought her home to see where I grew up. Mind you, she had no desire to see where I grew up. That should have been my first clue things wouldn't work out."

"She didn't want to see where you grew up? Did you want to show her that side of your life?" Aubrey asked.

"I don't know. Maybe deep inside I knew she wasn't the one."

"If she wasn't the one, why did you marry her?"

Laughing, I turned to her and winked. "That's the million-dollar question. Like I said, we got married for all the wrong reasons."

"What happened? Why did you get divorced?"

"Annulled. I had the marriage annulled."

"Okay, what made you do something so extreme?"

I inhaled a deep breath and held it for a few seconds before exhaling it. "When I got injured, things between us really changed. She kept asking to start a family and I wasn't ready. Something about it didn't feel right. Maybe it was because deep down inside, I knew the marriage wasn't really going to work for the long haul. There was always a part of her that resented the fact I was gone so much and she often told me. We fought a lot. I wasn't going to bring kids into a relationship like that."

Aubrey let out a gruff laugh. "Wait, she had to know what she was getting into. Especially if she dated you in college."

"I guess the money kept her somewhat happy." Thinking back on all of it, I felt myself getting angry. "Anyway, I was cleared to play again and was pretty jazzed about getting back onto the field. I had to wait one more game and then I was back at it. I asked the coach if I could fly home and be with Nicole for a long weekend. It meant I wouldn't be on the sideline of a game and I never missed a game, but if I wanted to make the marriage work, I thought a weekend alone together might do the trick. Especially if she knew I was missing a game. I decided to fly home and surprise her. I knew this was the last chance we had at attempting to make things work."

"Was she surprised?"

My stomach felt sick as the memory of that day came rushing back. "You could say. She was with my best friend who was fucking her in our bed."

Aubrey's hands covered her mouth. "What? Oh my God, Brett, that must have been terrible for you."

"Yeah it wasn't one of the finer moments of my life."

"Did you beat the hell out of your friend?"

I laughed and looked at her. "I hit him once, maybe twice. Nicole, of course, begged for forgiveness and said it was a weak moment and that it hadn't happened before. I believed her only because I knew she was most likely seduced by the bastard. I wore blinders when it came to our friendship. Only because he was like a brother. We grew up together. Played football together. I thought we had a bond."

"Why would your best friend seduce your wife, Brett? That's crazy!"

I was kind of surprised it hadn't hit Aubrey yet who the best friend was.

Turning to Aubrey, I replied, "Why don't you ask Ryan Dryer?"

Her mouth dropped open. "*Ryan* slept with Nicole?"

"Are you starting to get why I can't stand the motherfucker?"

Aubrey looked straight ahead as if trying to piece additional pieces of the puzzle together. "Oh my word. Why? Why would he do that to you?"

"Jealousy. Anger. He was still pissed I got drafted into the NFL and he didn't. With my whole football career, Ryan had always been just a few steps behind. It's the way it was. It was nothing I did. I was a stronger player. I was better at talking to girls, he wasn't. The night I met Nicole, we were both at a party. Ryan pointed her out, said she was cute. When we walked up to talk to her, he stood there like a lump on a log. I figured he wasn't really into her. She flirted with both of us. When he didn't bite, I did. The rest is history."

Aubrey sat there with a blank look on her face.

"So, Ryan basically went after your wife as a form of payback?"

With a slight nod, I replied, "Pretty much."

"But that can't be the reason you left the NFL."

"No, it wasn't. Once I was drafted, Ryan bought out one of the owners of the team and became part owner. I never really understood why he did it, but it soon became clear. He couldn't stand the thought of me succeeding at something and him not. So, with him being the owner of the team I played on, the last thing I was going to do was play for him. He knew it too. He agreed to pay out my contract if I agreed to not mention the affair. The only problem was he wouldn't release me to play for another team. I was stuck between a rock and a hard place. If I went public with the affair, I'd ruin Nicole's reputation. She was an elementary school teacher and that was the last thing she needed. Ryan knew that. She was as much a pawn in Ryan's deception as I was."

Aubrey's hand came up to her temples. "Wait. Why in the world would Ryan go through all that trouble?"

"Jealousy is a fucked-up thing, Bree. He knew I wouldn't play for him. He knew I wouldn't go public with the affair, and by him having the upper hand, he took away the one thing he wanted and I got."

"The NFL," she whispered.

"Yep."

We drove for a few minutes in silence.

"If Ryan was capable of going to such extremes to get you out of the NFL, do you think he would sit back quietly while you became one of the best college football coaches in the nation?"

I let out a laugh but then got where she was going with her statement. "Do you think he set up the whole thing with Emily?"

"Considering the trouble he went through to get you out of the NFL? Yes. I could totally see him setting up the whole thing with Emily."

I slammed on the brakes and pulled over to the side of the road. Getting out of the truck, I paced back and forth.

"Fucking hell. It's been right in front of me this whole damn time."

Aubrey grabbed my arm. "What has?"

"The benefit dinner that night I met Emily. Ryan was there and he was talking to her before she came up to me. I saw them standing in a corner and didn't think anything of it."

Her eyes grew wide. "Wait! The night I was out to dinner with him. He got up to go say hello to someone and left his phone. It rang and I saw the name. It said Emily Clarington."

"That's not Emily's last name, though."

It hit me as she grinned from ear to ear. "That's Emily's *real* last name, Brett. I need to call someone. Come on, let's get back into the truck."

I watched as Aubrey raced around the truck and jumped in. I followed and put my truck in drive and pulled out onto the highway.

"I have a signal! Thank you, God!" she called out.

She hit a few numbers and looked at me with a huge smile. "Michelle. Do you still have that private detective's number? Perfect. I need you to find out information on an Emily Clarington from Austin, Texas. Mid-twenties, I'm going to guess." I stole a peek at her as she gave the description of Emily to her friend Michelle. With a nod, she said, "Great. Tell him I'll make it worth his while if he gets me the information back as soon as possible. Okay. I might not have a signal so be sure to leave a message. Thanks, babe! Bye."

Hitting End on her phone, she punched me on the side of the arm. "We need to celebrate with music!" She reached over and started changing the channel on my satellite radio.

"Let's not jump ahead of ourselves, Bree."

It wasn't five seconds later and another eighties song was blasting.

"Oh, I love this song!"

"Who. Is. This?" I asked.

She looked at me with a gapped expression. "Brett Owens, do you know nothing about good music? This is Rick Astley!" She started belting out the song. I tried my best not to smile, but I soon found myself laughing as she jumped around and sang into a pretend microphone. I wonder if she knew she got half of the words wrong to the songs she sang. It didn't really matter, because every time she sang a wrong word I fell a little more for her.

As I drove into Marfa, I dared to let myself think of what life would be like with Aubrey Cain in it.

Chapter Twenty

Aubrey

BRETT LET ME listen to four songs from the eighties station before he took control and changed it. Soon we were both jamming out to Justin Timberlake's "Drink You Away." I knew there was another side to Brett Owens and it thrilled me more than I wanted to admit.

Once we pulled into Marfa, it felt as if I were on a tour. Brett showed me where he went to school, where they hung out on Friday nights after the football game, and promised to take me to see the famous Marfa lights.

"What exactly are the Marfa lights?" I inquired as he took my hand and helped me out of his truck.

When he slipped his arm around my waist, I tried not to think too much about it. We were comfortable with each other. That was normal when two people spent as much time together as we had. Besides, nothing else had happened between us other than the few kisses we shared.

The few mind-blowing, knock-me-out-of-my-socks kisses.

"Headlights from cars on the highway."

Hitting him on the stomach, we both chuckled. "Way to ruin it for me."

"Hey, they can be anything you want them to be. They're the magic lights of Marfa."

Adrenaline rushed through my veins filling me with hope. "Where are we going now?"

"My friend Chip owns a bar. I always stop in and see him when I'm in town."

Peeking up at him, I had to catch my breath. He looked so damn hot in that cowboy hat. I was positive my panties were soaking wet. I loved how he naturally fell into this role. It was him. Not that the Brett who I met in Austin wasn't him. That Brett was refined and focused. This Brett was relaxed. Carefree. Totally in the element that he loved and knew. I'd dare to say he loved this ranch more than football.

"Is there a place to two-step?"

Brett gazed at me and gave me sweet smile. "Chip's place. You like to two-step, sweetheart?"

Lord, please be with me because all my sense has been thrown out the door and I could give two shits that I was only here to write an article about this man. I wanted to know him for him. Not for what my boss wanted to read. "I love to two-step."

He tapped the tip of my nose with his finger. "I knew there was another reason I wanted to fuck you. Country girl at heart."

Shaking my head, I snarled my lip up at him. "You're an asshole."

Laughing, he led me up to the door of a country bar. "Come on, girl, let me show you how real Texans party."

It was only two in the afternoon, but I had a feeling what I was about to see is how Brett Owens partied.

The moment he walked in, the place went crazy with everyone jumping up and saying hi to Brett. He kept his arm around my waist which surprised me. Of course, every time a guy walked up to me it was hard not to notice him pull me closer into his side.

Oh, my. Mr. Owens was sending out a message loud and clear. Even when he introduced me, he made it sound like we were together. There was no mention of ESPN, work, or even football for that matter.

"Chip, I'd like you to meet Aubrey Cain."

Chip's face lit up. "It's a pleasure to meet you, Ms. Cain."

"Please, call me Aubrey."

He nodded and gave me a once over before turning back to Brett and slapping him on the back. I had no idea what that exchange was all about, but I let it go. I was giving myself one day of not worrying about what people thought, what my boss would say, or even that stupid ass article. Today was about me getting to know the real Brett and having a bit of fun.

Guiding me over to the bar, I glanced around. It was your typical country bar. Old, smelled like saw dust and beer, and brought a huge smile to my face. I could imagine all the hell Brett caused at this place.

Two beers were set in front of us. I picked mine up and took a drink. It was then I noticed a small handful of women in the corner staring at me.

Oh, great. I'm going to guess an old girlfriend was probably mixed into the group. Maybe a wanna-be girlfriend? Jesus, did no one leave this town after high school?

"So, is that your fan club in the corner shooting me daggers?" I asked as I leaned in to talk to Brett. The music was pretty loud so I had to put my mouth almost up to his ear.

His gaze lifted and searched quickly before he spotted the women. With a chuckle, he shook his head but didn't answer me.

For the next thirty minutes, I found myself glancing over to the women, wondering how many of them Brett actually slept with. I found my mood slipping further and further. Brett was lost in a conversation with Chip and another guy. From the bits and pieces I got from them, almost everyone left for college, but a lot came back to work in their community or on their parents' ranches. I also figured out it was Chip's birthday today and that was why the place was already packed in the middle of the afternoon.

His warm breath on my neck instantly made my insides quiver. "Why do you keep looking over there, Bree?"

Nonchalantly, I shrugged. "Just trying to figure out how many of them slept with you and which one took your virginity."

He looked over my shoulder and his face constricted. "None to both."

My lips cracked into a slight grin as I looked down, not wanting him to see I was pleased with his answer.

"I only slept with one girl before I left for college."

My brows pinched together. "One?"

"Does that surprise you?"

"Honestly, yes it does. Is she the one who took your virginity?"

He took my hand and pulled me off the bar stool, leading me to where everyone was dancing. "Yes, she was. Up in the hayloft of her father's barn with a chicken watching the whole time. Talk about performance anxiety."

I scrunched up my nose and giggled. "That doesn't sound like a great first time."

Pulling me close to him, I felt him pressing against my stomach. "It was forgettable to say the least. No offense to her, it's just, I don't think I've truly experienced my first time making love ... yet."

My mouth went dry and my breathing stalled. I forced out the name I was trying to say. "Nicole?"

His eyes softened and he slowly shook his head. "No, not even with Nicole. Maybe I'm not meant to find love."

An ache grew in the back of my throat as I got lost in his eyes. Not knowing what to say, I buried my face into his chest and let him lead me slowly around the dance floor.

The song changed and "Flatliner" started playing. I wasn't surprised how well of a dancer Brett was. He twirled me around that dance floor like we'd been dancing together for years. It seemed to me there wasn't anything this man didn't excel at. When someone walked up and asked to cut in, Brett hesitated, but then dropped his hold on me and motioned for the guy to take over. I stared at him as he walked toward the bar. One spin around the floor and I got another look at Brett only to see two girls standing there talking to him. I couldn't pull my stare off of them.

"So where you from, sweet thing?" Breaking my spell, I looked up at the cowboy. Geesh, they breed them good here in Marfa.

"Connecticut."

"How did you meet Brett?"

The last thing I wanted to do was tell people who I was. "We met at a restaurant in Austin." It was kind of the truth.

The guy glanced up. "Looks like Brett hasn't lost his touch with the ladies."

My gaze followed his. Brett was smiling at the two girls as one of them had her hand resting on his leg.

"What a bitch!" I hissed.

The guy looked at me with a surprised expression. "Did you say something?"

"I'm thirsty, would you mind if we stopped?"

"No, not at all. Thank you for the dance."

I nodded and replied, "Thank you."

Trying to keep these crazy feelings in check, I calmly walked over and stopped in front of the girls. "Excuse me, you're blocking my chair."

The redhead looked me up and down. "There's another seat on the other side of him."

I was positive I had a what-the-hell look on my face. My head turned to see Brett smiling.

Asshole.

Reaching around the girl, I picked up my drink and downed it.

Pushing the girl to the side, I set my bottle on the bar.

Another song played and the dark-haired girl grabbed Brett and yelled out, "Dance with me, Brett!"

Before I knew what was going on, they were both out on the dance floor dancing with him to Iggy Azalea's "Team."

The way they were all over him made me sick. Flagging Chip down, I held up my empty bottle of beer. Peeking over to them again, I noticed Brett wasn't touching either one of them, he actually looked pained to be out there. I turned away and grinned. I caught the eye of cowboy sitting at the end of the bar who winked. With a polite smile back at him, I looked at Chip and thanked him for the drink.

"So, I see the beauty, but I'm really itching to know what it is beyond that."

Wrinkling my brows, I asked, "Excuse me?"

Chip jerked his chin out toward Brett. "I've never, since I've known Brett Owens, seen him walk into any place with his arm wrapped around the waist of a girl with the clear intent on letting everyone know he was with you. I'm trying to figure out what makes you the one, Aubrey."

My stomach flipped. "The one?"

"Sweetheart, if you can't see the way that man looks at you like you're his everything, you need to open your eyes."

I let out a nervous laugh. "No, I think you're mistaken."

Chip slowly shook his head and replied, "If you say so." He turned and headed to the other end of the bar.

The one?

Impossible.

Brett vowed to keep his hands off of me, and as of yet, he really hadn't made any type of play toward me. No, if Brett really wanted me, he'd make the first move. Until then, I was going to keep things the way they were between us. Of course, a few kisses here and there would be nice.

Heat hit my body as two arms came on either side of me and gripped the bar. Brett had me pinned while his mouth brushed across my neck and up to my ear. "Save me, sweetheart."

Turning slightly to look into his eyes, I asked, "From?"

"The two vultures who are trying to get into my pants. What's wrong with women these days?"

Spinning around to face him, I smirked. "I thought that was something you liked, Mr. Owens."

He leaned closer, his lips inches from mine. "The only woman I want trying to get into my pants is the one I'm about to kiss."

When his lips touched mine, my heart dropped in my chest. If I didn't know better, I would think I was on a thrill ride. I forced myself not to moan into his mouth. "Locked Away" by R. City started and Brett took my hands, not breaking our kiss, and led me to the dance floor. When he finally tore his mouth from mine, I had to get my scattered thoughts together.

"Can you salsa?"

I laughed. "Yes. Can you?"

"Hell yes, I can."

The moment the beat started he moved his body in ways that should be illegal. We weren't really salsa dancing, but we certainly fell into a version of dirty dancing.

Each movement pushed my libido even higher as I rubbed my body against Brett. Just when I didn't think I could take any more, he would do a series of spins. Giving my aching body a break from the heat of his. I'd never had so much fun dancing in my entire life. Brett brought something out in me that I loved. It was easy with him.

I was positive my cheeks would freeze in the position of my smile. Leaning in closer, I shouted, "Where in the hell did you learn to dance?"

With a wink, he asked, "Where did you?"

Wrapping my arms around his neck, I answered, "My father!"

Brett laughed. "I need to meet this man. He teaches his daughter to barrel ride, two-step, and salsa dance? Tell me he likes football!"

With a huge grin, I answered, "Loves football!"

The song ended and immediately a slow country song started. Brett drew me against his body and we eased back into two-stepping to Chris Janson's "Holding Her."

My heart was racing and I wasn't sure if it was from all the dancing, or the way Brett was holding me in his arms.

Then the words to the song started and my breath hitched. We slowly moved across the floor as if it were just the two of us. The chorus started and Brett pulled me tighter to him. My eyes squeezed shut as I let the moment settle into my chest.

I was falling for Brett and there wasn't a damn thing I could do about it. Not that I even wanted to.

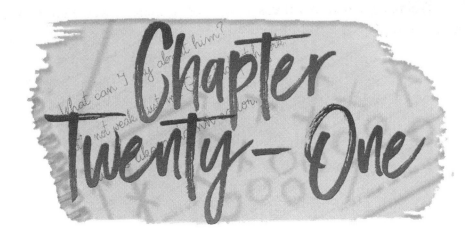

Chapter Twenty-One

Brett

I BURIED MY face in her hair and inhaled deeply, taking in her scent. Two months ago, I'd pick up a girl in a bar and fuck her just because I could. Now I was holding the most precious thing I'd ever held in my arms. I'd never felt such peace in my life. Everything was at a standstill, everything but my heart, which was falling more and more for Aubrey.

The song changed to a faster one but we continued dancing slowly. I'd have given anything to be alone with her. It was getting harder and harder to resist her pull.

Pulling back, she searched my face. "So where to next?"

Lifting my hand, I pushed a strand of hair behind her ear. "Ice cream?"

Her smile grew wide. "Ice cream?"

Sliding my hand around her neck, I pulled her closer to me. Before I kissed her, I whispered, "Not just any ice cream, Nancy's ice cream."

Aubrey giggled as I pressed my lips to hers. It was a short fast kiss. Taking her hand in mine, I guided her back to the bar. Tapping on it, I got Chip's attention.

"Tab?"

He rolled his eyes. "Dude, your tab is like six years old!"

"I'll settle it before I leave," I said, giving him a wink.

"Yeah, I've heard that before."

"It was great meeting you, Chip," Aubrey said as she leaned over the bar to shake Chip's hand.

"Trust me, the pleasure was all mine. Where y'all headed off to?"

"Murphy Street Raspa. Taking Aubrey to meet Nancy and get some ice cream."

Chip looked at me like I had grown two heads. "Who the hell are you and what have you done with Brett Owens?"

"Fuck you, asshole."

Pointing at me, Chip laughed. "There he is."

Walking out of Chip's place, I took Aubrey's hand in mine as we walked along the street.

"So what is this Murphy Street Raspa of which you speak? You mentioned ice cream."

With a chuckle, I turned to her. "Nancy owns the place. It's a gift store mixed with an ice cream place. She's owned it for years. She also has a limited lunch menu. We hung out there a lot when we were in high school."

"What was it like growing up in a town like Marfa?"

I shrugged. "Boring. I spent a lot of time at the ranch, but when I did come in to town, we'd almost always hit Nancy's place, and then Sonic." Letting out a laugh, I let some of the memories come back.

"It must have been hard having Ryan betray you like he did."

I couldn't even stand hearing his name. "Yeah well, life moves on and everything worked out for the best. I have a job I like, a life I'm happy with. I couldn't ask for more."

We stopped in front of Murphy's. Aubrey turned and looked at me. "What about a family? Kids? Don't you want those things?"

"They're not on my list of high priorities."

Her face fell and my chest tightened knowing what she was asking, and the answers I was giving her clearly weren't what she wanted to hear. "What about you?"

With a weak grin, she answered, "I do want to get married, and if I'm blessed with a baby that would be amazing. Truth be told, I thought I'd at least be half way there by now."

My heart leapt to my throat as fear gripped my chest and squeezed it.

"Is that Brett I see standing out here?"

For a moment, I couldn't pull my gaze away from Aubrey's. She was the one who broke the contact when she turned and looked at Nancy.

My eyes closed briefly before turning and smiling at the older lady coming out to greet us. I wasn't sure if I was glad she interrupted our conversation or not.

"Hey there, good looking," I uttered as I gathered her in a gentle hug.

Nancy slapped me lightly on the chest. "Oh, stop flirting with me, you handsome boy, you."

Aubrey laughed and watched the exchange between Nancy and myself. "Nancy, I'd like you to meet Aubrey Cain."

Standing back, Nancy looked every inch of Aubrey over. "Well aren't you a pretty thing." Peeking back at me, Nancy winked before wrapping her arm with Aubrey's and dragging her into the store.

"This building is over a hundred years old. It helps that we're next door to the famous Hotel Paisano. Now, you know, James Dean stayed at that hotel."

"No, I didn't know that. I love James Dean!" Aubrey exclaimed, glancing back over her shoulder at me.

"Oh, yes! Rock Hudson and Elizabeth Taylor also stayed there. But eventually they stayed at some fancier houses in town."

Aubrey sat at the counter while Nancy made her way to the other side. Sitting next to her, I couldn't shake the conversation we were just having.

"How exciting!" Aubrey exclaimed and I was starting to realize she really did think that was exciting.

"Your usual, Brett?"

With a nod, I replied, "Yes ma'am. Extra chocolate syrup."

Pulling her head back, Aubrey dropped her mouth in surprise. "I've yet to see you eat something unhealthy."

With a wink, I replied, "We're on vacation. Make it two, Nancy. Aubrey here needs to broaden her horizons."

While Nancy got busy making up the chocolate milkshakes, Aubrey glanced around the store. It was an eclectic store to say the least. One side was clothes, both men and women, the other more of a crafty home store, and in the middle sat a small nineteen-fifties-style counter.

Nancy set a large shake in front of me and grinned. "Now I'll make the other one."

Aubrey's eyes widened. "Wait! There is no way I can drink a whole shake like that." Her gaze lifted to mine. "Can we share?"

With a downward gaze to my shake, I looked back at her. "You want me to share this with you?"

With a chuckle, she nodded. "Yes! Brett, there is no way you can drink that whole shake." Reaching over, she grabbed a straw, opened it, dunked it in my beloved shake and went to town.

Sitting back, I watched her with agitation. Her gaze lifted to mine and I couldn't help but zero in how she was sucking on the straw. Nancy wandered off to help another customer. I leaned closer to Aubrey and said, "You have no idea how turned on I am right now. I'm not even mad you stole my shake."

Laughing, she pushed my shoulder back. "You're turned on watching me drink your shake, which by the way is amazing."

Dropping my mouth open, I exclaimed, "I know! That's why I wanted my own. And it was the sucking of the straw that got me."

Aubrey went back to drink the shake, but rolled her eyes at me. "Just drink it before I drink all of it!"

"You said you couldn't drink a whole one."

"Brett!"

"Fine," I said as I took a long drink. We soon found ourselves trying to race, sucking the thick milkshake through the straw.

Just when I was about to tap out from the worse ice cream headache of my life, Aubrey jumped back.

"Ice cream headache!" she gasped. "Oh. God. It's. Bad!"

Smiling, I took a quick break and watched as she stuck her thumb in her mouth and bent over.

"What in the hell are you doing?"

"Pwesthing my fumb to the woof of my mouwth."

By now, people were staring. Including Nancy who gave me a befuddled look. I shrugged and said, "She's had too much to drink."

Lifting her head, Aubrey shouted, "Bwett!"

"Oh, dear, Brett. Does she have a drinking problem?" Nancy questioned.

Aubrey and I both answered at once.

"No!"

"Yes," I said with a pout.

"Oh, you poor thing. Maybe you should take her next door so she can rest?"

I looked back at Aubrey who was now crossing her eyes and massaging her temples.

"I'm fine, I got an ice cream headache."

I slipped a twenty on the counter and kissed Nancy on the cheek. "See ya around, Nancy."

"Don't stay away so long, Brett Owens!"

"Yes, ma'am," I replied with a wink.

Reaching for Aubrey's hand, we walked out of the store and headed over to the hotel.

The second we stepped outside, she hit me on the arm. "I can't believe you told them I was drunk."

Laughing, I looked at her. "You sounded drunk. What in the hell where you even doing?"

"Haven't you ever heard of sticking your thumb to the roof of your mouth and pressing it there to stop an ice cream headache?"

I stared at her with a stony expression. "No. No I haven't."

She huffed and looked away. "You need a life, Brett Owens."

Walking into the lobby, Aubrey looked up and gasped. "This place is amazing! I can't believe I'm standing in the same spot as James Dean!"

I looked at the floor. "How do you know he stood in this spot?"

Looking at me with a dumbfounded look, she asked, "What?"

Damn it was so easy getting her riled up. "I don't know that he stood in this exact spot, but I'm sure he walked over it. He walked all over this hotel. Oh! I wonder what room he stayed in."

Snarling my lip, I asked, "Why?"

"I want to see it!"

"Again, why?"

An older lady walked up to us with a huge grin on her face. "Are you here visiting the hotel?"

Before I knew it, Aubrey launched into a whole thing about James Dean.

"Yes! I want to see everywhere James Dean was. Even the room he stayed in. If it's not booked." Spinning around to face me, her face lit up like a two-year-old in a toy store. "Can we book the room if isn't booked?"

My dick jumped. "For?"

Her eyes lit up then turned dark. "Just to sneak a peek. That's all."

Fuck that. If I was renting a room at this place, I planned on getting more out of it than a sneak peek.

"Sure, why not."

Before I knew it we were touring the hotel I had been in a million times. And I had booked a room. According to Aubrey, it wasn't just any room. It was *the room*.

The older lady's name turned out to be Liz, who was a little girl when James Dean and the whole crew were here. She was currently taking Aubrey, who had gone temporarily insane in the last thirty minutes, out to the fountain to show her exactly where James Dean sat.

"Brett, sit there."

I glanced to where Liz was pointing.

"Why?"

Aubrey jutted out her lip. "Please. I want to see you sit where James Dean sat."

Yet again, I found myself staring at Aubrey. I'd never felt my chest feel so light. Although the woman was crazy insane at the moment, I found myself loving every single second of it. Today had to be the best day of my life.

Little did I know, by me sitting on that ledge, I was about to change everything.

Chapter Twenty-Two

Aubrey

LIZ AND I both held our breath as Brett sat on the very spot James Dean sat.

"He's so much more handsome than James Dean," Liz whispered to me. I nodded in agreement.

Brett furrowed his brow as he looked between Liz and me. "Do I need to say a quote from the film or something?"

My heart melted on the spot. I'd never had a man do something for me simply to make me happy. Brett actually booked the room so I could see it, and he sat in the exact spot as James Dean with no arguing. Most guys would think it was stupid, but not Brett. He had a way of surprising me at every turn.

I laughed, "No, I never even saw the movie!"

"Well, we happen to have it if you'd like to watch in the room tonight."

My head turned back to Brett. "Well, I'm not sure we'll be keeping the room all night, but it might be kind of fun to watch it in the same room he stayed in."

Standing, Brett walked up to me and put his arm around my waist. Warmth radiated through my body. "Let's go see this famous room shall we, Liz?"

Liz smiled at Brett. "Well, come on!"

Making our way up to the historical room, my phone buzzed in my purse. Pulling it out, I saw it was a text from Michelle.

Michelle: Call me ASAP

I worried my lower lip because I knew it had to be about Emily. Peeking over to Brett, he wore a huge smile as Liz told him all about when they were filming the movie *Giant* here. I couldn't tell if he was just appeasing her, or if he was really interested.

"Here's your room. Is there anything I can show you or help with?" Liz asked while handing the DVD to Brett.

The way he looked at me made my heart skip a beat. He almost seemed nervous about going into the room alone with me. I couldn't help it; I smiled and winked at him, causing him to blush.

Brett Owens blushed.

"I think we're good for now. Do we need to make dinner reservations?" I inquired.

Liz grinned. "Oh, I can arrange for you to sit at the same table Jimmy sat at!"

"Oh, yay," Brett said, opening the door and rolling his eyes. I couldn't help but giggle.

Turning back to Liz, I replied, "That would be amazing. You wouldn't mind?"

Waving me off, she answered, "Heck no. You two have been fun. What time?"

Brett was already inside the room looking around. I glanced at him and then back to Liz. "I'm guessing I'll hog tie him to the bed and make him watch the movie, so maybe around seven-thirty?"

"You've got it! I'll see you both then. I'm here until eight."

With a huge grin, I hugged her. "Thank you, Liz, for showing us around and sharing all the fun facts."

"My pleasure. See you in a few hours."

Waving, I watched her walk down the hall. The second I shut the door, I was spun around and pinned to it.

My chest heaved as I looked into smoldering blue eyes. Oh … maybe coming up to the room gave Brett the wrong idea. A part of me hoped it had.

"Hog tie me to the bed huh?"

My mouth parted. "Um, I thought … well, I mean … we don't have to watch the movie if you don't want to."

"I kind of liked the idea of you getting a little 'fifty shades' on me."

My brow lifted. "Tell me you didn't read that book?"

Leaning in closer, he brushed his lips softly across my cheek. "Do you really think I need to read a book like that? I already know how to use my cock and make a woman come harder than she's ever come before."

My eyes closed and I asked in a breathy voice, "Brett, why do you talk that way?"

He placed a kiss on my neck. "Because I know deep down you like it."

I do. Lord knows I do.

My phone rang as I was about to admit I did like it.

I pulled it out of my purse and saw Michelle's name. "Oh shit! I forgot she sent me a text."

"Who?" Brett asked, pushing away from the door and walking over to the bed.

"Michelle," I said swiping my screen.

"Hello?"

"I wasn't sure if you got my text."

Glancing over at Brett, he seemed cool as a cucumber while I instantly started sweating. He was reading the back of the movie. I walked up and sat next to him.

"Sorry, I just got it. Did you find something out already?"

"Yes, I did. Are you sitting down?"

I swallowed hard. "Yes."

"Emily Clarington is from Austin, Texas. Twenty-six years old and the daughter of Mike and Ana Clarington."

"Okay."

"I sent you a picture of her. She matches your description, and get this, her daddy is a huge supporter of Senator Ryan Dryer. Looks like she has volunteered at many of his events and, at one time, she listed him as an employer. She graduated from Texas Tech with a degree in business management."

My breath caught and I jumped up. *Holy shit. Ryan?* It all made sense. Everything hit me all at once.

"Do you have any pictures of her with the senator?"

Brett's head jerked up.

"Yeah, I mean if you google her and his name together she's in a number of the photos. There's also one where they appear to be leaving a hotel together. I guess it was in a gossip magazine not too long ago."

I jumped and pumped my fist. "Michelle, I love you and the awesome private detective you have. Let me know what I owe him."

"Nah, he said this was easy. No charge. Did you get what you needed?"

Brett stood and looked at me. "Oh, I got more than I needed."

"What's this for anyway? Work?"

With a huge grin, I held up my finger to motion for Brett to hold on. I knew he was anxious to hear what Michelle's guy found out. Especially with me mentioning Ryan.

"No, this one was personal. Thanks so much babe, I've got to run."

"Okay, let me know if you need anything else."

My cheeks were hurting from smiling so big. I had to admit I was relieved with this information. Knowing Emily was tied to

Ryan, I was assuming he had set the whole thing up. I wouldn't have been surprised if he was the one who got her pregnant.

"Will you do me a favor and email me a couple of the photos with her and Dryer? Especially the one with them leaving the hotel."

Brett scrubbed his hands down his face. I could see the anger starting to build. He was piecing it together.

"Got to run, talk soon."

I hit End before she could respond.

"That motherfucker," Brett said.

Inhaling a deep breath, I took Brett's hand in mine and led him over to the bed. Sitting, I pulled him next to me. My email dinged and I opened the attachment Michelle had sent. The second I saw her picture, I let out the breath I was holding in.

Handing the phone to Brett, I waited for him to respond.

"He's setting me up." Slowly shaking his head, he looked at me. "Would he actually go that far to try and take me down like that?"

"Do you really need me to answer that?"

Brett stood and started pacing the room. I sat there and let him have a few minutes to soak all of it in. I couldn't imagine how he was feeling right now. With the way his fists were balled, I was thankful we were five hours away from Ryan or I'd be afraid Brett would go after him.

Stopping, he looked at me. "Can you determine the paternity before the baby is born?"

Pulling up Google on my phone, I typed it in. After visiting a few different websites, I looked up at him.

"Yes. They have a non-invasive test they can do."

Walking up to me, Brett reached down and pulled me up. "I have an idea." He cupped my face within his hands and kissed me. Pulling back, he smiled and my breath was stolen. "I think tonight we will be doing some serious celebrating."

Chapter Twenty-Three

Brett

AUBREY SEARCHED MY face.

"What's your idea?" she asked breathlessly. Damn if her kisses didn't leave me feeling the same way.

"I'm calling Emily."

She nodded. "Okay."

"Tell me everything Michelle said about her."

After Aubrey filled me in on what Michelle told her, I pulled my phone out and hit Emily's number.

My heart was racing and I had a feeling I knew how this call would turn out. At least I was hoping like hell I knew.

Aubrey chewed on her thumb nail as I waited for Emily to answer.

"Hey, miss me, Daddy?"

I wanted to gag.

"Emily, I've just gotten off the phone with my lawyer. We are going to arrange to have a doctor perform a paternity test now. He can schedule for Tuesday of next week. It's non-invasive, but it will be able to tell us if I'm the father of your baby."

The silence over the phone was a clear sign she was most likely freaking out right about now.

"Emily? Are you there?"

She cleared her throat. "You want me to let them stick a needle in me while I'm pregnant? Are you crazy? I already told you I haven't slept with anyone else."

"Not even Ryan Dryer? Because I have a picture of the two of you entering and leaving a hotel just a couple of months back."

Aubrey's eyes widened. I shrugged and covered the phone. "It's worth a try."

"How … how did you find out?"

My heart dropped. Holy shit. Could it really be that easy?

"It wasn't hard, Ms. Clarington. Funny thing is, my lawyer also found it interesting that you previously worked for the good senator and you've been in a relationship with him, which we both know is why you resigned from your position."

"I don't … I mean, I—"

"Will be charged with trying to extort money from me."

"What? No, wait. Please." She broke down crying on the phone. "He told me you would run scared. That once you found out I was pregnant, you'd offer me money to disappear. I wasn't supposed to ask for money, but I thought if I threw it out there you'd bite and offer to pay me off. He wanted you to lose your job."

I noted the recorder Aubrey was holding to my phone. "Who did?"

"Ryan! Ryan Dryer. It's his baby. I'm almost three months pregnant. He told me the night you and I first met that he needed me to sleep with you. It was only supposed to be that night. Something about wanting to take photos and say I was a student. He said you tried to frame him for your wife cheating on you and accused him of sleeping with her, and how he almost lost everything because of it. This was his way of getting back at you. He paid someone off at the university to put me into the system as a student. The photographer couldn't get any photos of us the first time we were together, so Ryan wanted me to make sure we hooked up again."

My head was spinning. "The pregnancy? Why come up with that story?"

"Because the photographer couldn't get any photos of us together the second time either. He was supposed to get a damaging photo and sell it, saying that you were sleeping with female students. When that didn't work and I found out I was pregnant, he came up with this plan. He thought for sure you'd never put your beloved university in harm's way. He promised it would be over quickly because you'd just step down, offer to pay me off, and that would it. But then you started talking about me moving in the same building as you and heading off to tell your parents about the baby. I panicked. I never wanted to do this, you have to believe me."

Anger raced through my veins. "Then why did you?"

The line was silent for a few moments. "Because I love him. I'd do anything for him."

My heart actually hurt for her. "I really feel sorry for you, Emily."

"Why?"

"Because you and your child are going to have to deal with a Ryan Dryer from now on. God help you both."

Hitting End, I dropped my hands to my knees.

"Holy shit." I sucked in a deep breath in and held it for a few seconds before exhaling.

"Ryan?"

My head snapped up. Aubrey was on the phone. What in the hell was she doing?

"I have two words for you. Emily Clarington."

Her gaze snapped over to mine.

"She's already confessed, and I have it all on tape. Now, let me make something very clear to you, and I need you to listen good. Your position means nothing. You see, I have a mother who is a senator and knows a hell of a lot more people than you. And my father, he's the best lawyer in Connecticut and as already gotten Brett in touch with a lawyer in Austin who is ready to take you down."

I stood up and stared at her. Who was this girl? Where did this Aubrey come from? Damn if she wasn't fucking hot as hell.

"You're going to tell me who you paid off at the university. Then you and your little pregnant momma are going to never speak to, or even look in the direction of, Brett Owens again."

Aubrey laughed. "Ryan, I'm not even the least bit scared of you. With one phone call to CNN, I can play this tape."

Aubrey hit play and let it go for about ten seconds.

With a huge grin, she said, "That would be the best thing for everyone don't you think?"

Aubrey rushed over to the desk and grabbed the pen and wrote down a name. "And you'll get that fixed as soon as we hang up? Perfect. No, Brett wants nothing from you but to let him be and he'll let you be."

"After I beat his ass," I mumbled.

Aubrey glared at me and held up her finger to quiet me.

"Okay, but I think we'll be hanging on to the tape, and you have my word, it won't get out unless you double cross us."

I stood there staring at this amazing woman. I'd never been so turned on in my life.

"Fine. Oh, one more thing, congratulations on the baby."

She tapped her phone and dropped it on the bed. Both hands came up to her mouth.

"I can't believe I did that!" she exclaimed jumping. "It was like I was a real investigative reporter! I could go after the mob now!"

"Let's slow down there, Jane Mayer."

Aubrey giggled and then calmed herself down.

"What did he say? What happened? He gave up without a fight?" I asked. Still trying to let it sink in I wasn't going to be a father.

Dropping her arms to her side, she said, "Apparently, Senator Dryer really likes being a senator. He gave me the name of the lady he got to add Emily into the system. He wanted the tape, but I told him no!"

Excitement danced in Aubrey's eyes. "Oh my gosh! That was the coolest thing ever! It was like a movie and I was a bad ass investigative reporter who just busted the bad guy!"

I laughed and pulled her into my arms. "You do realize you saved my ass."

With a huge grin, she replied, "I did, didn't I? Do you know what I want from you now?"

"Sex?" I asked as I wiggled my eyebrows.

"No."

The DVD of *Giant* appeared before my face. "After a celebration dance, we watch this."

"A celebration dance?"

She nodded. "Yep. I noticed they have an iPod station!"

Rushing over to her purse, she took her iPod out and plugged it into the docking station.

She hit play and spun around. "Baby One More Time" started and I couldn't help but laugh. "It's too small to dance in here."

Shaking her head, Aubrey grabbed my hands and started singing.

"I'm not dancing to Britney. Sorry, Bree."

Her lower lip jutted out as she danced around me. "Come on, it was me, after all, who solved the mystery!"

Damn this girl. All I wanted to do was pull her into my arms and show her how I felt about her. I tried hard not to laugh, but she brought out a side of me I kept hidden. She could make my worse day feel like it was the best day of my life.

"You know you want to! I see your hips moving!"

In that moment, I knew there wasn't anything I wouldn't do for Aubrey Cain. I'd do anything to see that smile.

The song changed and Florida Georgia Line's "H.O.L.Y." started. Aubrey stopped dancing and we stood there staring at each other.

Slowly walking up to me, she whispered, "Dance with me, Brett."

Pulling her into my arms, she buried her face in my chest as we slowly danced in the middle of the room.

My eyes closed as my heart fought with my head. I was tired of fighting. I wanted to make love to Aubrey more than I wanted air to breathe.

She lifted her head and stared into my eyes like she was peering deep into my soul.

"I'm afraid if I kiss you, I'll get so drunk on your lips I won't be able to stop myself, Bree."

Her mouth parted before her tongue swept across those soft lips. "I don't want you to stop yourself. My body is aching for you, Brett."

My hand lifted as I tucked a piece of her hair behind her ear. "I'm not sure I can give you what you want."

Her eyes pooled with water. "Love me for now."

I brushed my mouth over hers. "I don't want to hurt you."

She gripped my arms tighter. "I'm yours for tonight, Brett. Please."

Cupping her face within in my hands, I searched her eyes. They were dancing with desire. "Are you sure?"

"I've never been so sure of anything in my entire life."

I could no longer hold back. My lips smashed to hers as I kissed her like it was our last kiss. Her hands laced through my hair and grabbed a handful, pulling so hard I groaned into her mouth.

She was expecting me to fuck her. Fast and hard. That wasn't what I wanted with Aubrey. I wanted more. For the first time in my life, I needed *more*.

"I want to crawl inside of you and never leave," I murmured against her soft lips.

"Brett," she gasped as she ripped my T-shirt over my head. Her hand lightly moved across my bare chest, sending a wave of energy through my body. Lifting her gaze to mine, she whispered, "I've dreamed of this moment."

My hands shook as I lifted her long-sleeve shirt over her head and dropped it to the floor next to us. My throat grew tight as I stared at the white lace bra holding in those perfect-sized breasts. Her breath hitched as I ran my fingers along the edge of the delicate fabric.

Leaning over, I kissed her cleavage and whispered, "So perfect."

Aubrey's head dropped back, exposing her neck to me. My mouth placed a trail of kisses up her chest and to her neck. Her nails dug into my arms as she held on. Moving my lips to her ear, I spoke softly. "I want you to be sure."

"Brett, please. I need to feel your skin on mine."

Reaching around her back, I unclasped her bra. Aubrey moved her arms and let it fall to the floor. My chest heaved as I stared at her amazing body. Cupping her breasts in each hand, I placed my lips around one nipple and gently sucked.

"Oh, God," she mumbled.

Moving to the other nipple, I repeated the action, causing a low moan to vibrate from the back of her throat. I'd never gone this slow or taken this much care with a woman before. I wanted to learn how to love her until the morning light. Nothing else mattered in this world to me but the two of us in this moment.

"I've waited all my life for this, Bree."

Her eyes met mine and pulled me deeper into her soul. My shaking hands unbuttoned her jeans as she did the same with mine. Neither one of us breaking the connection of our stare. Pressing her lips together, she stepped back, kicked off her shoes and slowly slid her jeans down and off her legs. My heart slammed against my chest with a thud.

Jesus, I wouldn't last long buried inside of her. She left her panties on and glanced down, waiting for me to remove my own pants. I quickly stripped out of my boots and discarded my jeans on the floor next to hers. The only difference was I went commando and now stood before her completely naked.

"Oh. My. Goodness. Mr. Owens, you're going to make me very sore."

Grinning, I stepped closer to her and ran my fingers barely inside the waistband of her panties. Her breath caught as I got lost in her eyes.

"Lay down on the bed, Bree."

Chapter Twenty-Four

Aubrey

MY CHEST HEAVED as heat surged through my veins, leaving me dizzy with desire. Slowly walking backward, I bumped into the bed and quickly crawled on. All attempts of being sexy went out the door. All I could think about was his hands on my body. Caressing every single inch of me.

I wasn't sure what to expect from Brett. The way he took his time, as if he was worshiping me, had taken me off guard. His whispered words made me feel things I'd never felt before. My voice wavered as doubt rushed into my mind. What if I sucked? What if I couldn't please him like he wanted? "I'm … what if I … what if …"

He was over me in an instant, surrounding my body with his. "Don't," he whispered against my lips. As he pressed himself against my panties, my libido surged even higher.

"Yes," I hissed, totally forgetting all my insecurities with him against me.

Brett's mouth moved over mine, silencing me with his kiss. My hands moved lazily over his thick, built body as my heart quickened at the idea of him making love to me.

His hand slipped into my panties, causing me to lift my hips up, hungry for more.

I needed so much more.

He grazed over my lips and my breathing became labored. Each moment I anticipated his touch drove me closer and closer to the edge. I was almost positive I'd come the moment he slipped his fingers inside of me.

Taking his leg, he pushed mine out, opening myself to him more. One finger slipped in and Brett growled, causing me to hold my breath. Another finger found its way in and his words were buried by the pounding of my heartbeat in my ears.

The third finger filled me, causing me to let out a long soft moan which was mimicked by Brett.

"Jesus Christ. You're so wet."

My head was spinning as I lifted my hips more, silently begging him to give me the relief I wanted so desperately.

Brett was losing his patience and ripped my panties off in one movement. I gasped at the action and the way it made my body tingle. I wasn't sure how long I could last as he moved his fingers in and out of me in a slow torturous manner.

"Brett."

It was all I could manage to say. My orgasm was building quickly. His lips wrapped around a nipple and I lost it. My entire body shattered as the waves of pleasure rippled through me one after another.

My world went black. The only thing I heard was Brett's name from my mouth. I'd never in my life experienced something like that.

His words against my ear lured me back to the light. My lids opened as he brushed his fingers over my lips. "You falling apart on my fingers was the sexiest fucking thing I've ever seen."

My tongue ran over my lips as he grinned, his eyes darker than I've ever seen them. The way he regarded me was a mix of adoring and lust.

Brett took both of my hands and pushed them over me, pinning them to the bed. "Do you feel it between us?"

My head nodded. I felt the heat between the two of us, but I also felt something so much more and I hoped like hell he felt it too.

"Are you ready for me, Bree?"

"Yes!" I exclaimed.

His dick rubbed against my sensitive clit before he barely pushed in. My head was spinning and the only thing I could get out was one word.

"Condom?"

His grin made my stomach dip. "I put one on already, baby. I'd never do that to you."

My eyes widened in surprise. "When?"

With a slight laugh, he replied, "When you were still reveling in your orgasm."

His hand gripped my hands harder as he pushed himself slowly into me, his lips meeting mine at the same time.

Jesus. What is happening to me? The way he moved inside of me, had me desiring more. It was as if I was experiencing this for the first time.

His mouth moved along my neck while he pulled out and re-peated the heavenly movement again, this time going deeper.

"Fuck," he grunted. Both our bodies trembled at once. He moved a bit faster as he whispered, "I can't get deep enough inside of you."

His whispered words drove me insane as I felt the build up again. I'd never had an orgasm during sex.

Ever.

The way he moved so deliciously slow in and out was better than any dream I could ever have. He pressed his body against me more as he gazed into my eyes. "I want to touch you," I said.

The smile he gave me had me falling more for him. Letting go of my hands, I wrapped them around his body, pulling him closer to me. I didn't care that I was falling in love with him. This was the most amazing moment of my life. One I would remember for as long as I lived.

Resting his weight on his elbows, he grabbed a handful of hair and tugged.

"I don't want to lose control with you, but goddamn do I want to fuck you right now."

My heart pounded in my chest. I couldn't possibly take much more as he moved.

"But you deserve more than that. You deserve to be loved."

Before I could say anything, he pressed his lips to mine. It was sweet and filled with passion.

My legs wrapped around his body as we found our perfect rhythm. With Brett still kissing me, I felt my orgasm building. I swore it started in my toes and rushed up in one swift moment.

"Brett! I'm going to come," I cried out as he pushed in deeper and moaned. My body trembled as whispered names were spoken on kiss-swollen lips.

We had come together.

Two bodies became one.

And I was positive neither one of us would ever be the same again.

I wasn't sure how long we laid there, Brett still inside of me, as our breathing slowly steadied.

His baby blues where locked onto my eyes.

Breaking the stare, he searched my face as the silence between us was broken. "I don't want to move."

My chest tightened. "Then don't."

Brett buried his face into my neck. "What have you done to me, Bree?"

Tears burned my eyes. It hadn't been ten minutes and I already wanted him again. How would this work with us living so far apart? Stolen moments once a month, if we were lucky. Could that be enough for us? For him?

A tear slipped from my eye and rolled down my face.

It was almost like he knew, lifting his head, he watched it for a moment before kissing it away. "I don't want to think about what's waiting out there for us. The only thing I want to think about is you and me. Right now. Right here. Not about next week or next month."

I nodded. If only we could stay hidden in this hotel. I had no idea what the future was going to hold for us. That scared the hell out of me and I knew it did Brett as well. I could see it in his eyes. In that second, I made a decision. I was going to focus on the next few days with the man I'd just given my heart to and nothing else.

"Should we watch the movie?"

Brett chuckled. "I was thinking we should take a shower."

Lifting my brow, I asked, "Then the movie?"

A wicked grin grew across his face. "No baby, then I fuck you."

My lower stomach tightened. "Finally."

Brett pulled out of me, discarded the condom, and then slapped me on the ass before throwing me over his shoulder. "Finally, huh?"

"Well, all those whispered promises, I was beginning to wonder if it was all talk."

His fingers pushed between my legs, causing me to gasp. "You wanting fucking? I'll give you fucking, sweetheart."

Five minutes later, he made good on all of his whispered promises.

Chapter Twenty-Five

Brett

THIS WAS A dangerous game. One I had no plan for. I leaned my hand against the shower wall, dragging in breath after breath as I held Aubrey's shaking body. I'd never experienced anything like that with a woman before. Not even Nicole. That didn't even come close to what was racing through my body right now.

I let the one thought I'd been pushing away surface.

I was no good for Aubrey. She deserved someone who could give her everything she wanted. A husband. A family. A no-drama-filled life.

"Ohmygawd," she gasped. "How many orgasms is that?"

With a smile, I opened my eyes, looked at her, and winked. "I didn't know we were keeping track. I'd have tried harder."

She shook her head as the corner of her mouth rose into a sexy smile. "I've never had an orgasm during sex before, and I'm pretty sure that was the third one in the last hour."

My chest tightened. I didn't even want to think of another man inside of her. "Well, hopefully I've ruined you for life."

Her face beamed. "I believe you have, Mr. Owens."

Pressing my lips to hers, I laced my hand through her wet hair and gave it a tug. She opened her mouth to me as I took everything I could from her. Sucking in her lower lip, I gently bit on it as a sweet, low moan filled my body.

I wouldn't think about how right this felt or how I longed to stay here with her. Or how I'd never be able to make her happy. I was about to make a change in my life. A huge change and I knew Aubrey's dreams were important to her.

No. I'd take what I could from her now, and once we got back to Austin, I'd let her go. It would be the hardest thing I'd ever have to do it, but I'd do it.

Because I loved her.

Aubrey shoved another bite of steak into her mouth and moaned. My dick responded, which shocked the hell out of me. I was exhausted, I knew my cock had to be as well. But when it came to the woman sitting across the table from me, my body would do anything to be inside of her again.

"Good?" I asked with a chuckle.

She rolled her eyes up and slowly nodded. "Brett, this is amazing. The jalapeno gravy is the best thing I've ever eaten."

"You haven't had my mother's chile rellenos. Then you can say you've had the best thing you've ever eaten."

She wiggled her brows. "Do you think she'll make it while we're here?"

With a wide grin, I replied, "I know she will."

Taking a bite of my chicken, I took a chance and glanced around the restaurant. A part of me felt like someone was watching us, but I knew I was being paranoid. The whole thing with Emily and Ryan had thrown me and I wasn't so sure it was over like Aubrey thought it was. It all seemed too easy.

"How's that tasting, Brett?"

Looking at Marge, our waitress, I answered, "It's great, thanks."

She flashed a smile over to Aubrey and made her way to the next table.

"I guess living in a small town, everyone pretty much knows everyone?" Aubrey asked.

"Pretty much, but Marfa is bigger now than it was even just a few years back."

Placing her fork on her plate, Aubrey dabbed the corners of her mouth and sat back. "I'm full."

Her plate was empty. "Well shit, woman, you ate the whole damn thing."

"Sex makes me hungry. Amazing sex, and I'm starved."

Lifting my eyebrows, I asked, "I take it you were starved because you wouldn't get anything less than amazing with my cock?"

Her mouth fell as she leaned forward. "Oh. My. God. Brett Owens, your mouth!"

"Needs to be between your legs."

This time her eyes lit up and she didn't say anything.

"Want to be daring?"

She chewed on the corner of her lip as the slipped into deep thought. "Does it involve what you just said?" she asked in a hushed voice.

"You can say it, sweetheart."

Pressing her hands to her red cheeks, she mouthed the word, "No."

"I won't tell you until you tell me what you want me to do to you with my mouth."

"I can't," she declared with a giggle. Glancing around, she tried to hide the fact that she was turned on.

"Then we won't be daring."

Her lips opened slightly and I held my breath as I waited for her to speak.

"Your mouth—"

She paused.

"My mouth what?"

Closing her eyes, she snapped them back open. "Needs to be on my …"

"Is there anything else you'd like? Dessert maybe?"

My heart dropped as Marge walked up and interrupted Aubrey. She giggled and sat back. "The kind of dessert I want isn't being offered on your menu," she said with a pout.

That little stinker. My dick jumped and I quickly pulled out two hundred-dollar bills and left them on the table. "Keep the change. Everything was great, Marge."

With a stunned expression, Marge replied, "Oh, well gosh, thanks, but don't you even want to see your check?"

Reaching for Aubrey's hand, I hauled her up. "No thanks, we're in a bit of a hurry."

"Well, thank you for coming in," the waitress called out.

Laughing, Aubrey pulled against my hand. "Where are we going? You're going to pull my arm out of its socket, Brett."

We rounded the corner and walked down a small hallway. Stopping, I pushed her against the wall. "Say it."

"I … I'm not good at this," she chuckled as her cheeks turned the most beautiful pink.

"Say. It. And I'll give it to you, now."

With wide eyes, Aubrey glanced to her left and then right before settling her gaze back on me.

"I want … um …" Her eyes closed tightly for a moment before she snapped them open and talked. "I want your mouth between my legs."

"Do you want to come on my face?"

"Oh, gosh," she whispered.

"Do you?"

Nodding frantically, she gasped, "Yes. What do you do to me, Brett?"

Slipping my hand behind her neck, I pulled her lips short of mine. "Make you want things you've never wanted before."

Her stare fell to my lips as she softly spoke. "Yes."

I pulled back, leaving her longing for the kiss. Taking her hand, I guided her across the hall and into the small banquet room. I'd been in this room so many times for different reasons. This time, I was going to make a memory I was sure I'd never forget.

"No, no, no, no! Brett, this is a sunroom! Anyone can walk by and see us."

Wiggling my eyebrows, I replied, "That's what makes it daring."

"You're insane."

"No, I'm horny."

She shook her head. "Does your dick have the energizer bunny in there? How can you keep going?"

I leaned into her and pressed my hard cock against her. "I keep going, and going, and going. Until you beg me to stop."

"Well, we'll see about that."

"A challenge? You know how much I like them."

Aubrey smirked. "Don't forget, I won the last one."

Dropping to my knees, I unbuttoned her jeans. Her hands went to my hair as she ran them through it and tugged every so lightly. "You're not arguing with me anymore, sweetheart."

"Shut up and do it."

Making a tsk-ing sound, I replied, "So bossy. Will this be in the article? Coach Owens gives mind-blowing oral sex in public."

"Stop talking!"

With a chuckle, I plucked her sneaker off her right foot and pulled her jeans off. I loved that she was letting me do this. Lifting her leg, she moaned before I even touched her. I swallowed hard as I watched her touch her breasts through her T-shirt.

"God, what are you doing to me?" she whispered.

A part of me wanted to stop, I knew the more we were together, the closer we'd grow. The other part of me wanted her too much to stop.

Pressing my mouth over her pussy, I pushed my tongue inside of her as she grabbed my hair and pulled me closer.

It didn't take long before I won the challenge.

Chapter Twenty-Six

Aubrey

SITTING ON THE bed of Brett's truck, we watched the mysterious lights of Marfa. I leaned against his chest as he held me. It felt so right being in his arms. I didn't want to do it, but I dreamed of another life with Brett. Living on the ranch, sitting on the porch with a dog sitting next to us, all while I rocked a baby in my arms.

"What are you thinking about?" he asked, drawing me out of thoughts.

"How peaceful it is out here."

My heart hurt lying to him, but I knew Brett Owens was not the type to just walk away from a career he loved to become a husband and father. The dull headache was starting to form as I thought about what it would be like once we got back to Austin.

I had a career I loved and had worked my ass off for, and so did Brett. There was no way I could do a long distance relationship. Chewing on my lip, another light appeared. This one was bigger and there was no way it was from a car on the highway.

"There it is," he whispered. "Make your wish."

Closing my eyes, I made my wish. His hot breath against my skin made me shiver. "Did you make it?"

"I did," I said breathlessly. "Did you?"

He held me closer. "I did."

Neither one of us said a thing as we watched the light slowly fade to black.

I flinched when he spoke. "You ready to head back, we have a long drive."

"Yep. I'm so tired all of a sudden."

Brett slid out from under me and jumped out of the truck. Before I had a chance to jump down, he took me in his arms and carried me to the passenger side of the truck. My stomach dipped at the sweet gesture. As he sat me down on the seat and pulled my seatbelt over, I dared to think maybe we could make this work. Leaning in, he kissed me gently on the lips. "Thank you for today."

Lifting my hand up, I placed it on the side of his face. I was falling in love with Brett and I couldn't deny it.

"Thank you."

One more quick peck on the lips and Brett was making his way around the front of the truck. Once he pulled out onto the highway, I rested my head back and stared out the window. There was no way I could walk away from what we had started. Not with how I felt about Brett. I'd ask Joe about working from Austin. The days I traveled, Brett would be traveling with the team. The rest of the time, we could be together.

It could work if we tried.

I dared to let myself believe it as I drifted to sleep.

The light from the window caused me to squint my eyes shut. "Oh my gosh," I whispered, stretching and feeling the aches across my body. Smiling, I remembered exactly how I got those aches.

Sitting up, I ran my fingers over my lips. Brett had carried me upstairs after I had fallen asleep in the truck. I woke when he laid me in bed. We spent what seemed like hours kissing. What started as a goodnight kiss, ended up being a total make-out session. My lips still tingled and felt swollen.

I jumped up and headed into the bathroom that was attached to my room. After a quick shower, I brushed my teeth and pulled my hair up into a ponytail. One quick gander in the mirror and I decided to go with only mascara today and a light blush. My face seemed to be already flushed and I was sure it was from all the orgasms Brett pulled out of me yesterday. And Lord knows how I'll blush when I see his parents.

Walking over to my computer, I brought up my email. None of it was urgent, so I decided to head downstairs and find Brett.

It didn't take long to hear Birdy and Joseph's voices coming from the kitchen. Before I rounded the corner, I took in a deep breath and tried to act normal.

"Good morning," I said with a smile, but not a huge one. If I came in too happy, then they would know their son had his wicked way with me and I enjoyed every single second of it.

Birdy's gaze met mine. "Why, don't you look extra beautiful this morning."

Shit. They know.

"I slept great."

Oh, geesh, Aubrey. Why don't you just tell them the truth?

"It must be this country air," I quickly added.

With a wink, Birdy responded with, "Uh-huh. It's totally the air."

"There are some biscuits and fresh strawberries over there in the basket if you're interested, sweetheart."

My stomach rumbled. "Thank you, Joseph."

Taking a plate, I put a biscuit and a few strawberries on it. "Has Brett already eaten?"

Birdy was reading the morning paper. It was funny to me to see someone read the paper. It was becoming rarer. Usually people got their news from their phone, Facebook, or CNN. "Yes, he came down early and went for a run, then ate, and said he had some business to take care of with Mac."

I knew it wasn't any of my business, but I was still bothered by the exchange between the two of them yesterday. "Is everything okay between Mac and Brett? They seemed to be tense around each other yesterday."

Joseph sighed. "I'm afraid Mac has been taken on more and more here at the ranch and Brett isn't too happy about it."

Swallowing the berry, I asked, "Why not?"

Birdy glimpsed at Joseph, then me. She let out a small sigh and gave me a slight grin. "Brett loves football."

I nodded. "Yes, I know."

"He also loves this ranch. When he was a senior in high school, he announced he wasn't going to college."

A stunned expression covered my face. "What?"

"That's pretty much what my reaction was, times ten. We told him he had to follow his dreams and those dreams were college football and the NFL. He was torn because he wanted to stay here and ranch alongside his father."

Smiling, I wrapped my arms around myself. That sounded like the Brett I'd come to know.

Joseph cleared his throat. "I knew he had two dreams and if I kept my mouth shut, he'd have stayed here. I know my son." The sadness in Joseph's eyes was so evident. "I told him he needed to follow his dreams. He listened to me and did. Of course, they ended up a bit different, but in the long run, I think he's happier."

I wasn't so sure about Joseph's last statement.

"He loves his job at the university. I've seen him in action this last month. He's an amazing coach and person. You should both be very proud of him."

Birdy grinned practically from ear to ear. "I've never been so proud of him and what he has accomplished."

I silently said another prayer and thanked God for the way the whole Emily thing turned out.

"I've also seen another side of him here, though. He's so different. Completely at ease and happy. I've never had so much fun like I've had the last few days."

Birdy and Joseph smiled. "Well, I'm glad they sent you to do the article on him," Birdy said with a wink.

My heart skipped a beat. "Me too," I said, taking a sip of tea I had made.

The door to the kitchen jerked open, scaring all of us. Brett came storming in and slammed the door shut.

"Brett, what's wrong?" Birdy asked.

Ignoring his mother, he walked up to his dad. "How could you tell him the ranch would be his one day?"

Joseph drew his head back in surprise. "What and who are you talking about?"

"Mac! That's who I'm talking about, Dad. You told him I didn't want it and had no interest in running it. And he could have the place in Wyoming? What the fuck, Dad? You know how much I love that place."

Birdy jumped up. "Brett Owens, do not talk to your father that way."

Joseph held up his hands. "It's okay, he has a right to be angry."

My pulse was racing. I'd never seen Brett so upset.

"So you don't deny it."

Joseph expelled a short breath. "I don't deny saying he could run the ranch. I never said it would become his."

"Well he sure as hell thinks it will be."

Running his hand through his hair, Joseph looked hard at Brett. "You have a career, Brett. One that you love. I never wanted to make you think you had to pick, but anytime you want to come back you know this place is yours to run."

"And Wyoming?"

I felt like I was invading a private family meeting. I stood up and slowly retreated.

"I've already told you, I'm going to sell one of the ranches. I can't keep flying back and forth between the two."

A look of sickness washed over Brett's face. "You know how much I love that ranch up there, Dad."

My stomach dropped and I stopped walking. Last night Brett had talked about the summers and holidays they had spent up in Wyoming and how much he loved it. His dream had been to retire there some day. The way he described the house was amazing. I pictured it to be a log cabin mansion. Not unlike the one we were in right now. I knew this was killing him, his dad wanting to get rid of one of the ranches.

"Look, nothing is set in stone, and Mac is not taking anything from you."

"You're damn right he's not."

It was then Brett noticed me. He stopped talking and walked over to me, his face beaming with happiness. As if this whole conversation had never happened.

"Good morning. Did you sleep okay?"

I was completely taken aback as my stare drifted over Brett's shoulders to his two parents who were now standing there like lovestruck puppies listening to our exchange.

"I did. How about you?"

His eyes turned black and I knew he wanted to say something dirty but couldn't.

"It was uneventful. Do you have work to do or can you hang out with me and see what it takes to run a ranch?"

I needed to get working on the article, but decided spending time with Brett is what I really wanted to do.

"I'd love to see what *you all* do to make the ranch run."

Brett frowned. "Bree, were you just trying to say y'all?"

"Yeah. *You all.*"

Birdy giggled, "Lord, take the girl out to the barn and stop worrying about everything, Brett Owens. We'll talk later."

"Enjoy the day, *y'all*," Joseph said laughing.

Brett slid his arm around my waist "Come on, cowgirl, let's go muck some stalls."

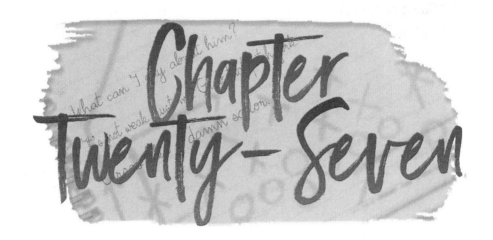

Chapter Twenty-Seven

Brett

MY HEART STOPPED when I realized Aubrey had been standing there. I didn't want her hearing me arguing with my father. Mac had a way of getting me worked up the last few days. The idea of him taking over the running of either ranch didn't sit well with me and I planned on talking to my father about it later. Maybe spending some time with Aubrey would calm me down.

Aubrey changed into jeans, a T-shirt, and boots and met me at the main stalls.

"So we're mucking out a stall you say? Such a romantic way to swoon a girl."

I lifted my head to see her standing in the entrance of the barn. "Hey, come meet, Kit, our new addition." Kit was a five-year old Palomino mare that I fell in love with the first time I saw her.

Making her way over, she stopped and gave me a smile that made my knees weak. Aubrey ran her hand along the back of Kit and then down each leg, lifting it to look at her hooves. I was pretty sure I fell in love with her even more watching her work with a horse.

"She's beautiful."

"I think so too. I found her online about a month ago, told my dad about her and he bought her. She arrived this morning."

Aubrey's face lit up. "Oh my gosh, what perfect timing for you to be here when she arrived."

I nodded. "Yeah, I think she'll be a perfect for my mom with her classes. She's a giant, but seems gentle."

The way she was eyeing the horse, I knew she wanted to ride her. "How about we muck out this stall that another horse was in and then we take her and another horse out?"

"Really? I absolutely love riding."

She set herself up for that one. "Good, you can ride me here in a bit."

With a wicked grin, she walked up to me. "Your shock factor is either getting weak, or I'm getting used to it."

Laughing, I kissed her quickly and slapped her on the ass. "It's not weak, trust me. Grab that pitch fork."

Aubrey grabbed the fork and went to town. Between the two of us, we had Kit's stall clean and ready for her when we got back from a ride. I watched as Aubrey folded the sides of the clean hay in against the wall.

If I didn't think someone would walk in, I would've taken her from behind and made her scream out my name.

"There. Looks perfect now."

Wiping her brow, she stepped out of the stall and made her way outside to Kit. One of the stablehands had already saddled up Kit and Spike. Aubrey climbed up on her and leaned over, whispering something in her ear and then gave her a pat on the neck. I'd noticed she had done the same thing with Joe and the other horses she'd rode.

We started walking toward a trail when I asked, "What do you say to the horse when you first get on?"

Peeking over at me, she smirked. "You want to know my secret. Hmm … I'm afraid I can't tell you. It's between the horse and me."

I rolled my eyes and huffed. "Whatever."

"Why, Mr. Owens, are you jealous of my mad riding skills?"

"You still haven't proved them to me."

She lifted a brow. "Is that a challenge?"

Knowing exactly where this would lead, I replied, "Yes. There's an open field up there. First person to get to the mesquite tree wins."

Scrunching her nose, she said, "I don't even know what a mesquite tree is! And how do I know if this horse is fast or not. I know Spike is!"

I couldn't help but laugh. Kicking Spike into a trot, I called back, "You're the horse whisperer, you'll figure it out."

The meadow opened up and I heard Aubrey call out to Kit. Following her lead, I pressed Spike to go faster. I let her run with me neck-and-neck before I whistled and gave my horse another squeeze of my legs and he took off. I made it past the mesquite tree with time to spare.

Coming to a stop in front of me, Aubrey was laughing. "You cheated. You knew this horse was not going to go that fast."

"Doesn't matter, you accepted. I'm the winner so you have to do what I say."

Her head leaned forward with a questioning look. "Um, when did we come up with that?"

"Just now. Get off your horse and follow me."

Aubrey slid off Kit. "Will they be okay?"

"Yeah, they'll be fine."

She looked nervous leaving them to graze in the field. Pulling her into my arms, I placed my finger under her chin and brought her eyes to mine. "I promise, they'll be fine."

With a grin, she took my hand and let me lead her down the trail. "It's kind of weird having this group of trees. Seems like it's so vastly bare out here."

"My grandfather used to call this his hidden oasis."

"Why?" she asked as I pushed the large tree limb out of the way, exposing the small cabin.

"Oh my goodness. How adorable. What is this place?"

"The original homestead. My father had it restored a few years back and my folks rent it out from time to time."

We made our way up the old stone stairs and I couldn't help but notice the huge smile on Aubrey's face. "Why are you smiling?"

Turning to me, she shook her head. "Because I'm happy, and I can honestly say I haven't been this happy in a long time."

I brought her hand up to my lips and kissed the back of it. "I feel the same way."

Pulling the keys from my pocket, I unlocked the door and stepped inside. There was nothing fancy about the cabin. It was one room. A queen-sized bed sat on the right side of the cabin. The middle held two small chairs and a coffee table. To the very left was a small kitchen and a table for two.

Shutting the door, I tugged Aubrey over to the bed and smiled. "Get undressed."

Covering her mouth, she looked at the bed and then me. "Are we ... we're doing something here?"

With a chuckle, I replied, "No, you're going to fuck me. Here."

"You bad boy, telling your parents you were showing me the ranch."

I started to undress, first kicking off my boots and then pulling my T-shirt over my head. Aubrey licked her lips as she watched.

"Are you going to stand there or are you getting undressed?"

She quickly shed her clothes and stood before me completely naked. Most women would want the lights out or they would jump under the covers before I could look at them, but not my Aubrey. Her body was amazing and she knew it. That, or she simply didn't give a shit. I was guessing it was a mix of both.

"Is there satellite TV in here?" She picked up the remote and I fell back on the bed. "I'm sure, but do you really want to watch TV?"

Flipping through the guide, I groaned when I saw what she pulled up.

Eighties music.

"No. I cannot have sex to this music."

Her hand went to her hip. She looked sexy as fuck.

"Oh, come on!"

"No! Put it on anything else but this. I mean, listen to how depressing this song is."

She looked back at the TV. "It's Cutting Crew! How could you not like them?"

I didn't say a word as she sighed and changed it. A pop song played. "This! Perfect."

"It's a remake of an old song!"

Laughing, I jumped up and grabbed her as she laughed. Throwing her on the bed, I crawled over her. "What an appropriate title of a song, 'Sex.'"

Teasing her entrance, she sucked in a breath. "I couldn't sleep last night."

Running my nose along her neck, I asked, "Why?"

With a low growl from the back of her throat, she said, "Because all I could think about was you inside of me and how amazing it was."

I pulled back and stared into those brown eyes. "It was amazing."

Aubrey frowned, "Did he say let's talk about pussy power in that song?"

Shrugging, I kissed her throat and down her chest. I had totally tuned the music out. "Are you ready to show me how good of a rider you are?"

Her face blushed. "What if I suck?"

Sitting back, I pulled her up. Brushing a piece of hair that had fallen from her ponytail out of the way, I answered her. "That's impossible."

She chewed on her lip as she glanced down at my dick. "I'm nervous," she giggled.

Damn, I couldn't get over this girl.

Leaning over, I grabbed my wallet from my back pocket and grabbed a condom. "I'd let you put it on, but I'm afraid I'd come the moment you touched me."

She pushed me back on the shoulder but glanced down and watched me roll the condom on. Laying back, I motioned with my head for her to crawl on. "I know you've been on top before, Bree."

A slight nod told me she had been, but probably not that often.

Moving over me, I reached up and fingered her, getting her ready for me. Her eyes turned almost black.

I had to force the words out of my mouth. She looked so hot. "Fuck me, Bree."

She slowly sank down a little. With a hiss, she lifted up and kept repeating the process until I filled her completely.

"Fuck yes, baby. You feel so good."

"Feels so deep and full," she whispered.

The way she rolled her hips slowly was driving me insane. My hands held her hips. "Bree, move."

Before I even knew what was happening she was calling out my name as she rode me fast and hard. I was on the verge of coming myself. Flipping her over, I fucked her from behind. Grabbing her hips and giving her what I knew we both wanted.

"Harder! Oh, God, yes," she cried out.

It didn't long for me to come. After getting my wits about me, I pulled out of her and got rid of the condom. Crawling back onto the bed, I pulled the covers up as she slid over to me.

"Can we stay here all day?" she asked while her fingers traced a circle over my chest.

My heartbeat quickened. "A part of me wishes we'd never leave."

She moved and rested her chin on her hand and looked into my eyes.

"You know we can't ignore it forever."

Holding her closer, I kissed her forehead. "I know, but I don't want to think about it now."

We spent the next hour talking about ESPN, my short stint in the NFL, and the article. Aubrey asked if I wanted to read it before she turned it in for Joe to read.

"Nah, I trust you."

Her crooked grin melted my heart. "That means a lot to me."

Another kiss on the forehead before I pushed out a deep breath. "We better get going. I'm sure the horses are ready for some water."

Aubrey jumped up. "Oh my gosh! I totally forgot about the horses!"

I'd never seen a girl get dressed so fast in my life.

"Hurry, Brett!" she called over her shoulder as we walked down the path toward the field. Sure enough, Spike and Kit were right there, just grazing.

"Oh! What good babies," Aubrey swooned. "I think they deserve a treat when we get back."

Climbing up on Spike, I patted the side of his neck as he bobbed his head. "A bath. They both stink."

I had no idea how Aubrey did it, but she brought out a totally different side of me I had buried long ago. I soon found myself at the barn, with Belinda Carlisle's "Mad About You" blasting on the satellite radio running around throwing soapy water at each other.

The more time I spent with her, the harder it was going to be letting her go.

I'd finally found the woman I wanted to make love to the rest of my life, and I couldn't have her.

Chapter Twenty-Eight

Aubrey

"SO, WHAT'S HE like in bed?"

Glancing around, I got up and shut the door to the library. "Oh my gosh. Why is it always about sex with you, Nelly?"

"Why do you ask me such stupid questions? Is the guy good in bed or not? It's a normal question."

Dropping on the couch, I sighed. "He's amazing. Like nothing I've ever experienced before."

"It's because he's a dirty talker. That's hot."

"He doesn't always talk dirty to me though. Especially when we're making love."

It had been three days since Brett and I had first slept together. Each moment we could sneak away, we did. The more we were together, the more I knew we could make a relationship work.

"How's this going to work with you living in different states?

Chewing on my thumb nail, I replied, "We haven't really talked about it."

"What? You're sleeping with the guy. No wait. You're sleeping with the guy you're supposed to be writing a huge article about, and you haven't talked to him about the future."

My stomach fell. I knew my sister was right. We were leaving tomorrow to head back to Austin. Brett and I were going to have to find the time to sit and talk about things.

"Hold on, my phone's beeping and it's Christine."

"Okay," I said as I stood up and walked over to the large window. My gaze immediately fell on Brett. He was walking up toward the house with his father. The conversation looked deep. I hoped they were able to settle things with the ranches. Brett wouldn't really admit it, but I knew his heart was more here working alongside his father than he wanted to admit. I could see it in his eyes.

"Bree?"

"Yep, I'm still here."

Nelly sniffled and my heart sank. Something was wrong. "What's wrong?"

"It's, Dad. He's had a heart attack."

Brett looked over and our eyes met. "Wh-what?"

"I'm so sorry to tell you like this, but the ambulance is rushing him from the gym now. Can you come home?"

My arm dropped as tears instantly fell down my cheeks. Brett stopped walking for a brief second before he took off running toward me.

Right before the darkness swept in, I heard Brett calling my name.

Daddy.

Brett walked up and handed me a coffee in a white Styrofoam cup and an apple. I didn't want either, but I knew if I didn't take it my mother would end up saying I needed something in my body.

Sitting next to me, Brett put his arm around my shoulders. The welcomed heat from his body felt good.

I turned to him and smiled weakly. "You don't have to stay. With everything over with Emily, I'm sure Pat expects you back at work."

"I've already talked to him. I told him I'll be back Sunday."

With a simple nod, I looked down at the tea. "You should drink it and eat that apple, or I'm afraid your mom will force it down your throat."

With a light chuckle, I took a bite of the apple. The crisp juice felt good on my lips and in my mouth. My stomach growled and I peeked up at Brett. He gave me a look that said I needed to eat.

Lifting his brow, he said, "Once they come out, I'm taking you to get something to eat."

My chest tightened. Brett had been so caring and attentive ever since I found out my father had a heart attack. I knew he had to be exhausted. He hadn't slept in I don't know how long. We had rushed back to Austin as quick as we could. After I broke down of course, and cried. Birdy was so sweet to me. She packed all of my stuff while I sat in a chair in my room and sobbed.

Brett's father booked us tickets on the first flight out to Connecticut, getting us in this morning right before they brought my father back for heart valve replacement surgery.

The door to the waiting room opened and the doctor came out. Everyone jumped up and rushed over to him. My sisters and I all stayed a few feet back as he talked to my mother.

"He's doing great. The valve is working perfectly. It's a long recovery for Jim, there is no doubt about that, but I'm very pleased with how the surgery went. He'll be in ICU for one to three days then moved to a regular room for another three days."

I was pretty sure everyone sighed in relief at once. "Thank you so much, doctor. I can't even begin to tell you how grateful we are for what you've done."

He smiled at my mother then looked at all of us. "Well, your husband is in great physical shape, he just had a faulty heart valve. As long as he keeps up a heart healthy diet and regular exercise, I don't see why he can't live a long healthy life."

My mother's hands covered her mouth. "Thank you. Thank you so much."

Brett reached out and shook the doctor's hand. "Thank you, Doctor, for the update."

"My pleasure, son. And I'll be rooting for Austin this fall."

Brett's face wore a surprised look on it. "Don't be surprised, Coach. I'm an alumni of the University of Austin."

With a slight laugh, Brett replied, "Well, thank you for your support, sir. I appreciate it."

"Great job coaching. We're lucky you're ours."

I wasn't sure why I thought that was so amazing, the way Brett went out of his way to thank the doctor. Maybe because my sister Christine's husband didn't. I was just as surprised as Brett that the doctor he knew who he was.

Turning to face everyone, my mother declared, "It'll a bit before we can see your dad. I think we should all get something to eat."

Everyone agreed, except for me. I knew Brett was exhausted. I was exhausted. "Mom, I'll grab something to eat on the way to my place, but we haven't showered or slept in a while. Would you mind?"

My mother glanced between me and Brett. I was positive she knew there was something going on between us. Really, why would he fly all the way here to be with me if I was only in a working relationship with him?

She walked up to me and kissed me on the cheek. "Of course, sweetheart. Get some food and a few hours of sleep. We'll have to go in one at a time, I'm sure anyway." Facing Brett, she pulled him into a hug and whispered something into his ear. He chuckled and nodded his head.

"Yes, ma'am," he said as she patted him on the arm.

Nelly walked up to me and hugged me. Putting her mouth to my ear she whispered, "Now that we know dad is okay, holy living shit. He's fucking gorgeous. No wonder you're hitting that."

Pushing her away, I glared at her. "Oh my God. Stop!"

She laughed and quickly kissed me on the cheek. "Don't be gone long. I don't think I can put up with grumpy, pregnant Christine and Marie the bridezilla."

Glancing over to my other two sisters, I covered my mouth to hide my giggle. They were both such drama queens. With everything.

"See you later, Brett!" Nelly exclaimed with a wink.

Wrapping his arm around my waist, Brett guided me to the elevator. "Your sister Nelly scares me."

I chortled as we stepped into the elevator. "You should be scared. She is attracted to anything with a dick."

"She looks at me like she wants to devour me."

He laced his fingers in mine, causing my stomach to drop. Maybe Brett did want the type of relationship I wanted. I hated the thought we would be separated, though. With my father's heart attack, I wasn't so sure about my idea of moving to Texas now.

By the time we hailed a cab, got in, and told him my address, I felt the lack of sleep hit me like a brick wall. Leaning my head on Brett's shoulder, I slowly felt my body relaxing.

I'd think about me and Brett later. For now, I needed to focus on my father.

Chapter Twenty-Nine

Brett

A UBREY WAS IN the shower so I stepped out onto her balcony to call Pat.

"How is she?" Pat inquired.

"Fine, I think. She's been really quiet. Like she's deep in thought."

"I'm sure that was a scare. Are you going to be okay leaving her?"

My chest hurt thinking about it, but I knew I had to. "Yep."

"You say that like you don't really believe it."

"I'll be fine. She's home with her family, and I know she wouldn't want it any other way."

Pat sighed. "Well, I'm glad we got the whole Emily thing taken care of."

Combing my fingers through my wet hair, I agreed. "You and me both. Now, if I see Ryan, I may want to beat the fuck out of him."

"Well don't. The last thing we need is that."

"I can't believe he used to be like a brother to me."

The tension was building as I fisted my left hand.

Heat from Aubrey's hand hit my back, causing me to instantly relax. "I better get going, Pat. I'll be back Sunday."

"All right. Give Aubrey my best and let her know Sharron and I will be praying for her father."

Turning, I held my arm up and Aubrey melted against my body. "I'll tell her. Thanks, Pat."

"Talk soon," Pat said. The line went silent as I pushed the phone into my pocket.

"Pat said they're keeping Jim in their prayers."

Aubrey wrapped her arms around my body tightly. "He's such a nice guy. I'll have to send him something for how nice he was while I was there and for letting you stay with me for a couple days."

Pushing her back some, I looked into her tired eyes. "You need to get some sleep, sweetheart."

Her teeth sank into her lip. "I know what would relax me."

With a smirk, I asked, "A foot massage?"

Her eyes turned dark. "Hmm … that would feel nice."

I reached down and lifted her up into my arms. Carrying her back into her living room, I placed her on the sofa.

"Lay down, sweetheart."

She did as I asked. Sitting, I lifted her feet and massaged them. The little noises that were coming from her lips had my dick growing hard. Shit, I wanted her, but I didn't want to force her into anything. I knew she was both emotionally and physically exhausted.

Ignoring the throbbing in my dick, I moved my hands up her legs. It didn't take long for her to fall asleep.

Dropping my head back, I felt my own eyes growing heavy. Sleep soon took over.

"Brett."

"Mmm," I moaned. I loved dreaming about Aubrey. The way she whispered my name against my lips. The heat from her breath was an instant turn on.

"Baby, are you awake?"

She was on me. Rubbing her tight pussy against my cock. Fuck, it felt so good.

"Brett, I need you to make love to me."

My eyes opened to see her staring at me.

"Bree," I whispered as I cupped her face in my hands. She was straddling me on the sofa, her wet heat separated by two thin layers of clothing.

My lips pressed to hers. She tugged my T-shirt over my head, breaking the kiss long enough for it to pass between our mouths.

"Please," she whimpered, pushing my shorts down, causing my dick to spring free. Her hand wrapped around it brought out a low deep growl from the back of my throat. Her finger lightly rubbed the top of my cock, lubricating it with my own desire. My hands went under the long T-shirt she had on as she pressed her lips against mine. I quickly discovered she wasn't wearing any panties.

"Fuck," I said pushing her back and lifting the long T-shirt over her head. Aubrey laid back as I crawled over her. I had never wanted to be inside her like I did in this moment. Her eyes were pleading with me and that turned me on more than anything.

"Tell me what you want, sweetheart."

She closed her eyes and lifted her hips. "Make love to me, Brett."

Slowly pushing into her, I about died. Our moans intertwined as I slowly made love to her. Her arms and legs wrapped around my body, as if she was trying to crawl inside of me. Little did she know I'd already let her in.

"Brett," she whispered as I pushed in deeper, slowly giving her everything I had, but in the most caring and adoring way I could. I'd never experienced this before.

We were not having sex, there was no fucking. We were one, together. My heart was beating hard in my chest. If I wasn't going so slow, I would think I was fucking her hard and fast. Each movement felt as if I was giving her more of me. My head was screaming for me to slow down with my feelings, but my heart wanted to give her more. So much more.

"I'm going to come," her voice stated with a tremble.

It was instant. Her pussy clamped down on my cock and I lost it. "Oh, God, Aubrey."

Something happened.

I'd never given a woman what I had given Aubrey. My complete heart.

My cock twitched inside of her as I kept my face buried in her neck. "Bree," I barely whispered.

Lifting up on my hands, my breath caught when I looked at her. A few tears rolled down her beautiful face.

"What's wrong?" I asked in a panicked voice.

She slowly nodded her head. "Nothing. That was the most beautiful thing I've ever experienced. I've fallen in love with you, Brett."

Swallowing hard, I felt my heart drop. Pulling out of her I looked down.

Holy fucking shit.

"No! What did I do?"

Aubrey looked down.

"I didn't wear a condom. How could I be so stupid? I've never forgotten to wear one. Ever!"

Jumping up, I headed into the bathroom, leaving Aubrey on the sofa. It was a dick move, but I was freaking out. I'd never had sex in my life without a condom. Even with Nicole.

Fuck. Fuck. Fuck.

I reached for the faucet and turned it on to hot as I grabbed a washcloth. Quickly cleaning myself off, I turned to go take care of Aubrey, but she was standing there, with her T-shirt on.

"I was … I was coming to clean you up."

There was no way I could read the look on her face. She reached for the cloth and cleaned herself before throwing it into the sink.

"Aubrey, I'm so sorry I was careless like that."

She walked away from me and into her bedroom. "I didn't notice either, Brett."

"Well, if I could go back in time, I ..."

Spinning around, she glared at me. "That was the most amazing moment of my life. Not to mention I put myself out there and told you I was falling in love with you, and what do you do? You freak out!"

"I didn't wear a condom!"

"I'm on the pill!"

Relief washed over my body.

"Thank you, God," I whispered as I covered my heart.

Her lip quivered. "Does the idea of that really make you sick, Brett?"

Pulling my head back, I stared at her. "What?"

"Nothing. I'm going back to the hospital."

Wait. What in the hell is happening right now?

"Aubrey, will you hold on one second," I said, taking her by the arm and gently turning her back to me. "Okay, I freaked out and I'm sorry. The moment we shared was amazing. Beyond amazing, but with everything that happened with Emily, I got spooked. Do you remember when I said I've never made love to anyone before? I can't say that anymore. Everything it happening so fast, my head is spinning."

Her eyes filled with tears. "What do you want, Brett?"

I looked at her with a confused expression. "What do you mean?"

Pointing between the two of us, she replied, "With us. What are you wanting between us?"

My mouth opened, but nothing came out.

"I want you and only you, Brett."

The room felt like it was spinning. "I want you too, Bree."

"But are you willing to give up your playboy ways and be exclusive?"

My head was pounding. "Why do we have to talk about this now?"

"When would we talk about it?"

"I don't know, Aubrey. You're hitting me with this out of the blue. What do you want from me?"

A tear slipped away and slowly made a trail down her cheek. My instinct was to reach out and wipe it away.

"I want you, Brett. Exclusively."

Fucking hell. I'd been down this path before with Nicole. "Aubrey, you live here and I live in Austin. I'm not going to make you do something that wouldn't be good for your career."

She shook her head. "I can't move to Austin, not with my father having a heart attack."

My hands scrubbed down my face as I let out a laugh. "Why is it so important we decide on this now?"

"Why can't you say you'll be mine exclusively and that we'll figure something out?"

Narrowing my brows, all I heard was Nicole's voice in my head, accusing me of cheating. "Why don't you trust me?"

When she didn't answer, I walked over to the bag I brought. Grabbing a pair of jeans, I slipped them on.

"I do trust you, and I'm sorry I'm pushing you. I'm overly emotional, and I don't know why I'm acting like such a baby. I'm sorry."

The hurt in her voice was practically screaming in my head. Everything was racing through my thoughts. My parents and the ranch, Mac trying to take it out from under me, the university counting on me for another championship. To top it all off, I was freaked out about what had happened between me and Aubrey. Aubrey saying that she loved me didn't help any. Even though I felt the same way, I wasn't sure I was ready to admit it to her. Everything was happening too fast. How could I commit to a future with Aubrey, when I had no idea where my own future was going?

When would I have time to see her? Once the season started, we'd both be traveling.

I absentmindedly pulled my shirt over my head as I tried to figure this out.

"Brett? Did you hear me?"

Looking up at her, I nodded. "Yeah. This isn't going to work."

Her face fell. "Wh-what?"

"I don't think I can give you what you want."

"Please don't do this, Brett. I said I was being overly emotional."

Walking up to her, I placed my hand on the side of her face. It tore me apart knowing she wanted something I wasn't sure I could give her. "I can't give you the things I know you want. I think deep down you know that. Marriage and kids are not on my radar right now, and you said that was something you wanted. I don't know where my life is headed, Bree. I can't promise you that, at least not now."

Another tear slipped from her eye. Leaning over, I brushed it away with my lips.

"Brett, we can make it work. I know we can."

Pulling her into my arms, I kissed the top of her head. "Your dad is going to have a long recovery, and I know you're not going to leave him, Bree. I'm not sure I can do the distance thing again. We'd never see each other."

Her head fell to my chest as she cried. Holding her tighter, I pressed my lips to the top of her head. I loved her. There was no denying that. I'd never in my life had another woman make me feel the way Aubrey did. *Why would I just walk away from this without trying? She is the best thing that has ever happened to me.*

"I'd never do anything to hurt you."

"I know," she mumbled and nodded.

Swallowing hard, I knew I had to be truthful. I owed it to her. "But, I love you too, and fuck if I don't want to let you go."

Her face drew back. "What are you saying?"

One second I was saying it wouldn't work, and the next I was scared shitless I'd lose the only woman I'd ever loved. "I don't know how it will work, Bree. All I know is I can't walk away from you and the way you make me feel. If you're willing to give this distance thing a try, I am. I've never experienced these feelings with anyone else before, and although it scares the piss out of me, it also makes me feel alive. This time we've spent together has changed me. For the better. But I need to be upfront with you and honest. I want to give us a go, but I'm not ready for marriage or a family."

She swallowed hard. I was sure her mind was racing, and I wouldn't blame her if she told me to leave.

With a smile so beautiful it made my stomach drop, she softly spoke. "I don't want you to let me go either."

Feeling the instant relief, I grinned and placed a soft kiss on her lips.

"Then I won't."

Chapter Thirty

Brett

TROY SAT IN the chair across from my desk. The look on his face pissed me off, and I knew why he was here. "You're miserable."

"I am not," I stated, shifting paper around on my desk.

With a huff, he asked, "When did you see her last?"

"Two weeks ago."

He leaned forward. "Two weeks. If this is how you're going to be with two weeks, imagine what a month or more will feel like."

"It's won't be that long."

Laughing, he dropped back in his seat. "Brett, I don't mean to cross a line, but I remember what happened with Nicole."

Piercing his eyes with mine, I gritted my teeth together. "This is *nothing* like that."

"Really? Because if my memory serves me right, you said you would never again be in a relationship that kept you away from the person. And look where you're at."

"This is different."

"Why?"

Frustration laced my voice as I said, "Because I love her."

His eyes grew wide. "And you didn't love Nicole?"

"Not like this."

He nodded his head. "That's interesting."

Letting out a sigh, I asked, "Troy, don't you have work to do or something?"

With a shrug he replied, "Nope. But I am going out tonight. Say you'll come."

"No thanks," I answered, filing some papers away in the desk drawer.

Troy stood. "I'm going with my sister and her friend. It's completely innocent and I really don't want to be the only guy with these two. I *need* someone to talk to."

"Where?"

He smiled wide. "I'll make it easy. Second Street bar and grill. All you have to do is walk across the street. You'll like Cass, she's super smart and engaged, so no chance of her hitting on you."

My phone buzzed with a text from Aubrey.

Finally. I hadn't heard from her all day.

Bree: Hey! Sorry it's been a crazy day. How's yours going?

Me: Long. Troy wants me to go to dinner with his sister and her friend. He needs me there so he has someone to talk to.

Bree: You should go! Get a free meal out of him!

Me: Both girls have boyfriends.

Bree: Brett ... I trust you. Have to run. I love you!

Me: I love you too.

"You do know it's rude to text your hot girlfriend while I'm sitting here."

Not bothering to glance up at him, I replied, "Fine, but you're buying my dinner."

"It's a deal."

Lifting my hand, I gave him the finger. "Now leave my office."

Walking into the restaurant, I looked around for Troy. My heart was heavy.

I missed Aubrey. I hated this long distance shit. It had only been two weeks, yet it felt like two years.

Troy stood and waved me over. With a grin, I headed their way.

"Hey, sorry I'm a little late. I helped the doorman with something."

Both girls looked up at me and smiled. I'd met Kim, Troy's sister, plenty of times. Reaching my hand over to her, I said, "Hey, Kim. How's it going?"

"It's going. Brett, this is my best friend Cass."

I repeated the gesture with Cass before sitting down.

It didn't take long to fall into an easy conversation with Cass. She was raised on a cattle ranch, had a degree in sports medicine, and loved football.

About an hour after dinner, my phone buzzed.

Pulling it out of my pocket, I grinned like a fool when I saw her name.

"Must be a girlfriend," Cass teased.

"Yeah, Aubrey. She's a reporter for ESPN."

She lifted her brows. "Oh, that's cool. What a fun job."

Opening the text, I stared at it.

Aubrey: Do you remember where we first met?

Quickly turning around, I saw her standing at the bar. I was positive the smile on my face lit up the entire room.

Dropping my napkin on the table, I stood. Turning to look at the two girls and Troy, I said, "Thank you so much for the wonderful company, but I'm going to excuse myself."

"Thanks for joining us, Brett," Troy said standing and shaking my hand.

"Good evening ladies. Cass, it was nice getting to know you, I hope you like Austin."

She returned my smile with one of her own. "Thanks, Brett. The pleasure was all mine."

Making my way through the sea of people and tables, I finally stood in front of her.

She glanced over my shoulder. "Seems like you made an impression on someone."

Looking back, Cass was watching us. She looked away when I caught her stare. Shrugging it off, I focused back on Aubrey.

"Nah. She's engaged and getting married in a few weeks. This is a nice surprise. What are you doing here?" I asked with a huge grin.

Her face blushed and my cock twitched. "Well, it's Memorial Day weekend, I have Friday and Monday off and I need a head shot of you for the article. I didn't want to use the school's."

Lacing my hand around her neck, I pulled her to me, kissing her on the lips.

"I don't really care why you're here, I'm glad to see you."

My fingers laced with hers as I pulled her through the restaurant. Once we got outside, I pulled her into my arms and kissed her properly. She moaned into my mouth and it filled my body with heat.

"I've missed your kisses," she gasped when we finally pulled our mouths off each other.

"Fuck, I've missed you, sweetheart. Come on, I need my cock in you like yesterday."

We hadn't brought up the fact that we made love with no condom. Aubrey said she was on the pill so I tried hard not to worry too much about it.

"How's your dad doing?" I asked as we walked the short distance back to my place.

"Good. He's going stir-crazy, though, being in the house."

Laughing, I shook my head. "I bet. But he's taking it easy and all of that?"

"Oh yeah. My mother is making sure Dad follows the doctor's orders."

I looked over at her. Damn if she wasn't the most beautiful thing in the world.

She grinned. "I turned the articles all in. Joe loves them so far."

"I never had any doubt."

Her face turned red again as we walked through the doors to my building and straight to the elevator. I needed to get her up to my place before I ended up fucking her in the elevator.

We stood in silence, the sexual build-up growing between the two of us. The thought of being inside of her for the next four days drove me insane.

The doors opened and we stepped in. I could practically smell her lust as the metal box slowly started its way up.

Reaching over, I hit stop.

"What are you doing?" Aubrey asked with a confused face.

I pushed her against the wall as my hands went under her dress, finding a thin layer of lace separating me from her sweet, delicious pussy.

Dropping to my knees, I pushed the fabric to the side and licked between those soft pink lips.

"Jesus, Brett!" she gasped.

It didn't take long for her fingers to lace through my hair, pulling me in closer to the spot she needed for her release.

"What do you do to me?" she panted right before she came.

Standing, I cupped her face in my hands. "Fuck, if you don't taste like heaven."

Her chest was heaving. "I need you, Brett."

With a quick step back, I hit the button and the elevator jerked to life again.

"Trust me, baby, I'm about to give you all of me."

Chapter Thirty-One

Aubrey

WHITE LIGHTS DANCED behind my eyelids as I came down from one of the most intense orgasms of my life.

Brett had fucked me like he never had before, each movement was hard and fast, like he couldn't get enough of me.

I loved it.

Needed it.

Desired it.

He continued to thrust into me, hard and fast.

"Bree," he called out as his body shuddered and he came hard. I had to admit, I was a bit bummed out when I saw him cover himself with a condom. A part of me knew it was the right thing to do, but I also couldn't stop thinking about how he felt inside of me with nothing between us.

He laid on top of me as he caught his breath. "I'm sorry," he gasped.

My fingers moved lazily over his back. "What for?"

"For being rough with you. You deserved to be loved on, not fucked two shades to Sunday."

With a chuckle, I wrapped my arms and legs around him, feeling him still moving in side of me. "I loved it. It was exactly what I needed."

Pulling out of me, Brett quickly got up and headed to the bathroom. Leaving me alone in his bed.

I followed him into the bathroom. "I'm sorry," he said again. My heart dropped. Why was he apologizing?

"Why are you saying you're sorry? Brett, it was amazing."

He quickly cleaned himself off, then wiped gently between my legs. "I wanted to be slow, enjoy every inch of you, yet I acted like a sex-crazed maniac who needed his piece of meat."

He buried his face into my stomach. Something else was bothering him. I'd been around Brett enough to know when he had something weighing on his mind.

Dropping down to my knees, I looked into his blue eyes. "Brett, don't make what we shared into something bad. It was real, raw, and filled with passion."

He smiled an evil smile and my lower stomach tugged with desire. "You like when I fuck you, sweetheart?"

Brett would forever rock my world with his dirty mouth. It no longer stunned me, but filled me with a lust I'd never knew was possible. How I longed to hear him whisper those forbidden words in my ear.

Digging my teeth into my lip, I whispered, "Yes."

"Tell me."

Never in my wildest imagination would I ever dream I'd be saying what I was about to say to a man.

"I like it when you fuck me. And when you tell me you're going to fuck me, and all the delicious ways you're going to do it."

Every word I said was true. Of course, I loved the sweet and gentle Brett. But the other side of him brought out something in me I never knew existed. And I loved it.

Brett's eyes turned dark, and my body trembled. He cupped my face within in his hands and I waited for the impact of his kiss.

But he stared into my eyes for what seemed like forever before he gently pressed his lips to mine. The kiss was soft, sweet, and utterly romantic. All the things you wouldn't expect from Brett but I'd come to know and love.

He slowly stood, bringing me along with him, not breaking our connection at all. Walking me backward, I hit the counter and came to a stop.

Pulling his lips away, I saw something in his eyes. Something so deep and profound, it nearly brought me to tears. Lifting me in his arms, he walked us back to the bed and gently laid me down.

My eyes drifted to his hard length and I whimpered slightly, knowing I was going to be filled with him again. He reached for a condom and, again, my heart broke slightly. That hidden knowledge he didn't want kids bothered me more than I was willing to admit. For now, though, I wouldn't think about it. All I needed was Brett.

Once he sheathed himself, he slowly pushed inside of me, drawing out a low growl from the back of his throat that vibrated through my entire body.

Taking my hands, he held them above my head as he made love to me. My mind drifted to the day he said he didn't make love. That he hadn't found the one person he felt he could make love to.

And here he was.

Making love to me.

It was almost too much for me to take as I stared into his eyes. Brett Owens had taken my heart and I was positive he would own it for the rest of my life. He moved and hit the spot only he seemed to know.

With a gasp, I felt myself falling apart as he pushed his lips to mine and we came together.

The last two days had been pure bliss. I'd never had so much fun in my life as when I spent time with Brett. Today we rented bicycles and were riding around Lady Bird Lake. Mine had a basket attached to it and I imagined it to be like something my grandmother would have rode when she was my age.

"How about there?" Brett asked, pointing to a large oak. Smiling, I followed him over to the large tree. Brett spread out the blanket as I placed our lunch down on it.

If someone had told me a few months ago I'd be having a picnic under a tree with Brett Owens, I would have laughed in their face.

Chicken salad sandwiches, fresh fruit, and a bottle of wine.

Perfection couldn't describe it.

Pulling out the plastic cups, Brett poured us each a glass of wine. Handing me mine, he winked. "How do you feel about public sex?"

I choked on my drink. "Excuse me?"

"You know. This tree, you up against it, my cock pounding your sweet, tight pussy." He wiggled his eyebrows as I stared at him. Bastard. He still could shock me.

I was about to say something when a female voice interrupted my thoughts.

"Brett? Oh my gosh, Brett it really is you!"

My gaze lifted to see a beautiful blonde standing before us.

Brett jumped up. "Nicole?"

My heart dropped. His ex.

"My goodness you look great!" she stated as her eyes roamed his body. Clearly she still desired him with the way she eye-fucked him.

Brett looked stunned. As if he wasn't sure how he should be reacting. "I thought you moved?"

"I did, but decided I missed Austin too much. I thought about calling, but I know how we left things, so I wasn't sure if that was the right thing to do."

My heart felt pained as I watched him with her. This was the woman he married. A woman he claimed he wasn't even sure he loved … yet he married her. The fact that he didn't want that with me suddenly hit me full force. All those thoughts rained down on me all at once.

I wanted marriage. I wanted a family. I wanted all of that with Brett. But he didn't feel the same. What made him want it with her … but not me?

Nicole glanced down to me, which seemed to cause Brett to snap out of his moment of utter shock.

"Um, Nicole, this is my girlfriend, Aubrey. Aubrey, this is Nicole."

Standing, I felt like I had won a small victory since he hadn't introduced her as his ex-wife but made sure she knew I was his girlfriend. *But would I always be just the girlfriend?*

Nicole held her hand out and gave me a fake smile. "It's nice meeting you."

I could hear the hate in her voice as she stared at me. "Same here, Nicole."

You could practically cut the tension in the air with a knife. She looked me over and then glanced down to the picnic.

"Well, it seems like you found the girl to bring out the romantic in you." She looked between us and back to me. Was Brett not romantic with his own wife? "You're a very lucky girl. I should know, I've been in your shoes."

Frowning, I stared at her. Who says something like that? Brett cleared his throat, causing her to look back at him.

"Well, it was great seeing you again, Brett. Maybe we can get together for lunch sometime."

"I don't think so, Nic."

Ugh. He had a nickname for her.

Her eyes looked sad. "Brett, I need you to know something."

My heart started pounding as I wondered what in the hell she could possibly have to say.

"If I could go back, I would give you the things you wanted."

Brett grunted. "If you'll excuse us, we're having lunch."

He took Nicole by the arm and walked her away from me. He said something to her then turned and made his way back over to me. I wasn't sure why, but I was frozen in my place as I watched her retreating.

What had she meant by if she could give him the things he wanted. Kids? Was that what she was talking about? The thought made me sick, especially knowing he didn't want that with me.

"Bree? Are you going to sit back down?"

Snapping out of my daze, I sank to the blanket. Brett took a drink of wine and said, "Sorry about that. I never imagined I'd be running into her again."

I tried so hard to push it all from my mind, but I couldn't. Brett had given me conditions up front with our relationship. I knew he didn't want marriage or a family. Yet, the idea of letting him go, at that time, was too painful and I went along with it. Content to just wait. But how long could I wait? I wasn't getting any younger.

"Will you ever want to marry me?"

Brett looked at me with a stunned expression. "What?"

"It's not a hard question, Brett."

He narrowed his brows. "We've already talked about this. I'm not ready for that kind of commitment yet."

"What if I am?"

His mouth opened, but he quickly shut it. "What did she mean she would have given you everything you asked for? Why were you ready for marriage and a family with her, but not me?"

Brett let out a frustrated groan as he laced his fingers through his messy dark hair. "Aubrey, things with you are very different than how they were with Nicole."

"So are you saying you don't love me enough to marry me and want kids, but you did with her?"

"No! I'm not saying that all. Where I'm at right now in my life, I can't commit to marriage and kids. I mean look at us. We don't even live in the same fucking town. How often will we see each other? Every few weeks? What do you want, to get married and pop out a baby and then what? Leave her with someone else to take care of her while we work our asses off and travel every week. Is that what you want?"

My stomach flipped. He said her. A little girl. I imagined holding a baby in my arms as I rocked on the front porch.

Tears threatened to spill from my eyes as I responded. "Yes. That is what I want, Brett. I thought I could wait, but I need to know that it's something you'll want as well."

A look of horror flashed over his face. "Bree, I don't ... I can't. I don't even know where my own life is going right now, and to bring a wife and child into a future I'm not even sure is not fair to you."

Standing, I swallowed hard. "What are we doing? It's clear you're uncertain about our future, and maybe this long distance thing wasn't a great idea. I guess I didn't realize I needed more from you."

Brett jumped up. "What? Aubrey, why are you all of sudden giving me an ultimatum? We just started dating for Christ's sake, and you want me to marry you and have a kid? Why can't we work on this? Us?"

I shook my head. "I'm not asking you to do that right now! I'm asking you to tell me there is a possibility of it, Brett."

"Is this because of Nicole and what she said? That part of my life was another world. Aubrey, I can't decide what my future is going to be right now. Not with everything up in the air."

"What's up in the air, Brett? What are you not telling me?"

He shook his head. "I don't want to talk about it."

My mouth fell open. "You don't want to talk about it? Well whatever it is that you don't want to talk about it is affecting my future as well, and fuck if I don't want to talk about."

"Bree, why all of sudden are you doing this?"

My chin trembled. "Maybe because I realize I want things you don't."

Brett's eyes searched my face. "I can't give you what you so clearly want right now, so maybe your right."

My stomach dropped and dread filled my body. "So that's it. Are we breaking up?"

He didn't utter a word as he stared into my eyes. It was as if he was having an internal struggle, and I wanted to grab him and scream for him to tell me what he was thinking. But he stood there … not saying a word.

Forcing myself not to cry, I replied, "I'll take that as a yes."

I quickly got on the bike and peddled away from the one man I knew I loved more than the air I breathed. The only man I've ever gotten drunk from his kisses.

The worse part was, he didn't even try to come after me.

He let me go.

Knowing I wasn't even worth a fight was the ultimate slap in the face.

Chapter Thirty-Two

Brett

One month later – End of June

S TARING OUT OVER the mountains of Wyoming, I took in a slow deep breath and exhaled. The very last bit of snow barely sat atop the mountains. I loved this place. More than I ever wanted to admit. My eyes had been opened to what my heart truly wanted. One was in reach, the other I let go without even trying to fight for her.

"Your mom said you'd be here."

Turning, I gave Annie a weak grin.

"Hey, Annie."

Her horse stopped next to mine where she remained quiet for a few minutes.

"Want to talk about it?"

"Not really," I replied.

She chuckled. There was no way she was going to let this go. I'd known Annie since I could remember coming up here. Her dad was the ranch foreman and was getting ready to retire. The main reason my father was thinking of either selling or having Mac run this place. Fuck that. I'd never let Mac touch this place. This was mine. I just never realized how much it was mine until the idea of it being gone was pushed in my face, by none other than by Mac himself. I loved the ranch in Texas, but there was something about Wyoming. The mountains, the streams, the fresh air.

I loved it here more than any place on earth.

"Well, we're going to talk about it. I've known you my whole life, Brett. And I've never seen you this depressed. Why did you let her go?"

My head snapped over to look at her. "Been talking to my Mom?"

With a wide grin, she nodded.

"What all has she told you?"

Annie looked straight ahead. "That she'd never seen you so happy before. And how amazing Aubrey is."

"She is amazing."

I could feel the heat of her stare. "So why did you let her go, Brett?"

I slowly shook my head. "Because she wanted things I couldn't give her right now."

"Such as?"

"Marriage, a family."

Annie chuckled. "Brett, I know you want those things too."

Letting out a frustrated groan, I turned to her. "How can I promise her a future when I have no clue what mine is going to be? Will I be coaching in Austin next year or will I be living here in Wyoming? I have no clue. A part of me has always known I would be taking over the ranch, either this one or the one in Texas. Do you really think she is going to want to be married to someone who runs a cattle ranch? And with dad not feeling well lately, it might be sooner rather than later. With her job and how much she travels, we'd never see each other. I've already tried that before, remember? And that wasn't with me living in the middle of Wyoming. You can't come and go very easily here, Annie, and you know it."

Annie nodded. "I do remember. If my memory is right, you also didn't love Nicole like you love Aubrey."

I knew she was right. "She has her whole life ahead of her, Annie. I can't expect her to let me whisk her away from her family, friends, and her career, while I take care of the ranch. I love her too much for that. Besides, the last time I felt pressured into marriage look what happened."

"If you truly loved her, you would have let her make that decision for herself, Brett Owens. You're being an asshole. A stubborn asshole. I'm guessing she isn't asking you to marry her right now, but to know that it's something in the future. That isn't so much to ask for."

Shooting her a go-to-hell look, I huffed. "Her father just had a heart attack. She got a huge promotion at work and she's working on trying to get on the NFL sideline. I won't take that away from her, and I won't live two separate lives. I thought at first, maybe if she moved to Austin, we could make it work. Then everything changed. I started questioning if football was really what I wanted to do with the rest of my life, and I'm worried."

"Your dad?"

With a grim look on my face I turned back to the mountains. "I have a bad feeling and I can't shake it. It's been with me since I brought Aubrey to Marfa."

"Have you talked to him?"

I shook my head. "No. Not about that." Letting out a frustrated sigh, I mumbled. "Fuck. When I brought Aubrey home to Marfa, something in me changed, Annie. I realized how much I missed the ranch. How much I missed working with my dad. Maybe that's why I avoided going home, because I knew deep down it was what I truly wanted."

"Brett, don't you think maybe it had something to do with Aubrey being with you there as well?"

With a shrug, I answered. "Maybe. But I love football. Fuck, I love it. I love coaching. Putting on those headsets and feeling the excitement from the crowd. It's a rush."

"Then don't give it up."

Turning to her, I felt my test tighten. "For once in my life, there are other things more important than football."

She smiled. "The ranch?"

"And, something else I'm afraid I lost before I ever really had her. Aubrey."

Walking into my father's office, I smiled at the view in front of me. The back wall was almost floor to ceiling windows. The view to the mountains looked like a picture.

The moment I found out Mac was trying to push his way in further with the ranch, I made it known to my father, I wanted that job. Not Mac. Both of these ranches were in my blood. I'd been putting football above my family for far too long. Things were about to change.

"How you feeling?" I asked, making my way over to one of the chairs in front of his desk.

Glancing up, he grinned. "I'm feeling fine."

My father had beat prostate cancer not too long ago so anytime he wasn't feeling well, I worried.

I took a seat. "Have you thought anymore about what we talked about last night?"

Leaning back in his chair, he looked at me. "I have. Brett, you're talking about walking away from something you have dreamed about and worked your ass off for. Why? Because your worried Mac is going to move in." He moved forward and stared into my eyes. "Son, this ranch is yours. The ranch in Texas is yours.

Anytime you want it, but don't do this because you think I'm not capable of handling it anymore or someone is going to take it out from under you."

I shook my head. "I don't think that, Dad. What I know, is that I've been denying something that has been a part of my life since I can remember. Football was my dream. I won't deny that, and I made it the NFL and chose to leave. I made it as a college football coach and took my school to the National Championship three years in a row. I've lived football for so long, Dad. The endless driving you and Mom did for select playing. Walking away from a family tradition. I love football, yes, but I've ignored the two people who mean the most to me."

"Is this because Mac said you weren't here during the cancer? From what I understand, the two of you really went after each other."

Shifting uncomfortably in my seat, I replied, "It has something to do with it, yes. But that's not the only reason. Being in Marfa a few weeks back opened my eyes to how much I want this life."

He lifted his brow. "And what about Aubrey?"

My heart felt like someone gripped it with a vice. "I can't think about that right now. What I need to be thinking about is if I'm going to be coaching college football next year, or running one of these ranches."

The look on my father's face turned serious. "Brett, I really think we need to sell one. The job of running two cattle ranches has been crazy, and the only reason I could do it was because Dalton was running this ranch. Besides you, he is the only person I trust taking on this place full-time. With him retiring, I don't think I could trust it to anyone else."

With a nod, I looked down and thought about what my father had said. I knew what I had to do. I needed to put my parents first, above all else.

"You've always talked about living up here in the summer and Hawaii in the winter."

Letting out a roar of laughter, he agreed. "Yes, that's been a dream of your mother's and mine for a while."

"Sell the Marfa ranch, I'll run this one and you and mom can do just that. Dad, you've been working these ranches since you were twelve-years old. It's time to take a break."

He furrowed his brows and gave me a hardened stare. "You would be able to walk away from everything you built?"

"Yes, because I'd be walking toward everything you built and grandad built, and his dad! This ranch has been in our family a hell of a lot longer than the Marfa ranch. I've always talked about living here, Dad."

His face softened. I could see the years of hard work in his eyes. He was tired. He'd work himself into the grave if he thought he had to.

"Sell the Marfa ranch, huh?"

With a nod, I stood. "I've been thinking about what Annie told me about the ranch across from the Salt River."

"The McEwen's place."

"It's for sale. We sell Marfa, invest that money into that place. It's only four thousand acres, but they've got a lot of pasture land that they are growing alfalfa on. He's been talking about subdividing it."

My father's eyes widened in horror. We're a little under two hours from Jackson Hole. The idea of growth wasn't that far off. The longer I could put it off, though, the better.

"We buy it, we keep it ranch land," my father replied, deep in thought.

Smiling, I replied, "Yes, sir."

His blue eyes met mine. "Don't do this because you think it's what I want you to do."

It felt hard to breathe. How did I explain it to my father I had a bad feeling something was about to turn all of our lives upside down? It was time for me to step up to the plate and do what I knew deep in my heart I was meant to do.

"I'm doing this because it's what I want to do. This place is as much in my blood as it is yours."

Slightly bobbing his head in thought, he turned and looked out the wall of windows. "Would make a beautiful place for a wedding."

My heart ached. How could I ever ask Aubrey to move to Wyoming? In the middle of nowhere with the closest airport two hours away. I had laid in bed the last few weeks trying to decide if I should call her, or let her go. In the end ... I made the decision I thought was best for her.

Finally finding my voice, I agreed with my father. "It would indeed make a beautiful place for a wedding."

Turning, he reached down and picked up a magazine and handed it to me.

"*ESPN*'s Magazine. The college football preview. She did a great job."

Looking down, I saw her name.

Brett Owens.
The University of Austin's secret weapon.

By Aubrey Cain
Correspondent

Chapter Thirty-Three

Aubrey

SITTING IN JOE'S office, my knee bounced up and down at a fast rate. I wasn't sure if I was nervous or it was from lack of sleep. I'd hardly slept a full night since the day I left Austin two months ago. I walked away from the love of my life and there wasn't a day that went by I didn't regret it. Although my sister Nelly insists I couldn't fall in love that fast. I was almost positive I fell in love with him that day on the sideline when he smiled at me.

My gaze drifted down to the *ESPN* magazine on my boss's desk. Brett's picture on the cover caused my heart to ache.

He hadn't even called or texted about it. It came out last month and not a word from him.

Silence.

Pat had called me, though. He told me how wonderful the article was and thanked me for the good reporting I had done.

The door opened, pulling me from my thoughts. Joe walked in with another guy. He was about my age, cute, and a smile that would make any girl blush. Not this girl, though. I couldn't seem to make myself move on even two months later. It was clear with no communication from Brett that we were over. Maybe he got back together with Nicole. The thought made me nauseous.

Every night before I went to bed, I searched the Internet for any signs of Brett. Each night turned up nothing. According to Michelle, it was rumored Brett Owens had hung up his bachelor days and was living pretty much out of the limelight.

"Thanks for clearing your day, Aubrey. I know you're heading out tomorrow."

My stomach dropped thinking about tomorrow. I was scheduled to fly back to cover the charity football game that Brett's foundation was doing. It was the kids versus the University of Austin football players. Joe wanted me to do a follow-up piece.

With a quick nod, I forced a grin. "Not a problem."

"I'd like for you to meet Logan Hill. He's an analyst for the NFL."

My heart started pounding. Maybe Joe was impressed with my piece and he was starting to second-guess keeping me in college. Standing, I reached for Logan's hand. "It's a pleasure meeting you, Mr. Hill."

"Likewise. Please call me Logan."

Trying not to let myself jump ahead, I grinned.

"I have to say, I'm impressed with your article on the University of Austin and Brett Owens. That must have been hell spending so much time with a man like Brett."

Anger engulfed me immediately. "Mr. Owens is a very respected and well-loved coach. Not only by his team, but his staff and the university as well. I was honored to get to cover both the university and Coach Owens."

Joe and Logan seemed to be caught off guard by my response. Matter of fact, so was I. The way I was so quick to come to Brett's defense had Joe giving me a questioning look. He never once asked how I got along with Brett. I'm sure he knew something had happened between us, but he never brought it up.

"I didn't mean he wasn't well respected. I guess I've heard things about him."

Forcing a smile, I sat back down. "Well, we shouldn't always believe what we hear."

Damn it, Aubrey. What in the hell are you doing?

Joe coughed and Logan laughed. Turning back to Joe, he said, "I like her. She'll fit right in."

I sat up straighter. *Oh. Shit. Don't jump ahead. Do not jump ahead.*

"Fit right in?" I asked nonchalantly.

Joe held up his hands. "Don't get your knickers in a twist. Logan here read your piece and was impressed. He wanted to know why you were covering college football and not NFL."

Glaring at Joe, I wanted to tell Logan exactly why I was covering college football, but I kept my mouth shut. The last thing I needed was to piss Joe off any more than I already had.

"I told him I didn't think you were ready, but with the great job you did on Owens and The U of A, we might have to reconsider where you'll be next year."

My breath hitched and I cursed myself. *Play it cool. Save the excitement for when you leave.*

"Well, I'm sure this year my experience on the sideline of the college teams will be a great learning experience. One that I hope takes me to the next level."

Jesus, why did that sound so rehearsed? Did I even believe that anymore? I used to love my job … now it felt as if I was going through the motions. The passion I used to feel was slowly slipping away.

Logan stood behind Joe. He wore a huge smile on his face. Almost as if he knew I didn't belong on the college level.

Truth be told. I wasn't sure where I belonged any more. The only place I longed to be was in the arms of one said, Brett Owens.

"You had dinner with him?" Michelle asked as we made our way through the Austin airport. She'd been bugging me about Logan Hill since we left for our five a.m. flight this morning. I lucked out when she fell asleep almost as soon as she buckled her seat belt. One of the perks of my job was that we got to fly first class. Michelle was out before the mimosa was even finished.

"Yes, I had dinner with him. It's not that big of a deal."

I could feel her look of disapproval so I avoided direct contact with her. "What about Brett?"

Coming to a stop, I turned to her. "Brett? You mean the guy who let me walk away from him when I said I wanted marriage and kids in my future? The guy who hasn't even bothered to check and see if I'm alive or not? Fuck. Brett."

Her eyes widened in shock. "Ouch."

Spinning on my heels, I marched toward the exit door. A part of me knew I had backed Brett into a corner that day. It was so out of left field for me to demand that from him. We'd only been dating for a small amount of time and here I was talking marriage and kids.

Ugh. What in the hell was I thinking?

Jealousy. I was jealous of Nicole. Bottom line.

"He called me."

All the air left my lungs in one nanosecond. I stopped walking and waited for her to come up to me.

"I wanted to tell you, but he asked me not to."

I fought like hell to keep my feelings in check. "What did he want?" I asked in a whispered voice.

"He said he wanted to see how you were and to ask about your dad."

My entire body shuddered. Opening my eyes, I turned to her. "That was it?"

Michelle swallowed hard. "Kind of."

"Kind of?" I asked, my heart feeling like it was being ripped from my chest. Why hadn't he called me? He could have asked me how my father was doing.

"He, um, well he told me he regretted letting you walk away that day, but he knew it was the best thing for you. He mumbled something about not keeping you back from the things you wanted."

A tear trailed down my cheek. "He'll never change his mind about marriage or a family will he?" I asked as I sob escaped from my lips.

With a slight shrug, she replied, "I don't know if that's it, Bree. I mean, don't you think you might have been putting a lot of pressure on that seeing as you guys were just starting your relationship?"

Wiping my tears away, I stood up straighter. Ouch. The truth hurt even more coming from my best friend's mouth.

"Well, whatever it is, marriage, kids, career, he doesn't seem to think I can handle it. So either way, it doesn't matter right?"

I went to walk when she took me by the arm. "Doesn't it?"

Thinking back to last night's dinner with Logan, I realized for the first time in two months I actually felt alive again. Logan lived in the same town as me. We worked for the same company. It was convenient.

Swallowing hard, I forced the next three words from my mouth. "No. It doesn't."

My phone rang. Reaching into my purse, I grinned when I saw his name. Looking directly at Michelle, I answered it. "Hey, Logan. How's it going?"

Her eyes turned sad before she turned and walked ahead of me. My hands started shaking and I covered my mouth to keep my emotions in check.

"Hey. So, I have tickets to this great outdoor play Tuesday night. Are you free?"

Dragging in a deep breath, I slipped into the cab Michelle had gotten for us. I could decide right now to go another few months crying myself to sleep wondering if I had pressured Brett or if we really truly didn't have a future together, or I could move on from him. My heart told me one thing, while my head told me another.

My heart lost.

"I am free. It sounds like a lot of fun. I'll be back in town Sunday morning."

"Oh, fast in and out, huh?"

Forcing out the words, I answered, "Yep. Nothing really in Austin to keep me there longer."

"How about dinner then, Sunday night?"

"Sounds great. I'll call you when I land."

After saying our goodbyes, I slipped my phone back into my purse. Sneaking a look at Michelle, she had her head turned away as she looked out the window.

I knew what I was doing was the right thing to do. Brett didn't want the same future I did. Maybe Logan would.

"What brings you two lovely ladies to Austin?"

The cab driver's friendly voice pulled me from my thoughts. "I'm covering a benefit football game at the University of Austin," I answered, looking over at Michelle, who was still ignoring me.

"Ahh, Brett Owens' foundation. *Bright Futures.*"

Hearing his name pained my heart. How long would it truly take to get over him? I'd never felt this way about anyone ever before. Not even, Cliff. "Yes."

"We're very proud of Coach Owens in this town."

I nodded. "Yes. I know."

"He's a good man. I got to meet him once."

Michelle turned her head. "Oh yeah? How?"

The cab driver stopped at a light and turned back to smile at us. "It was Thanksgiving. He came to the shelter I work at and helped hand out meals to the homeless. Good man. He does it every year."

Now it was my turn to stare out the window as Michelle replied, "That was very thoughtful of him to do that."

"This morning he was at Dell Children's hospital. His family donated a large sum of money for help in getting some piece of equipment for them. I wish I could remember what it was."

My head snapped forward. "Really?" I asked.

"Yes. His parents were in town, maybe you'll meet them at the game!"

"I've already met them. Very nice couple and so is Coach Owens. I've done an article on him."

"Oh," he replied. "Then you know how lucky we are to have Coach Owens. He not only loves the U of A, he loves helping our community."

With a barely-there nod, I responded, "Yes. I know how lucky you are."

Chapter Thirty-Four

Brett

I WAS COACHING the *Bright Futures* team and Troy was coaching the college team. It was flag football, but I wouldn't be surprised if my little guys here took an opportunity to try and tackle one of the big leagues.

We all gathered in the locker room as we got ready to play. "Remember who I always say the winner is?"

The room all answered back, "We are, Coach."

"Why?"

"Because we try."

I nodded. "That's all I ask for. If you try the hardest you can, you're already a winner. What's the main thing I want you to do today?"

They erupted in cheer. "Have fun, Coach Owens."

Smiling, I replied, "Have fun. The rest is just bonus. Now let's do a group hug."

The kids jumped up and gathered around in a circle. Wrapping arms around each other, we dropped our heads. The air in the room felt charged as I quickly looked up.

Standing in the door was Aubrey, and next to her, Michelle Brown. My stunned stare bounced between them both before they landed on those warm brown eyes. My stomach dropped at the sight of her. What was she doing here?

"You gonna pray or what, Coach Owens?"

I opened my mouth, but nothing would come out. It was the first time I'd seen her in two months. Fighting the urge to rush over to her, I looked away and over to Pat.

He saw the pleading look in my eyes and jumped into action. "Um, that's my job today, y'all."

Bowing my head again, I didn't hear a damn word Pat said. All I could hear was the sound of my heart pounding in my ears.

Aubrey looked beautiful. Her eyes were filled with such sadness and it killed me knowing I caused that.

"Coach Owens, you have anything else to say?" Pat asked, dragging me away from my thoughts.

"Ah ... no. I said all I'm going to say. Let's go out there and be safe first and foremost, and let's have some fun!"

Clapping my hands, I motioned for the kids to head on out of the locker room.

My heart stopped when I heard her call my name. Glancing over my shoulder, I forced myself to stop.

Michelle walked by me first. "Hey, Brett."

Nodding my head, I mumbled, "Hey, Michelle. Good seeing you."

Aubrey stopped directly in front of me. "I take it from the look on your face they failed to tell you I was coming to interview you?"

Fighting the urge to pull her into my arms, I replied, "No. I wasn't aware you would be here."

"Oh," was all she said in return.

"The piece is out. Why another interview?"

She smiled and my heart broke in half. Fuck, I'd missed that smile.

"It's a follow-up piece since the first one was such a hit."

I wanted to tell her everything. Tell her my father sold the ranch in Marfa, tell her I would only be coaching one more season. There were so many things I wanted to say to her. I wanted her to go with me to Wyoming. I wanted to be with her. Only her. If she needed a promise of marriage, I'd give it to her now.

My mouth opened as I was about to pour my heart out to her.

Her eyes had lit up for one brief moment. Almost as if she knew I was about to open the flood gates of emotions.

"Coach Owens! Come on!" Turning, I saw Chuck, one of the kids, had his head poked in the door, motioning for me to hurry.

Looking back at Aubrey, I forced a grin. "Good to see you again, Bree."

The way her body slumped, I knew that was not what she was hoping for. She grinned and started heading out of the room. The second the door shut I closed my eyes, counted to ten, and then punched one of the lockers.

Fucking asshole.

The game was over and, of course, team *Bright Futures* had won. I'd successfully kept my focus on the field and off of Aubrey. She sat with Pat, and the last thing I saw was her beautiful smile as she cheered the kids on.

I was glad she was happy. Unlike me. I'd spent the last two months practically hiding in my condo.

"We won! Coach, we won!" Chuck shouted as he ran over to me. Little Casey was right behind him. She'd recently been adopted by her foster parents and I could see what a positive effect of being with a loving family had had on her.

"We did it, Coach Owens," Casey exclaimed, waving her pom-poms all around.

Leaning down, I looked them both in the eyes and beamed with pride. "You did it. I'm so proud of all of you."

I had asked for the cameras to give me ten minutes after the game before they came rushing over for all the political shit to start. Ever since that article, I'd been hit up to do more and more interviews. I turned them all down. They would get their news from me later in the season.

After talking with the kids, I stood and turned to face the media. Aubrey was standing next to Pat and, of course, she got first dibs. *ESPN* and all that shit.

Taking a deep breath, I walked over to her. Glancing over her shoulder to the camera man, she pointed and then turned to me. This would be the first time she had officially interviewed me on camera.

"I'm here with the University of Austin's head football coach, Brett Owens."

She turned and smiled at me. "Coach Owens, we just saw your team from *Bright Futures* beat the University of Austin's football team. How proud are you of this amazing team you've built with *Bright Futures*?"

I was so fucking tired of playing this game. Putting on the show I was expected to give, I grinned. "Very proud. These kids have all come from different backgrounds and situations, but the football and cheer programs let them have some needed fun while building character, as well. And they learn team work and what it means to be there for each other."

"It's more than that, though isn't it, Coach? They're learning life lessons not only from you, but from the whole U of A football team."

With a nod, I responded. "Yeah, the whole team comes out and helps with these kids and something magical happens. I think it's a life lesson all the way around for everyone."

"Coach, I know it's not a requirement for your college football players to volunteer with these kids, but every single guy on the team does. That has to make you proud of your guys and what they are doing, not only on the field, but off as well."

"Very proud. I've got a great group of young men who make me proud to say I'm their head football coach."

"Speaking of the U of A football team, have you put the stress of spring practice and who would be your starting quarterback behind you? And what are you focusing on for that first game with Notre Dame?"

My hand stabbed through my hair. I couldn't help but notice how it caused Aubrey to catch her breath. "Yeah, I mean all the drama surrounding the starting quarterback was hyped up more by the media then me or my staff. We had two great kids who, honestly, are both good enough to be the starting quarterback. At this point, I'm not ruling anything out. Our focus right now is staying healthy and going out there and doing what I know we can do. And that's win."

She lifted her eyebrows. "Does that mean you'll change your mind before the opening game against Notre Dame on who will be starting as quarterback?"

"I'm not sure what I'll do, we're still a month out from that."

Aubrey nodded. "Number twenty-seven still seems to be favoring that right knee. How confident are you that he'll be healed up and ready for that season opener?"

With a smirk, I responded, "He'll be ready. No doubt about that."

"How do you feel about your defensive line? Last year there was some talk it would be weaker with you losing half of it to graduating seniors and the draft."

Taking in a deep breath, I glanced over to the next reporter. That was my way of saying I was ready to move on. Every good sideline reporter knew when the coach was ready to keep it moving. It wasn't her questions that was getting to me. It was the smell of her goddamn perfume. And the fact that I wanted to kiss her. Take her back to my office and fuck the living hell out of her.

"I feel great about our defensive line. It's stronger than ever. Thanks, Aubrey."

"Thank you so much, Coach Owens, for your time. Good luck this season and, of course, with *Bright Futures*."

With a quick wink, I replied, "Thanks."

Taking a step away, Aubrey dropped her mic and stared at me. Our gaze locked for a moment before the next reporter stepped up and the whole process started over again.

I had no fucking clue how I made it through the next thirty minutes. The moment the last reporter thanked me, I turned and headed over to both teams. After a quick talk, I grabbed my bag and headed out of the stadium. The sooner I got the hell out of here, the better.

Chapter Thirty-Five

Aubrey

October

MY CHIN RESTED on my knees as I looked out over the lake. My parents had rented a lake house for everyone to celebrate Marie and Harry's upcoming wedding. I had cut a deal with Holly Richards for her to cover my game the weekend of my sister's wedding. In exchange, I had to go to some function at the end of the college season. I had half-heartily listened to her when she said what it was. All I knew was it meant being off for my sister's wedding, and I wouldn't have to hear my mother complaining about me missing it for a football game.

"You're deep in thought."

Glancing up, I grinned as my mother handed me beer. "Thanks."

"Where you thinking about Brett?"

I quickly darted my eyes back to the water. "Mom, please. Don't do this again."

I'd told my mother everything about what happened with Senator Dryer and Brett. She had offered to dig up dirt on Ryan, but I declined. The next day she told me she had called Brett. He declined as well. Seems like he'll talk to anyone but me.

"Fine. We won't talk about Brett."

"Thank you. Because in case you forgot, I'm dating Logan."

My sisters walked up and gathered around us. Marie sat first. "What are we talking about?"

Letting out a chuckle, my mother answered, "Well, we are certainly *not* talking about Brett Owens."

Marie placed her hand over her chest. "Oh, god. That fine piece of male meat. Damn, Bree, you messed up big time with that one."

I hit her leg. "Shut up. We should be talking about your wedding."

Nelly plopped onto my lap, making me grunt. "Hell no. I want to hear more about hottie Brett. Tell us how good the sex was, Bree!"

Shooting her a dirty look, I pleaded, "Please, have you all forgotten that I have a boyfriend who happens to be here?" I glared at my mother, after all, it was because of her we were even saying Brett's name.

She shrugged and took a drink of her wine.

Nelly let out a roar of laughter. "Oh, yeah, because you'd much rather shag him over Brett."

I gave Nelly a good push, causing her to hit the ground with a thud. She laughed and jumped up. She tried like hell to pull me out of the chair and into the lake.

"Girls! Stop it right now before someone gets hurt," my mother called out.

Christine rubbed her very pregnant belly as she laughed. "You'll make me go into labor and I really want to enjoy this vacation, so knock it off, you two."

Nelly gave me a look like she had won as she let her hold of my wrist go, sending me back down into my chair. "Wait until later," I threatened.

She lifted her hands and said, "Oh, I'm shaking!"

"Will you girls stop it," our mother pleaded, turning to Christine. "Darling, are you feeling okay?"

With a sweet smile, my older sister nodded her head. "I feel amazing, Mom."

My chest tightened as I glanced down at her hand rubbing over my sweet little niece or nephew. My sister and Ralph had decided to not find out the sex of their second child. It drove my mother insane because all she wanted to do was shop for her future grandchild.

I couldn't take my eyes off her hand, resting on her unborn child.

"Did I tell you Harry and I decided to try right away for a baby?" Marie said. Everyone started cheering, especially my mother.

"Oh, thank you, Lord. Another grandbaby!"

Marie grinned from ear to ear.

"Our kids can grow up together, Marie!" Christine said.

With the threat of tears looming, I glanced back out of the water. The boat the guys had taken out earlier came into view. Nelly's boyfriend of two months was at the wheel.

"I hope Ben knows how to drive that thing," I verbalized, knowing it would goad Nelly on.

She didn't utter a word. As they got closer, Logan held up a handful of fish.

"Looks like we won't starve tonight ladies," Mom said as she stood up and waved. "Come on girls, let's go say hi to our guys."

Everyone else stood, well everyone but Christine. Chuckling, I helped her out of the chair. They all headed over to the dock, but I was frozen in place. For some reason, my heart ached.

"Bree? Baby, are you okay?"

Facing my mother, I plastered on that famous fake smile I had nailed so many years ago. "I'm fine."

Lifting her brow, she tilted her head. "Is everything okay with you and Logan?"

"Yeah. I mean, I think so," I replied with a slight shrug.

Tears built in my eyes as my mother pulled me into her arms. I knew she liked Logan, but even she told me one night when she had drunk too much wine, she liked Brett better.

So. Did. I.

Pushing me back, she looked at me. "It's not fair to him if you don't care for him like he cares for you."

I nodded. "I do care about him, Mom. I'm emotional this week-end, that's all. You know. Marie getting married, Christine having a baby. All of that."

"It will happen when God wants it to happen for you, Bree."

My eyes closed. "I know, Mom." My chin trembled. "I thought it would be with him and I forced the idea on him. I drove him away from me because I got jealous! Like a stupid little teenage girl."

She pulled me into her arms. "Oh, darling, I saw the way Brett looked at you. He loved you and you can't keep beating yourself up. You both really need to talk to each other for Pete's sake."

"You're probably right."

"Am I interrupting?"

I jerked back and wiped my tears away at the sound of Logan's voice. "No! Not at all."

He looked at me funny. Something in his eyes was different, and I hoped like hell he hadn't heard what my mother had said. Nelly told me I was crazy when I started dating Logan. He was the re-bound guy. The rule was, fuck him, then leave him. The only prob-lem was, Logan and I hadn't even slept together yet. He had been so patient with me. I never told him about Brett, but he knew I was coming off a broken heart.

"Happy tears," I replied as I glanced back at my mother. She wore a fake smile and I was sure Logan knew I was lying.

"You caught some fish I see," I remarked, changing the subject.

His chest puffed out. It didn't take much to get Logan's ego going. "I did. Your dad said I'm a natural fisherman."

My mother laughed. "If he thinks he can drag you out on that
boat all day, he'll tell you whatever you want to hear."

Logan tossed his head back and laughed. "I figured as much."

Draping his arm around my shoulders, we walked to the boat.
Everything seemed to be fine with Logan. Thank goodness he didn't
overhear my mother and me talking.

Dad and Harry were carrying the fish off the boat. Logan
dropped his arm from me and grabbed the ice chest.

"Where are you going next weekend?" Christine asked me out
of the blue.

I hadn't wanted to think about the game next Saturday. It meant
seeing Brett again and having to interview him again like nothing in
the world was wrong.

"Oklahoma. They're playing Austin."

Logan dropped his arm from my shoulder and reached for my
hand as he said, "I heard your friend Brett Owens is engaged—"

I stopped walking and looked at him. "What?" My heart started
racing. This was not happening.

Oh. God. He really didn't want to marry me. It was *me* all along.
I wasn't good enough for him. Maybe it was all a game to him.
Something from his playbook to get me to sleep with him. My head
started spinning.

No. No! Brett wouldn't do that.

Nelly walked up to me and wrapped her arm around mine. "Oh
my gosh, I totally forgot to tell you what I did for the shower."

Quickly pulling me ahead of everyone, she whispered, "Breathe.
Bree, you have to breathe."

Everything was spinning. "He's engaged. Nelly, he's engaged?"

Leaning in closer to me, she whispered, "You don't know that
for sure. Just please don't freak out in front of Logan."

The moment we walked into the library of the house we were
staying in, I broke down into tears.

"He's engaged, Nelly!" I cried out.

She quickly sat at the computer and began typing. The knock at the door caused me to jump.

"Aubrey? Is everything okay?"

I couldn't even talk. "All is fine, Logan! I'm just showing her something. We'll be right out in a few minutes."

"Okay, but you I think misunderstood me. I—"

Walking up to the door, I tried like hell to keep my voice normal. "It's all good, babe! We'll be right out, Nelly remembered to tell me something about the shower."

"O-okay."

Quickly walking over to Nelly, I leaned over and looked at the Google results.

She clicked on a link. "See. You freaked out over nothing. If you had let him finish talking, he would have said this."

I scanned the article, looking for a picture of the bitch Brett had given his heart to.

Nelly pointed and I read the title out loud, "Is Brett Owens engaging the idea of NFL? It's a subject something the University of Austin is keeping hush hush about. It's big enough, though, that it is taking Owens away from this weekend's game in Oklahoma. Leaving the newly appointed assistant coach, Troy Rogers, to hopefully lead the team to victory."

I let out the breath I had been holding.

"Jesus! Why would he quote the damn article title! What is the matter with him?" I whispered as Nelly started laughing. "It's like he did it on purpose."

"You should have seen your face!"

Narrowing my left eye at her, I shot her the finger. "Fuck you, Nelly!"

She lifted her hand and wiped her tears from her face. "Oh, man, you still have it bad for Brett Owens, sis. Let's hope your poor boyfriend didn't pick up on that little freak out moment."

Nelly did another google search. "Doesn't look like he is dating anyone."

Standing, she gave me a stern look. "Seriously, Bree. You need to move on or go after Brett. But this is insane."

I ran my hands down my face. I knew she was right. The second option wasn't even really an option. Brett didn't want me, and I wasn't going to throw myself at him, or any man, for that matter. "There's only one thing I can do to get over, Brett." I said.

Nelly's face dropped. "You still haven't?"

Shaking my head, I replied. "No."

"Oh, Bree. How has Logan stayed with you for so long when he isn't getting any?"

My chin trembled. "Cause he's a good guy."

Taking my hand in hers, she nodded. "He is. But he isn't Brett. Are you truly ready to move on?"

Sniffling, I dropped my face into my hands. All I needed was to cry it out, then I'd be ready to move on.

That meant giving a part of myself to Logan. A part I knew in my heart would always belong to one man.

Chapter Thirty-Six

Brett

"*THE CANCER'S BACK.*"

Three words I never wanted to hear.

Sitting in the chair, I stared out over the mountains. My father was having surgery tomorrow in Jackson Hole to remove his prostate. I didn't care that it meant missing a game. I was going to be here for him no matter what. This time around with the cancer, things were going to be different. My parents were in a different state and all new doctors. I vowed I'd be here for them.

"Look at that snow coming down," Annie said.

With a grunt, I took a drink of my beer.

"Daddy is predicating this to be a hard winter."

I sat in silence as she talked about nothing. Half her words went in one ear and right back out the other.

"Is there anyone you want me to call?"

My head snapped over to her. "Like who?"

With a shrug, she replied, "I don't know. Somebody you'd like to let know about your dad."

"Everyone who needs to know, knows."

The way she was staring at me pissed me off. I smiled and then finished my beer. "I need to get to sleep. The surgery is at nine tomorrow, and I have a two hour drive."

"I can take you, if you don't want to go to sleep yet. Maybe you'd like to drown your sorrows in another six pack of beer."

Standing, I ignored her comment. "Night, Annie."

I headed out of my father's office and to the stairs.

"You think once you get up there it will be any better?"

"It will."

"How do you know that, Brett?"

Stopping, I turned and looked down at Annie. She was standing at the bottom of the stairs. "What do you want from me? Because if you want me to open and confess to you how brokenhearted I am, you'll be waiting a long time." I smiled and took a few steps back down the stairs. "If you want me to rip that dress over your head and fuck you, I can do that too if it would get you to shut up. Might even make me forget this for a few minutes."

The look on Annie's face was one I couldn't read. We'd been friends forever. She was like a sister to me. This was the first time I'd ever said anything sexual to her. I knew it was a shit thing to say, especially since she had recently left her cheating bastard of a husband.

"Is that what you need, Brett? To fuck someone so you can feel better?"

"Why? You offering?"

"What if I said yes? Maybe I need a senseless fuck right about now too. I mean, my husband did it, why shouldn't I?"

I swallowed hard. Could I do it? Fuck Annie?

Rushing down the steps, I grabbed her and kissed her. Walking her back, I pushed her against the wall and went to grab a breast but stopped. Quickly taking a step back, I wiped my mouth off.

"Thank God!" Annie gasped.

"Gross! Son-of-a-bitch!" I said as trembled at the thought of what I had done.

With a look of horror over her face, she shook her head. "That was disgusting."

"Hey!" I exclaimed.

Snarling her lip, she punched me on the chest. "What in the fuck did you that for? Blah!"

She frantically wiped her tongue off with her fingers.

"It wasn't that bad, well except for the part where it felt like I was kissing my own sister."

Annie shuddered. "I'll give you one thing, your dirty talk and that kiss … I see why you're a manwhore, but don't you ever try to kiss me again, or I'll cut your dick off."

There was the girl I talked into jumping out of the barn loft together and we both broke one of our legs. My best friend who I taught how to gut a deer and convinced her into tasting the blood, after all it was what real hunters did on their first kill.

Letting out a frustrated groan, I sat down on the bottom step. Annie sat next to me.

"Since I first met you, Brett, you have captivated me. Not because of your looks or charm. It was your love of living life. You were unstoppable. The dreams you had for yourself kept you soaring. Sometimes leaving your head up in the clouds."

Turning to look at her, she frowned. "You have to let her decide for herself, Brett. You're cutting her out of your life without so much as giving her the chance to know why."

Glancing down to the floor, I nodded. "Annie, do you remember that baby deer we found?"

With a chuckle, she bumped my shoulder. "Yes. We nursed it back to health."

With a grin, I thought back to how much Annie loved that fawn. "You remember the day we let it go? What my father said to us?"

Her smile faded. "If we loved it, we had to let it go."

"I love her too much to ask her to walk away from her dreams."

She shook her head. "I get that, Brett. But that was a deer! This is the woman you love and I know she loves you. You have to let her decide if she's going to walk away or not."

Leaning over, I kissed her on the forehead. "I'm exhausted, Annie. The only thing I can think about right now is Dad."

Standing, she reached for my hand. "Promise me you'll call her, Brett. Call her and let her know what's happening with your dad at the very least."

Feeling my chest squeeze, I knew she was right. Maybe what I thought was the right thing to do, was really just me being scared of my feelings for Aubrey. She freaked me the fuck out by pushing me into answering her marriage and family question. Even though deep down inside I knew she was the only woman I'd ever truly love.

"I'll call her right now."

Jumping up, she threw her arms around me. Whispering in my ear, she said, "Use that dirty talk on her."

Laughing, I pushed her back and headed up stairs. After shutting my bedroom door, I took out my phone and pulled up Aubrey's name.

Hitting her number, I took a deep breath.

When her voicemail started, I closed my eyes. The sound of her voice felt like a warm blanket covering my body.

Fuck, I missed her.

"Leave your message after the beep."

"Hey … Aubrey, it's Brett. I um … miss you. I'm in Wyoming. It's my dad. Anyway, I don't want to tell you in a voicemail. If you get a chance, will you give me a call back? Thanks."

Hitting End, I set my phone on the side table and crawled into bed. I did what I told Annie I would do. Now the ball was in Aubrey's court. How she played it was totally up to her.

"Brett? Darling, why don't you head on over to the hotel and get some sleep?"

Stretching, I caught my mother's gaze. She looked tired.

"Nah, I nodded off for a few minutes, but I'm good, Mom. Why don't you head on over and get some sleep?"

"Why don't you both leave and get some sleep?"

Jumping up, I followed my mother over to the side of my dad's bed. "Hey, sweetheart, how are you feeling?"

My father's blue eyes met mine. "Thirsty."

"I'll go get some cold water."

Quickly making my way out of the room, I ran into the night nurse. "Hey, I was coming in there to check on everyone."

With a huge grin, I said, "He woke up and is thirsty."

"Ice chips first, then water."

I lifted my brows. "He's going to be pissed ... you know that, right?"

Scrunching her nose up, she shrugged. "Then I'll be the bad guy. You get the chips and I'll deliver the news."

With a chuckle, I made my way into the small kitchen area and got a cup full of ice chips. Joanne was the night nurse and had been so kind to Mom and me. Before walking back out, I checked my phone. I'd called Aubrey last night and still hadn't heard back from her. The ache in my chest and the silence on my phone was the tell-tale sign she was most likely over me.

Sighing, I pushed it back into my pocket and made my way to my father's room. By the time I got back, the doctor was already there, speaking to my parents.

"I feel really good about the surgery. We did preliminary tests on the surrounding tissue and there are no signs the cancer has spread."

It felt as if a weight was lifted from my shoulders. Peeking over to my mother, I saw her let out the breath she had been holding.

"I hope you are planning on taking it easy for a few weeks," the doctor said, looking directly at my father.

Guilt washed over my body knowing I would be heading back to Texas in a few days.

My father looked at me, almost as if he knew what was going through my mind.

"I plan on resting, don't worry. I've asked my foreman to take over *everything* until Brett finishes out his season."

The doctor looked at me. "You're leaving Austin?"

Swallowing hard, I nodded. "Yes, sir. My place is next to my father, doing what's in my blood. Ranching."

He grinned. "Well, I'm sure they'll miss you. You've done a fine job done there, Brett. Who knows, you might get into coaching again someday."

With a quick nod, I replied, "Thank you, sir. I appreciate it. I guess you can never say never."

He chuckled and agreed. "That's right. Okay, get some rest, Joseph. I'll be back in tomorrow morning."

After the room cleared out, it was only the two of us. Sitting, I scrubbed my hands down my face and took in a deep breath.

"Don't give up your life because of this, son."

Dropping my hands to my sides, I looked at my father. "I'm not giving up my life, Dad. I promise you that. It took me a bit of time to figure out what I truly loved in life. For years I've been living this sort of, Peter Pan existence. It was football and sex. That's all I cared about."

He narrowed his eyes. "Don't let your mother know all that gossip about you was true."

With a curt laugh, I shook my head. "Then Aubrey came into my life, and my world literally was turned upside down in a matter of weeks."

"Have you talked to her?"

"I called her. Left a message, but she hasn't called me back. I don't blame her, really. I acted like a dick. It's been months since she left."

My father reached his hand out, prompting me to take it. "Well, it takes two to tango. I'm sure you both did and said things you wish you could take back. Don't worry, son. She'll call. Don't give up."

Trying to smile, I didn't feel as confident as my father. I knew Aubrey, and I knew she always had her phone with her and she would have called by now, especially with me missing the game. Trying to push the sick feeling in my stomach away, I changed the subject.

"So, are you ready for me to work side by side with you, old man?"

"I've never been more ready, son."

The way his face lit up, I knew I was making the right decision. Not only for me, but for my father.

My phone buzzed and I looked down to see Troy was calling. "Dad, let me grab this."

He closed his eyes and I hoped the few moments of peace would allow him to fall back asleep.

Walking out into the hall, I answered the call.

"Hey, Troy. What's up?"

"Nothing, I wanted to check in and see how your dad was doing."

My heart warmed at the kind gesture. I didn't have a whole lot of friends. Really, I only had two I fully trusted. Troy and Pat. I knew I was leaving my team in good hands with Troy. "He's doing great. It looks like the cancer didn't spread, but we'll know for sure when the rest of the tests come back."

"That's great news, Brett. I'm really happy for y'all."

I could hear something was off in his voice. "What's wrong?"

Clearing his throat, he replied, "I wasn't sure if I should tell you or not."

My heart dropped. "Did someone get hurt? I'll kill someone if they got hurt."

"It's not about the team. It's something I heard about Aubrey."

My breath hitched. "Aubrey?"

"Yeah, apparently she's dating someone."

It felt like I had been hit by a truck. I felt dizzy and had to grab onto the wall to hold myself up.

"Wh-what? How do you know?"

"I overheard someone saying she was dating some NFL analyst who also worked at *ESPN*. Dude, I wasn't sure if I should tell you, but I know if it were me, I'd want to know."

The air in my lungs felt heavy. Joanne walked up with a smile on her face. It dropped the moment she saw me. "Brett, are you okay?"

"Who's that?" Troy asked.

"The nurse," I mumbled.

My head was spinning.

Aubrey's dating someone. That explains why she didn't call me back.

She's moved on.

Holy shit. I waited too long.

She's. Moved. On.

Chapter Thirty-Seven

Aubrey

November

S ITTING IN THE conference room, I sent Michelle a text.

Me: Will you grab me a coffee? I have a feeling this is going to be long.
Michelle: Done.

I'd been the first one in the room and was able to get caught up on a few emails. I'd sent one to Pat, in an attempt to find out anything about Brett and why he had missed that game against Oklahoma last month. No one had any clue as to why he missed it. The U of A was keeping it tight-lipped, which led me to believe Brett was looking at moving to the NFL. I knew he was highly sought after by a few team owners. I'd attempted to call him a number of times, but guilt swept over me every time I tried.

My gaze lifted as Holly and Jen walked into the room. Two other sideline reporters. Both were laughing.

"Hey girls," I said with a grin.

Holly waved and slid down onto a chair. "Hi, Aubrey! How's it going?"

Jen sat opposite of her on the other side of the table. "Hey, Aubrey, you ready for the holidays?"

Nodding, I answered, "Yes. I'm mostly excited to spend some time with my new baby nephew. He'll be a month old next week."

Both women smiled at me before I went back to reading an email.

"So, guess who's back to his normal self again?" Holly remarked.

Jen asked, "Who?"

"Brett Owens."

My head snapped up. Both of them were taking out their laptops and didn't notice my reaction.

Jen chuckled. "For a while there, the rumors were he had finally settled down."

Holly typed in her password and replied, "Well, he must not be anymore. After my interview with him, he asked if I wanted to grab dinner. Then he said something pretty naughty and I'll admit it, I blushed. I don't know how you dealt with him for so long, Aubrey. The man is sex on a stick."

Jen leaned forward and I found myself doing the same thing. "What did he say?" Jen asked.

Holly looked between us and giggled. "He asked if I wanted to a part of a threesome, me, him, and Kasey Vaugh from *Fox Sports*."

My stomach turned.

"No way," Jen gasped with a chuckle.

Jen looked at me. "How many times did he ask you that, Aubrey?"

Trying to recover from my shocked state, I focused on keeping my voice straight. "Um, never. He never said anything like that to me."

With a wave of her hands, Holly laughed. "Well, he was clearly kidding, but let me tell you, for a second, I honestly thought about it!"

Both of them busted out laughing. "How ... how do you know he was um ... he was kidding?"

Holly glanced over to me. "Oh, he leaned closer and said he was totally kidding. But not about dinner. I declined, though. I did see him talking to Kasey, though. They actually left together, so I'm sure she got her some of that."

She wiggled her eyebrows and I quickly stood up. "Excuse me for a moment."

Quickly leaving the room, I almost ran into Michelle with our coffees. "What's the matter with you?" she asked as I placed my hand over my mouth and ran to the restroom.

Five minutes later, I heard the door open.

"He didn't sleep with Kasey."

Wiping my tears away, I tried to talk normal. "I don't care if he did."

"Uh-huh. Well according to Holly and Jen, you looked like you just lost your favorite dog. Now they're both asking if something happened between the two of you."

Stepping out of the stall, I glared at her. "You didn't tell them did you?"

Pinching her eyebrows together, she answered, "Of course I didn't."

I stepped around her and went to the sink. Staring at myself in the mirror, I shook my head. "I'm so stupid. How could I honestly think I'd get over the only man I've ever truly loved by sleeping with another guy?"

Michelle leaned next to the sink and I was instantly brought back to the day I found out I was going to be interviewing Brett. I had come full circle.

"How are things going with you and Logan by the way?"

Tears built in my eyes and I forced myself not to go there. Michelle never liked Logan or me dating him. She never could understand why Brett and I didn't talk about our feelings. Something I questioned for the last few months. Were we both stubborn or just plain stupid?

"They're okay. Things changed after we slept together."

Turning to face me, she leaned her hip on the sink. "What do you mean?"

Pressing my lips together, I fought to keep my voice sounding strong. "I don't know, Michelle. I really thought I was going to be able to move on. Taking my relationship with Logan to the next level seemed like the right thing to do at the time. We had been dating a few months, he was super patient, it was a romantic setting. I mean, I was staying in the same house as my parents, but we snuck off to the pool house and… and …"

Lifting her brows, she asked, "And?"

"At one point, I almost asked him to stop. I felt guilty, like I was cheating on Brett. It was awkward, nothing like…"

"Brett? Well my God, girl. Have you forgotten what Brett looks like? How he made you feel? Did Logan not make you feel anything like that? He must have made you feel something if you took it to the next level."

Wiping the tear that slipped from my eye away, I shook my head frantically. "Nothing. I've been trying so hard to feel something stronger. Anything. I feel like I've simply settled."

With a frown, Michelle pushed off the sink. "Then break up with him."

"I care about him, don't get me wrong. And when I think I've moved past Brett, something or someone reminds me about him and I feel like I'm right back to that day in the park."

"He hasn't tried to call or text?"

Biting my lip, I felt my chin tremble. "No," I whispered.

"Have you tried calling him?"

My head dropped. "No," I whispered. "I've felt too guilty."

The door to the bathroom opened and Holly poked her head in.

I had quickly wiped my tears away and plastered on a fake smile. "Hey, Joe's ready to start."

Smoothing out my pencil skirt, I looked in the mirror and adjusted my hair. My eyes were bloodshot red now. Great. Holly walked up to me and placed her hand on my shoulder. "Aubrey, he didn't sleep with Kasey. She showed up at the hotel bar and said Brett freaked out on her. He kissed her, but then pulled away and said he couldn't do it. He ended up leaving her in the hallway of the hotel. They didn't even make it to the room."

My heart raced in my chest.

Hugging her, I whispered, "Thanks, Holly."

I followed my co-workers back into the conference room and put on my *everything is fine* face. Joe talked about the upcoming championship games, as well as the holidays. I'd be covering the University of Austin against Baylor game. That was a given. I simply nodded and acted like I was taking down notes.

The only thing on my mind was why Brett turned Kasey Vaugh down and what would he think of me if he knew I had been in a relationship for a few months and had slept with Logan. Granted, we'd only slept together the one time. I'd used every excuse under the sun not to sleep with him again. I had a feeling he knew something was wrong.

I knew what I had to do.

As much as it would hurt me to let go of such a great guy, I knew I didn't love Logan and I couldn't see a future with him.

Looking down at the piece of paper, I held my breath at the note I wrote.

Break up with Logan before Dallas.

"Rick, we need to make sure we get up there and get to Owens before *Fox* does," I said.

Nodding, Rick took another bite of salmon. "Got it. Jesus, Aubrey, can you not just enjoy the fancy dinner we're at? We can go over all this tomorrow before the game."

With a frustrated groan, I rolled my eyes. I hated these dinners. It was nothing but *ESPN* big shots, a few NFL players, and some coaches. If one more football player hit on me, I swear I was going to kick someone in the balls.

Glancing around the room, I smiled politely when Joel Nickerson, the Denver quarterback winked at me.

Ugh.

This was my payback from asking Holly to cover my game during my sister's wedding. I wasn't really so sure Marie was worth this.

"You know how I feel about these dinners," I sighed. We attended so many functions I had started to lose count on which one was which.

Rick laughed. "Yep, I know. Tomorrow you'll be on the sidelines doing what you love most."

His words felt like someone has punched me in the stomach. Was this what I loved most? I didn't know anymore. Logan had all but told me I'd be moved up to the NFL next year. But why? Because I had slept with him, or because I had earned it? Did I even want that anymore? A year ago, I would have said hell yes.

Now? Now, I wasn't sure what I wanted.

I absentmindedly said, "Yeah. Doing what I love most. What dinner is this anyway?"

Rick chuckled. "Shit, Aubrey. You should know what freaking dinner we're at. It's the college coaches' dinner."

My stomach dropped. *Why did I think that was next week?*

Quickly glancing around, I said, "I'm going to mingle for a bit, Rick."

He lifted his hand to dismiss me as he reached for another hors d'oeuvre that the waiter walking by had on his tray. "I'll be here … eating."

With a chortle, I made my way through people. Instead of going out and buying a gown for the dinner, I wore the simple curve-hugging dress I had worn in my sister's wedding. It was beige and I could have kissed Marie when she picked out dresses I knew I could get a second or third use out of.

"Aubrey, it's good seeing you."

With a wide grin, I stopped and said hello to the Oklahoma State football coach. My heart raced slightly knowing Brett would be here. What if he was with a date? How would I react?

I quickly scanned the room again.

"How are you liking sideline reporting?"

Not finding anyone from the University of Austin, I frowned. Their championship game was tomorrow here in Dallas. I knew they had to be here.

"Aubrey? Did you hear me?"

Turning back to the coach, I swallowed hard. "I, um, I'm enjoying it a lot."

"Well you're good at it. I've heard great things about you."

I was honestly touched by his words. It had taken me a long time to earn respect from a lot of the coaches. I knew my article on the University of Austin and Brett had earned me a lot more respect. "Thank you, Coach Simmons. It's been a great learning experience."

He threw his head back and laughed. "I bet. How was it working so closely with Coach Owens? He's set to make some big announcement tonight."

My breath caught in my throat. "He's here?"

Looking at me like I'd lost my damn mind, Coach Simmons replied, "Well, of course, he is. Aubrey, are you feeling okay?"

Forcing a smile, I replied, "Yes. I think I'm a little jet lagged, that's all."

Goosebumps covered my body. It felt as if the whole energy in the room changed.

Brett never showed up on time. He was always late. I felt him before I even saw him. Looking over Coach Simmons' shoulder, I found him. Standing there in a tux looking handsome as hell was Brett. My blood rushed through my veins, leaving me dizzy.

Brett looked directly at me. Catching my breath, we stared into each other's eyes. Turning back to the person he was talking to, he shook their hand and then made his way over to me.

Licking my lips, I concentrated on my breathing.

"Coach Simmons, how are you this evening?"

"Ah, speak of the devil. I was just talking about you to Ms. Cain here."

Brett moved his gaze over to me. The way he looked me over had my body shivering with desire.

"Aubrey, you look beautiful tonight."

My words were stuck in my throat. Opening my mouth, I tried to speak, but nothing would come out.

Coach Simmons cleared his throat, pulling me out of my daze. "Thank you, Brett. You look very handsome as well," I finally replied.

"It looks like the two of you need to catch up. I'll talk with you soon, Owens."

Brett shook the other coach's hand and watched him for a few moments as he walked away.

Glancing back at me, his face dropped. "You never returned my call."

My heart stopped. It actually felt like it stopped beating as I stared at him with a dumbfounded look. Brett called me? When? "What ... what call?"

Brett rubbed the back of his neck and forced a grin. "It doesn't matter."

"It matters to me. I never got a call from you, Brett. Did you leave a message? Was it at work or on my cell?"

Brett pinched his brows together. "It was early November. I called your cell phone and asked you to call me."

I was positive my heart rate had tripled in the last ten seconds. "Brett, I never got a message from you. I swear."

He opened his mouth to say something, then shut it. I wasn't going to let him do this to me again. We were going to talk and I didn't give a shit where we were.

"Say it, Brett. Say what you want to say because I can see it in your eyes. Please don't walk away again without saying what you want to say."

The way his blue eyes lit up, I couldn't help but feel the familiar pull in my lower stomach. How stupid was I to think I'd ever be able to get over him?

"You want me to just say it?"

"Yes! I want you to just say it, no matter if it's good or bad."

Taking a step closer to me, he leaned in. His stare dropped to my lips, causing me to take in a sharp breath. Our gazes locked again.

"I was stupid. Blind to see what was in front of me and too scared to admit I wanted the same thing as you."

A small gasp slipped from my mouth.

"Tell me you could walk away from all of this to be with me. Marry me, Bree. Right now, tonight."

My jaw dropped. *Was I hearing him right?* "Wh-what?"

There was no way. I had to be dreaming. All those nights I cried myself to sleep praying I'd hear those words from Brett's lips.

"Don't think about it, it's either yes or no."

Placing my hand up to my face, I let out a confused laugh. "Have you been drinking?" I asked, looking down at the drink in his hand.

"No. It's ice water."

I dipped my finger into it and tasted it.

Water.

"Wait. Brett, I'm so confused. What are you saying?"

"I'm saying marry me, Bree, and come to—"

Someone placed their hands on my arms. Warm breath tickled my cheek as lips pressed against my skin.

"Hey, baby. Surprise, I made it after all."

A look of horror moved across Brett's face. My head was spinning. The room felt like it was tilting back and forth as I tried to make sense of Brett's proposal.

Brett was asking me to marry him and go to Austin.

Taking a few steps away, Brett's eyes moved from mine to the person standing behind me. The same person who had kissed me.

"I'm sorry. I didn't realize you were with someone. If you'll excuse me."

It felt like I was planted in cement. His words took forever to register in my mind.

Shaking my head, I called out his name. "Brett! Wait!"

Someone grabbed my arm. "Honey, let him go."

Honey?

Spinning around, I stood face to face with Logan.

"Logan? What are you doing here?"

His smile faded. A look of anger moved across his face but was gone as soon as it had appeared. "I wanted to surprise you. Looks like I did." He glanced over my shoulder, causing me to look in the direction he was shooting daggers.

Brett was talking to Pat. His fingers, pushing through his hair. He was agitated. Upset.

He asked me to marry him. And I didn't say anything. I asked him if he was drinking.

"Oh. My. God," I whispered.

Turning back to Logan, I pulled my arm from his grasp. "I need to talk to Brett."

"I would let him go. According to one of his players, he's about to make his announcement."

"What? What announcement?"

Logan gave me a smile. It was almost as evil as his eyes looked.

Why was I standing here talking to him? I needed to talk to Brett.

I made my way through the people and over to Brett. Reaching for his arm, I called out his name. He moved before I could reach him. People were standing all around him as a man's voice filled the room.

"I'd like to introduce to you someone who has made a huge impact in college football the last few years. He's asked for a few minutes of everyone's time."

Before I had a chance to make it to Pat, I was pulled to a stop. "Aubrey, what on earth are you doing?"

"I need to talk to, Brett. Logan, I'm sorry, I didn't realize you would be here and well, I, um." My breathing was labored as I fought for air. If I hadn't known better, I would have thought I just ran ten miles.

People started clapping, causing me to jump.

"Well you can't talk to him right now, Aubrey. He's about to speak."

My heart jumped to my throat as I turned and looked at Brett standing at the podium. Pat was standing next to him as well as Troy Rogers.

Something was wrong. Why were they all standing up there together?

"Thank you for letting me have a few moments of your time. The last six months have seen a lot of change for me. I've discovered some things about myself that I had buried deep inside of me and different events in my life have brought them to light."

My hand covered my stomach as I concentrated on breathing normal. Maybe Brett had a moment of freaking out? If he was announcing a move to the NFL, Lord knows what was going on in his head. Maybe his proposal was a reaction to being nervous about his announcement.

"After much thought and talking it over with the University of Austin and my family, I've decided to step down as head coach of the University of Austin's football team. Troy Rogers will be acting coach starting after the conference championship game. I have every confidence that if we are blessed with a win, Troy will be able to take our guys all the way to a win in January."

Someone called out from the crowd, "Who in the NFL won you, Owens?"

Everyone laughed as I frantically searched to see who had asked the question before looking back at Brett. His smile was forced. His body tense. He was about to deliver a blow.

"I won't be moving up to the NFL." Gasps could be heard throughout the room. My hand covered my mouth as I tried to make sense out of what I was hearing.

"I wanted y'all to know first. The official announcement is being sent to the media now and should hit tonight's news. I wish each and every one of you the best of luck. Thank you for making the last few years such a great experience. I'll treasure it always."

Brett quickly walked off the stage and started toward the door. I was quickly lost in the crowd while I tried to push my way through. "Brett!" I cried out. "Brett!"

He didn't bother to stop walking. By the time I made it to the door and rushed outside, he was gone.

I pulled in a deep breath and held it for a few moments before releasing it along with a sob.

"What in the hell just happened?" I whispered.

Chapter Thirty-Eight

Aubrey

I TOSSED MY phone onto the bed. Brett must have turned his phone off. Every time I called it, it went straight to voice mail.

Sitting on the end of the bed, I dropped back and stared up at the ceiling.

His words replayed in my mind, like they had all night.

"Don't think about it, it's either yes or no. Marry me."

The knock on my hotel door had me jumping up and racing over to it. Looking out, I saw it was Logan. I was seething mad.

Pulling the door open, I glared at him.

"Aubrey, we need to talk."

I held up my hand, blocking him from coming into my room. "No, Logan. We don't. I told you before I left Connecticut, that this was not working. I made it very clear to you that we were through, yet you showed up at the dinner like that conversation never happened. Trying to mark your territory in front of Brett. Why?"

Logan laughed. "Do you really think I was going to let you walk away? Aubrey, if you gave us a chance you'd see how great we could be together. You need to put this silly notion to rest of you and Brett Owens having something together."

Narrowing my brow, I looked at him with a scowled expression. "What do you mean, this silly notion of me and Brett Owens?"

He tried to reach for me, but I stepped back. In that moment, everything became so clear. All of it seemed to make sense all at once.

"You erased his message, didn't you?"

"What?"

"Brett's message. He called and left me a message. You erased it. Why?"

He shook his head. "He's not good enough for you. He's a fucking player, and if you think for one moment he would be true to you, you are insane."

My hand covered my mouth. "Oh. My. God. It was at the lake. The weekend he missed the game. I walked into the room and you were holding my cell phone. You said you needed it to make a call, but you had erased his message. You saw he called, listened to his message, and deleted it. You bastard."

Logan closed his eyes and pressed his lips together.

"I slept with you that night. If I had gotten that message …"

His eyes popped open and he gave me a stone-cold look. "You would have run to him. Like a little lost puppy. The way you reacted when you thought he was engaged made me realize how stuck on him you still were. I needed to do something to push you along."

Anger raced through my veins like ice water. "How dare you even try to tell me what I would have done?"

He let out a gruff laugh. "Well, I know you wouldn't have slept with me had you known your fuck buddy had called you. Yeah, I know all about your little love affair you had with him. Joe told me all about it. Said it was probably the only way you could get anything out of Owens was by letting him fuck you."

My hand came up and slapped Logan as hard as I could.

"Brett Owens is ten times the gentleman you or Joe could ever wish to be. I'll regret the night I slept with you until the day I die. There was a reason we only slept together once."

Logan rubbed his cheek. "You don't really mean that. You're angry and upset, and I apologize for what I said."

I started to close the hotel door when Logan stopped it with his foot. "Leave me alone Logan or I'll call the police."

"No. We're going to talk this over. Now move away from the door and let me in."

Logan pushed at the door and then in a flash he was gone. I quickly looked to see him on the ground with Rick standing over him.

"I believe the lady said no. I suggest you do as she asked."

Logan jumped up, glancing between both of us. Without so much as a word, he stalked off toward the elevator. Once he was in it and the doors closed, I let out the breath I had been holding.

Rick walked up to me. "Aubrey, are you okay?"

Holding the door open with my foot, I grabbed Rick and engulfed him in a hug. "Thank you! Thank you so much!"

He laughed. "Well, when I heard what he had said to you, I got pissed and decided it was time for him to leave. I never did like that asshole anyway."

Hugging him again, I pushed out a relieved sigh. "Let's get ready for the game. I'll meet you in the lobby in an hour."

"Sounds good," he replied.

Walking back into the room, I picked up my phone. Hitting Nelly's number, I took in a deep breath, and slowly exhaled it.

"Hey sis. I thought you'd be getting ready for the big game."

"I need to, but first, I need your advice on something."

"Remember, get over there as fast as you can."

I nodded, even though I knew they couldn't see me.

"Aubrey?"

"I got it," I snapped back at Joe. He had been talking into my ear for the last ten minutes. Each time I heard his voice I grew angrier. How dare he gossip to Logan about me and Brett. Lord knows who else he's ran his mouth off to.

My gaze drifted over to Brett. He was dressed in khaki dress pants and a white polo shirt. He was shouting into the mic that was attached to his headphones. I couldn't help but smile. Nothing he made him look as sexy as when he was on the sidelines of a game. My heart dropped as I watched him.

One peek up into the stands was all it took to see his many fans holding up their signs. I had to agree with them. Brett Owens was the hottest coach in college football.

Grinning, I looked back at him. Austin was up by three touchdowns, yet he was standing there screaming at the ref. His headphones off and his hand running through that dark hair of his.

My lower stomach pulled with desire. How foolish was I to think I could ever get over this man. I loved him. Everything about him.

The clock ticked down and the crowd went wild. The University of Austin won the championship. They would be heading to the national championship game in January.

Without Brett Owens as their head football coach.

Making my way through the crowd, I was relentless as I pushed people out of my way. I wasn't normally so pushy, but I had to get to him. Rick was right on my trail.

"He knows you're first."

"I got it," I replied again to Joe.

"Hard hitting questions. Find out why he's leaving."

"Yep. I know what I'm doing."

Brett was smiling as he shook hands with the opposing team's coach. They hugged, exchanged words, and went their separate ways. It was as if he knew I was there. Brett turned and looked directly at me. I stopped walking when I saw he was making his way to me.

"Remember, be sure to ask him—"

"Shut the fuck up, Joe, would you?!" I shouted as Rick laughed.

Thirty seconds later, Brett was standing in front of me. I wanted to jump into his arms and tell him I loved him. Tell him how sorry I was I pushed him. Tell him I didn't need promises of marriage. I only needed him.

"We're on in ten," I said to Brett in a nervous voice. He simply nodded, thanked someone who congratulated him, and waited for me to start talking.

"Thanks, Dan. Well, Coach Owens, that was an incredible victory. Were you worried at all that your offensive line wouldn't come around? The first half they struggled with moving the ball down the field."

"What in the fuck kind of question is that?" Joe shouted in my ear.

Brett smiled. "I wasn't the least bit worried. I know these guys and what they're capable of. They were just warming up."

I smiled bigger. "Are you happy with your defensive line going into the national championship? You yourself have mentioned the line is plagued with injuries."

Looking into my eyes, he replied, "Time heals all wounds. We'll be fine."

I was momentarily stunned. Was he talking about the team … or us?

"Why are you leaving, Brett?" I asked. It was more of question from me to him. Not the *ESPN* reporter to the best college football coach out there.

"My father's cancer has come back."

Tears built as I pressed my lips together, I fought for something to say. He saw I was having trouble, and kept talking. "Last spring, someone I love very much opened my eyes to a world I forgot I belonged to. A world I long to be in and I was confused. Would they want to be a part of that world with me? I wasn't sure. I ended up pushing them away because I was afraid they wouldn't want the same future I had to offer."

"What in the hell is he talking about?" Joe asked in my ear.

"You should have asked them. You might have been surprised," I answered as I looked into his beautiful blue eyes.

Brett looked down and then back at me.

Nodding my head, I asked, "So this is your last game?"

"Yes."

"And, um, will you be a part of the hiring of the new coach?"

Brett grinned. "Well I'm hoping they'll listen to what I have to say, but you never know, right?"

"They'll listen."

Joe started screaming in my ear. "What in the fuck are you two talking about?! Goddamn it, Aubrey, ask him about his father's cancer. Will he be coming back to coaching after things settle down? Report! Do your damn job!"

Pulling my ear piece out of my ear, I softly spoke. "Thank you, Coach, for taking the time to talk to us and please know everyone at *ESPN* will keep your father in our thoughts and prayers. And don't give up."

His eyes glistened with tears as he nodded and turned to the next reporter. I took a few steps back and watched him for a few moments. I prayed he knew I was talking about us. As much as I wanted to run into his arms and ask him if he was serious about marrying me, I knew I had other things I needed to take care of first.

We waited this long, we'd have to wait a bit longer.

The next reporter asked Brett about his decision to leave Austin. "It's been a hard decision to make, one that affected a lot of people I love and care about. But in the grand scheme of things, it's best for me and the team if I step down."

Rick touched my arm, causing me to jump. "You ready?"

"Yeah, I'm ready."

Walking off the field, I glanced over my shoulder. Even through the crowd of people, Brett's eyes captured mine. They looked so sad. Those hauntingly beautiful blue eyes. I seared them into my memory as I looked straight ahead, following Rick off the field. I had a flight back home at eight in the morning. The faster I got home, the better.

Chapter Thirty-Nine

Brett

Christmas Eve

MY MOTHER STOOD back and stared at the tree. "You broke it, Brett."

With a stunned look, I answered, "I didn't break it. It didn't work in the first place."

"It worked last Christmas," she replied.

My father sat in his chair reading something on his phone. "Dad, are you going to put your phone down and tell her this didn't work last year?"

Glancing up, he pinched his brows together. "I'm pretty sure it worked last year."

"What?" my mouth gaped open. "Dad! You know this stupid thing didn't light up last year."

With a smack on the back of my head, I cried out. "Ouch!"

"Don't talk about the angel like that. She has been on this tree since your first Christmas, Brett Owens."

"Exactly! It's time to put something else up, Mom. Start a new tradition."

My father stood. "I like that. Starting new traditions. How about we start with opening a bottle of wine."

"What for?" my mother asked.

"Do we need a reason to drink wine?" my father asked.

Frowning, I looked at him. "You only drink wine when you want to celebrate something."

"I'm alive. The cancer didn't spread. It wasn't an evasive cancer … my wife is beautiful. It's Christmas Eve … shall I go on?"

With a laugh, I walked up to him and put my hand on his shoulder. "No. You had me at *I'm alive*. I'll go open a bottle. Sit back down, Dad, and take it easy."

With a wide grin, he did as I asked. My mother flopped down on the loveseat and stared at the ten-foot Christmas tree in the family room. The picture window behind it showed a clear view out the west pasture to the mountain range. The light dusting of snow fall was perfect.

"It's beautiful," she softly said.

She was right. It was beautiful.

I had loved being in Wyoming in the winter. We always came up here for Christmas. Every summer, every Christmas. They said it was going to be a bad winter, but so far it wasn't too bad. It was like Wyoming knew the Owens were here full-time. It was easing us in.

Walking into the kitchen, I glanced around. *What in the hell was I going to do in this giant house by myself?* Once my father's treatment ended, they talked about heading to Florida for a month for some R-and-R. I knew what it really was though. My father was showing me he trusted me enough to leave the ranch in my hands.

The smile on my face was hard to hide. As much as I loved football, I loved being here with my mother and father.

Pouring the last glass, I set the bottle of wine down. There was only one thing missing.

Aubrey.

I hadn't heard from her since the day after the interview. She sent me an email that simply said she needed two weeks to get some things settled. In that email she also told me she was not with Logan, they had broken up before she came to Dallas. My impromptu proposal probably wasn't the best thing to hit her with. To my defense, she told me to tell her what I was thinking. I had no idea what things she had to settle. It was rumored she was moving up to the NFL. Maybe it had something to do with that.

Grabbing a tray, I put the wine glasses on it and headed into the family room. I came to a stop when I saw the sight before me. My mother was curled up fast asleep on the loveseat and my father was lost in a book.

"You still want that wine?"

With a glance in my direction, he dropped his book some and replied, "Yes. Will you set it there on the side table for me, son?"

I set his glass down. "I'll put Mom's over here."

Every night since I got back home, I had gone out and sat under the black sky. The stars dotted the sky and made me think of Aubrey and us sitting in the back of my truck looking up at the Marfa sky.

He grunted and went back to reading.

"I think I'm going to go sit out back."

"Sounds good, Brett. It's snowing, though, don't stay out there for too long."

With a weak smile, I replied, "I won't, Dad."

Walking down the back steps, I headed out to the patio to take a seat in one of the chairs. It was already covered with a light coating of snow. Wiping it off, I sat down and dropped my head back. The feel of the cold flakes hitting my face was refreshing.

Pulling my phone out of my pocket, I pulled up her name. It was two weeks. I wasn't waiting another second longer.

Taking in a deep breath, I typed out a message to her.

Me: Merry Christmas, Aubrey.

It was less than a minute and she replied, causing me to smile.

Bree: It's not Christmas yet.

I let out a small chuckle.

Me: Merry Christmas Eve
Bree: What's on your list for Santa this year?

My heart ached. I wanted to tell her that she was the only thing on my list.

Me: Tell me what's on yours and I'll tell you what's on mine

She didn't reply right away and it pained my heart more than I wanted to admit.

I'd never felt love before Aubrey. This time, I was going to fight for her. I needed to let her know how much I loved her.

My phone dinged with a message. Glancing down, I smiled when I saw her name.

Bree: I only asked for one thing. And I'm looking at it right now

Lifting my brows, I was curious.

Me: Early Christmas present, huh?
Bree: I hope so

My eyes burned with the threat of tears. Dropping my head back, I cried out, "Fuck. Fucking idiot, why did you let her walk away?"

Quickly wiping away the tears that trailed down my face, I sent her another text.

Me: I don't know if this matters now or not, but I've never loved anyone like I love you, Bree. I'm sorry I let you walk away.

Bree: Ask me again

Narrowing my brow, I leaned forward in the chair. My heart was pounding so loudly in my ears I could hardly hear myself think.

My breathing was labored as I typed out the question.

Me: Will you marry me and come to Wyoming to be with me?

I stared at the phone for what felt like forever. My entire body came to life as I held my breath. She was here.

Aubrey was here.

"Yes. I'll marry you, and yes to Wyoming, too."

With a smile, I stood and turned around. Aubrey stood before me looking like an angel. The white snow fell lightly around my beautiful princess.

"But I'll only do it on one condition."

"Anything," I answered.

"Dance with me," she answered with a smile.

Laughing, I made my way over to her. "There's no music."

The way her warm brown eyes caught the starlight had my heart dropping to my stomach.

"Oh, Mr. Owens, there's always music."

The speakers that were on the back porch crackled. Glancing up, I saw Annie standing there. She hit a button and the song poured out of the speakers.

Phil Collins' "One More Night" softly filled the air.

Aubrey walked up and placed her hands on my chest. Her head dropped and I knew she was crying. Lifting her chin up so her gaze met mine, I leaned down and kissed her tears away.

Wrapping her up in my arms, we danced slowly, neither one of us saying a word.

As we held each other tightly, I prayed like hell I wasn't dreaming. Aubrey pulled back and looked into my eyes.

"I told you what was on my list, now have to tell me what's on yours."

Taking a step back, I placed my hand on the side of her face. "The only thing I had on my list was to see your face and hear your voice."

Her teeth sank into her lip before she scrunched her nose up and giggled. "Are you about to talk dirty to me?"

I reached into my pocket and pulled out the ring box I had been carrying around with me for the last four months. I'd seen the ring in a jewelry store when I was trying to find a birthday present for my mother. The second I saw the princess cut diamond in the antique setting, I knew I had to have it for Aubrey. Even though I wasn't sure what the future held, I knew that was her ring.

Aubrey sucked in a breath of air as I dropped to one knee. My hands were shaking as I opened the box and she instantly started crying.

"If you want me to talk dirty to you I can, but I was kind of hoping to be a bit more romantic when I asked the only women I've ever given my heart and soul to for her hand in marriage."

Covering her mouth, she dropped down to her knees and threw her body into mine. I wasn't sure how long we knelt there, holding each other as the snow fell lightly around us. I didn't care either. She was back in my arms and I was never letting her go again.

Finally, we let go and looked into each other's eyes. "I love you, Brett. I never stopped loving you."

My hands gently cupped her face. I brushed my lips softly across hers. "I never stopped loving you, and I'm sorry for acting like an ass. I should have given you the choice, but I was so afraid you'd give up what you love."

She searched my face. "That night you asked me to marry you—"

I pressed my lips to hers, taking what was mine in a slow passionate kiss. Nothing else mattered besides the fact that she was here with me.

Breaking the kiss, I leaned my forehead against hers. "It doesn't matter. It's all in the past and I only want to think about our future. All the other shit we'll work out later, Bree. I'd rather have you part-time, then not at all."

It felt as if the world stopped when she smiled at me. "Brett, I need to say this because I want you to know why it took me until Christmas Eve to get to you."

A stray strand of hair hung over her eyes. Sliding it behind her ear, I softly spoke, "Maybe we should head in where it's not wet and snowing."

With a giggle, she nodded. I stood and took her hand in mine. Guiding her to the house she quietly said, "And I thought the house in Marfa was amazing. And big!"

Laughing, I turned to her. "Well, looks like it's on you and me to fill it up."

Squeezing my hand, she grinned from ear to ear as her eyes glistened from the tears she was trying to hold back.

The second we stepped into the house, my mother pulled Aubrey into her arms and started crying. My father grabbed my shoulder and gave me a good squeeze. "Do you have any idea how hard it was for your mother to pretend to be sleeping? We knew that was the only way to get you to go outside."

I shook my head. "You were all in on this?"

He gave me a wink. "Blame your beautiful fiancée, it was her idea."

Taking a peek over to Aubrey, I could feel my heart filling with even more love for her. Annie was hugging her as they both giggled and bragged about pulling it off.

Shit, I really hope this isn't a dream.

"There's hot chocolate in the library if you want to head in there and get warm. I've also started a fire for you," Annie said with a beaming face. She made her way over to me and leaned in close. "She's beautiful. You're a lucky son-of-a-bitch, and don't mess this up again!"

I watched as my mother wrapped her arm around Aubrey's and started toward the library.

Focusing back on Annie, I winked. "She is, I know I am, and trust me—... I won't."

Taking in a deep breath, I followed behind my mother and my beautiful bride to be.

Reaching, I hit my leg as hard as I could.

With a smile, I whispered, "Not dreaming."

Chapter Forty

Brett

MY MOTHER WORE a huge smile on her face as she made her way to the doors of the library. "Your father and I are heading up to bed so you will have the house to yourselves. Merry Christmas, kids."

Aubrey's cheeks turned a bright red as she laced her fingers with mine. "Goodnight, Birdy. Merry Christmas."

The door latched shut and I pulled her into my arms. "We can talk later, right now we have a lot of sex to make up for."

Her mouth opened as she searched for the words to say. When I saw the tear, I wasn't sure what to do.

"I slept with Logan."

It felt like a knife was pushed into my chest. I knew we hadn't been together, and I knew she was dating someone, so why her words felt like someone just shot me in the gut, I don't know.

She wiped her tears away. "It was only one time and the entire time it felt so wrong. I thought if I took the next step with him, I'd forget about us. Then the night you announced you were leaving and you asked me to marry you … I was so caught off-guard because I didn't think that was something you wanted with me. I was confused, but I had already broken up with Logan."

My eyes narrowed. "But he was there."

"I know! And when he showed up and acted like everything was okay with that stunt he pulled kissing me on the cheek, it all started to make sense. Logan had been drip feeding me things about you. He knew we had a relationship before because Joe had told him. The night I slept with him was the same day he misled me into thinking you were engaged."

Jerking my head back, I asked, "Engaged?"

She waved her hands to dismiss it. "It's a long story. At any rate, it all became so clear to me the night of the dinner. The reason I never got your message was because Logan erased it from my voicemail. He ended up admitting to it."

Another sob slipped from between her soft pink lips. "If I had gotten that message, I'd have never slept with him and he knew it. I'm so sorry, Brett. Can you ever forgive me?"

With a wide smile, I rubbed my thumb across her soft cheek. "Aubrey, you don't need my forgiveness because you didn't do anything wrong. I won't lie and say that if I ever see him again I'm going rip his head off, but baby, there is nothing for me to forgive."

She chewed on her lip. "Did you … I mean … were you with anyone while we were apart?"

My hand slipped behind her neck. "I came close to being with Kasey Vaugh from *Fox Sports*. I made it to the outside of the hotel room before I turned and walked away."

More tears trailed down her face. "If you keep crying you'll fill up the room with your tears."

Aubrey looked at the floor and then back into my eyes. "Make love to me, Brett. I've missed you so much."

Reaching out, I picked her up into my arms and carried her over to the front of the fire. Gently setting her back on her feet, I lifted her sweater over her head. My dick throbbed in my pants when I saw her nipples stretching against the lace of her bra. As I ran my fingers over each, she moaned lightly and arched her back.

One quick movement of my fingers, and the bra was on the floor as I cupped her perfect breasts in my hands. My mouth descended on one nipple while I squeezed the other between my finger and thumb.

"Yes, oh God, yes," Aubrey panted.

I had to fight the urge to rip her jeans off and just fuck her. I wanted so badly to be inside of her.

"Slow, Brett, please go slow. I want to enjoy every single feel of your touch."

With a grin, I dropped to my knees and unbuttoned her pants while she kicked off her sneakers. Grabbing the waistband, I slowly pulled them down as she shimmed out of her pants. Tossing them to the side, I pressed my lips onto her light blue lace panties. Sucking in a breath, I slowly blew it back out as I cupped her ass in my hands.

With a moan, she said my name and pushed herself into me, her hands pulling my hair and fueling me on. "More," she gasped.

Not being able to take the fabric between us, I pushed her panties off. Gently kissing above her soft pink lips, I moved slowly up her body until I was standing.

She was completely naked, her breathing heavy as she gazed into my eyes.

I stripped quickly out of my clothes and pulled her warm body against mine.

"Aubrey," I whispered before my lips crushed to hers. We couldn't get close enough to each other as we quickly got lost in the kiss. Bringing her down, she laid back on the soft white rug as the fire crackled and gave off more heat.

Slipping my fingers inside of her, she lifted her hips and mumbled something I couldn't make out.

"Fuck, you're so wet. Do you want me?" I asked as I ran my lips across her neck.

"More than you know."

With a smile, I nipped at her earlobe. "Tell me what you want."

Her head thrashed back and forth. Her desire growing by the second as I pumped my fingers in and out of her.

"You. Brett, I want *you*! It's always been you."

Pulling my fingers out, I said, "Look at me, Bree."

Her eyes snapped open and her lips parted as I pushed my fingers into my mouth and moaned. Taking them out, I slipped them back inside as she gasped. "You taste so sweet."

Licking her lips, her gaze fell to my mouth. Leaning in, I kissed her hard and fast as I worked her with my fingers.

I could feel her pussy pulsing as I built up her orgasm.

"So close," she whispered. "Brett … I'm almost … oh God."

My first instinct was to grab a condom and put it on. But I wanted to feel all of her. I wanted to pour myself into her. Leaning over, I whispered against her ear as I stopped moving my hand, "Condom?"

Her eyes opened and she wore a look of horror. "He wore a condom, I swear."

Fuck. That wasn't what I was asking and for a moment, my cock felt like it went down some.

With grin, I whispered, "No baby, do you want me to wear one?"

"Oh," she softly mumbled. She chewed on her lower lip and slowly shook her head.

"Good, because neither do I."

Aubrey smiled and my heart melted.

Moving my fingers again, she was even more wet as she continued to stare into my eyes. Her body was getting close so I pulled my fingers out of her and moved over her.

"Brett," she gasped as I teased her with the head of my cock.

"I don't want you coming unless I'm balls deep inside of you," I whispered, pushing into her hard and fast.

"That's it," she cried out, her nails digging into my back while she wrapped her legs around me. "Changed. My. Mind. Don't go slow. I don't want slow right now."

With a grin, I grabbed her ass with both hands and gave her what she wanted.

"Fucking hell, you're so tight. Baby, you feel so damn good."

"So. Close. Oh, God."

"Tell. Me. What. You. Want," I panted as I fucked her harder, hitting the spot I knew would push her over the edge.

Even though I knew my parents were clear across the house, we both whispered. I wanted to scream out, though. It felt so damn good being inside of her.

Pushing in harder, I demanded, "Tell. Me."

"You. Harder. Oh, God, Brett!"

Covering her mouth with her hand to drown out her moans, she arched her back and pulsed around my cock as she came. It didn't take long before my own orgasm built. I poured myself into her as I dropped my face into her neck and whispered her name off my lips. I came so hard and for so long I swore I saw fucking stars. There was only one Christmas present I wanted to give to Aubrey. The one thing I knew she longed for. The one thing I longed for, but was too afraid to admit to until this very moment.

When I finally stopped moving, she wrapped her arms around me tighter. I wanted to stay deep inside of her. The two of us connected as one. Even when I thought I was fucking her, I was making love to her. What we shared was amazing. It was rare and I knew it.

After a few minutes, I pulled out of her and rolled onto my back and reached for my T-shirt. Quickly cleaning myself off and then moving to clean Aubrey.

Gazing into her eyes, I smiled. "I missed you ... so much."

Her hand caressed the side of my face. "I missed you too."

After folding up the T-shirt, I set it to the side and laid back down. Pulling Aubrey closer to me. She rolled on her side with her left leg thrown over my body and her head on my chest.

We laid there in silence for a few more minutes, neither one of us saying a word.

"I needed a few weeks to take care of things before I came out here. The one thing that was most important to me was for you to know how much I wanted to be with you. When I called your mother and spoke with her, I realized why you pushed me away."

Closing my eyes, I felt the heat from her stare.

"I know what I did by pressuring you was wrong."

I shook my head and she placed her finger over my lips. "We were both stupid. But I've always known what I wanted."

Peeking at her, I asked, "What did you want?"

"You. This. Waking up and falling asleep every single day next to the man I loved. Feeling your hand on my stomach as our child grew inside of me."

My eyes burned as I held my tears back and placed my hand over her stomach.

"Your career, Bree. Wyoming isn't really the easiest place to fly in and out of."

She giggled and moved to where she was looking right at me. "No, it's not, but you should have let me decide that, Brett. We have to promise each other that we'll be honest with one another. If something scares us or bothers us, we have to communicate it."

"I'm scared of you being gone. Of us living two separate lives, but I realized I'd rather have that over a life of living without you."

Aubrey sat up and smiled. "The last few weeks I've been taking care of some things I needed to deal with before I made the long hike up here to the mountains."

My heart was racing. I had no idea what she was about to say, but I had a feeling everything was going to change.

"I spent some much needed time with my sisters. Nelly's getting married."

With wide eyes, I replied, "No shit?"

"Yep. Marie found out she's pregnant, and Christine found out she no longer wants three kids and told Ralph he needed to fix that situation."

Screwing my face, I whispered, "Ouch."

"There were a few other things I did."

I forced myself to swallow. "What were they?"

"I put my condo up for sale, gave my two week notice to *ESPN*, and loaded all my favorite eighties songs onto an iPod for you."

Sitting up, I looked at her with a stunned expression. "Bree, you quit your job?"

She nodded her head. "Just like you discovered this is where you belonged, I discovered *this* was where I belonged." Placing her hand over my heart, she pressed her lips together as I let her words sink in. "What I thought I wanted, wasn't at all what I wanted. Even if you hadn't asked me to marry you, Brett, I would have followed you to the ends of the earth. All that I need is your love. Forever and always."

Pulling her onto my lap, she straddled me. Her warm pussy pressed against my cock as it stirred back to life.

"Aubrey, you have my heart, always and forever. I swear to you. I'm going to make all of your dreams come true."

Kissing her gently on the lips, I rested my forehead to hers. "I hope one of them starts tonight," I whispered.

"Me, too," she replied with a giggle.

"God, I love you."

"I love you too, Brett."

Her fingers twirled around in my hair as she leaned against me. My dick jumped each time she moved.

"He's ready," I said, laying her back onto the carpet.

"For?" she inquired with a smile so breathtaking I found it hard to breathe.

"To hopefully keep trying to give you your first Christmas present."

Pushing slowly into her, I never took my eyes off of hers as we made love.

I knew this night would be a night we would never forget. I might not get her pregnant tonight, but hell if I wouldn't try every single night until I did.

Everything in my life was exactly how it was supposed to be. Well, almost everything.

Chapter Forty-One

Aubrey

Two years later

"**B**RETT! WE'RE GOING to be late," I called out.

Rushing into the kitchen, he came to a stop and smiled. "Looking at the two of you, I can't seem to catch my breath. So beautiful."

Smiling, I shook my head and whispered, "Charmer."

Charlotte squealed in delight at the sight of her father. She had Brett wrapped around her little finger and, at fifteen months old, she already knew how to toy with his emotions.

"Oh, baby girl! Daddy is so happy to see you too." Scooping her from her high chair, he kissed her all over her cheeks and neck, causing her to giggle even more. Spinning her around, Brett told her a story.

"Once upon a time, there was a beautiful princess who got dressed in the most beautiful white wedding gown the prince had ever seen."

I stood and brought the plate of food to the sink while I listened to Brett tell our daughter about our wedding day while he spun her around again.

"She just ate, Prince Owens. If you make her sick, I'll smack you."

Charlotte and Brett laughed as he tossed her around with ease.

Finally holding her to the side, he kissed her nose and said, "My girl doesn't get sick with a little bit of playing, do you, Char?"

Again, she gave him a huge smile and giggled. Oh, she was as much of a charmer as her daddy.

"The prince had never seen a princess so beautiful. She was the fairest in the land. And trust Daddy when I say I searched the land over and over."

Glaring at him, I folded my arms over my chest.

Brett gave me a wink and kept talking.

"The prince ..."

"Handsome prince," I injected.

"The handsome prince waited outside for his beautiful princess to walk down the aisle to him with all of their family and friends surrounding them. He was afraid she would trip because she kept looking at the mountains behind the handsome prince."

"The sun was making them glitter, you have to tell her that part," I giggled.

Looking at me, he shook his head. "This is my story, you tell it your way, I'll tell it mine."

Charlotte laughed again and I couldn't help but shake my head at the sight of my husband holding our daughter and talking about our wedding day. My heart was overflowing with love.

"Well, you'll be happy to know, Princess Bree didn't trip, Charlotte. It was a good thing, too, since you were growing in her belly at the time."

My hand covered my mouth and I was suddenly overcome with emotion.

"She made it to her prince, they exchanged vows that she forced the prince to write…"

I reached over and slapped him, making Charlotte laugh again.

"They kissed and lived happily ever after."

Charlotte only heard kiss and grabbed Brett's face and planted a wet sloppy kiss right on his lips.

"Oh, how I love your slobbery kisses," Brett stated as he curled his lip up at me and wiped his mouth off. "She gets her kissing from you."

Birdy walked into the kitchen carrying a giant basket. "I've got snacks in here in case you want some, Aubrey. I know how your cravings have been lately."

Setting the basket down, Birdy took Charlotte from Brett's arms. "I'll get her coat on, we don't want to be late."

A warm feeling settled into my chest as I watched my mother-in-law whisk my daughter off to get her dressed to go.

My body trembled as Brett wrapped his arms around me and rubbed his hands softly over my very swollen nine-month pregnant belly.

Pressing his hard dick into my back side, I dropped my head to his chest. "Yes. Please. Make this baby come out," I begged.

His hand somehow masterfully found its way under my dress, into my panties, and to my clit where he softly massaged it. I was so horny during this pregnancy all he had to do was look at me and I'd come.

"Brett, we can't."

"We can." His hot breath against my neck as he whispered in my ear, "Do you want my cock?"

"Yes," I gasped.

"We'll be late for the play and my mother is going to walk back in any second."

My head rocked back and forth against his chest. "I don't care."

"Do you need to be satisfied, baby?"

"Yes, but we … we have to … go … the kids."

Brett had been asked to coach a special league football team for boys in fourth and fifth grade and he loved it. I don't think I'd ever seen him so happy as when he was on that field with those boys. Not even when he was coaching for the University of Austin. And he looked hot as hell out there coaching. Something about it turned me on. I was pretty sure that's how I got pregnant this time around. The back seat of his truck after a spring practice.

Lust was beginning to cloud my good judgement. We needed to get to the play. Half of the boys who played on the football team Brett coached were in the Christmas play at the elementary school.

"Ah, the kids. Can't let the kids down," Brett whispered.

Of course, Brett wasn't the only one who had found something he was passionate about. After I had Charlotte, I quickly fell in love with making her outfits. My hobby soon turned into other moms asking for outfits, and now Birdy and I owned a small little children's boutique in downtown Thayne. It was perfect for me. I could bring Charlotte into the shop since we had a small nursery area set up in the office. Working alongside Birdy was also a dream come true. She pretty much ran the store while I kept up with inventory. It gave her something to do, and allowed me to do something I loved.

"No, we can't let them down," I uttered, turning to face him. My pregnant stomach separating us.

Brett flashed me a sexy smile. "I can go fast."

Hitting him on the chest, I said, "Stop it before your mother hears you."

Wiggling his eyebrows, he leaned in and sucked my lip into his mouth and moaned.

I could hear Charlotte giggling as Birdy walked into the kitchen.

"Do you kids want to meet me at the play?"

Brett and I both looked at her. She slung the diaper bag over her shoulder and stopped. "What? What's wrong?"

"Did you offer to meet us there?" Brett asked.

Birdy nodded. "Yeah, you still have to load those gifts into the car to drop off at the shelter. You better get a move on, though. Your father and I will take Charlotte, get there early and get settled into our seats."

God, how I loved having my in-laws right here. My parents came to visit as much as they could. They even talked about buying a place outside of Jackson Hole. I really hoped they did. My whole family was set to come and spend a week with us after we had the baby.

"Sounds good, Mom. We're right behind you."

Trying to keep a straight face, I smiled as she brought Charlotte over to us. "Give Mommy and Daddy kisses bye-bye."

After kissing our daughter, we watched as Birdy headed out the door.

With a low growl from the back of his throat, Brett took my hand and led me to the master bedroom. After Brett and his father bought the adjacent ranch, Birdy and Joseph moved into that house, leaving us with this beautiful log home that Brett had spent so many summers and holiday's making memories. I loved that we continued to make new memories.

Shutting the door to our bedroom, he led me to the bed.

"I've got something new for you today."

Laughing, I stripped out of my clothes, the anticipation of Brett filling me causing my heart to race.

"Ah, a new play from the playbook huh?" I asked, attempting to lay down and not feel like a whale.

He crawled over me and rolled me on to my side.

Moving his mouth to my ear, he said in a sexy voice, "And this one is guaranteed to score a touchdown."

Laughing, I glanced up at him. "By touchdown you mean put me into labor ... right?"

I was two days past my due date and so ready to have this baby.

Before Brett even had time to do anything, I felt a warm wetness between my legs.

"Damn baby, you that horny?"

Oh. My. God.

Trying to sit up, I struggled for a few seconds before Brett realized what I was doing and helped me up into a sitting position.

My breathing picked up as I let out a nervous chuckle.

"You'll have to tuck that play away for another day, baby."

His eyes widened as he jumped up. "What? Are you? Are we? Holy shit!"

Laughing, I placed my hand on my stomach while Brett did the same. His eyes filling with tears as he whispered, "Our baby boy."

With a smile, I nodded.

"He's on his way."

Acknowledgments

Darrin and Lauren – For your patience with me as I wrote this book and finished it up. Thank you for always standing by me and supporting me in all I do. I love you both to the moon and back.

Danielle – For giving me the idea to write this book!

Laura and Kristin – Thank you for always beta reading for me. I love that you two are the first set of eyes on my babies!

Erin – Thank you for doing such a great job editing this book. You made some great suggestions. You are the best! Are you ready for the next one?!

Holly – Thank you for proofing! I have loved working with you and can't wait to work with you again!

Julie – Thank you for always making the inside of my book so beautiful. You're the best!

Sara – Your covers are amazing. Thank you for bringing Brett Aubrey to life with this amazing cover.

Everyone who picks ups and reads this book, shares it, tells a friend about it … THANK YOU! Your support means the world to me!

About The Author

Kelly Elliott is a New York Times and USA Today bestselling contemporary romance author. Since finishing her bestselling Wanted series, Kelly continues to spread her wings while remaining true to her roots and giving readers stories rich with hot protective men, strong women and beautiful surroundings.

Kelly lives in central Texas with her husband, daughter, and two pups. When she's not writing, Kelly enjoys reading and spending time with her family.

To find out more about Kelly and her books, you can find her through her website.

www.kellyelliottauthor.com

Stand Alones

The Journey Home
Finding Forever (Co-written with Kristin Mayer, previously titled *Predestined Hearts*.)
Who We Were (Available on audio book)
Stay With Me
Searching For Harmony
Made For You (Releasing fall 2016)

Wanted Series

Book 1– *Wanted*
Book 2 – *Saved*
Book 3 – *Faithful*
Book 3.5 – *Believe*
Book 4 – *Cherished*
Book 5 Prequel – *A Forever Love*
Entire series available on audio book

The Wanted Short Stories

Love Wanted in Texas Series
Spin off series to the WANTED Series

Book 1 – *Without You*
Book 2 – *Saving You*
Book 3 – *Holding You*
Book 4 – *Finding You*

Book 5 – *Chasing You*
Book 6 – *Loving You*
Entire series available on audio book
Please note *Loving You* combines the last book of the *Broken* and *Love Wanted* in Texas series.

Broken Series

Book 1 – *Broken*
Book 2 – *Broken Dreams*
Book 3 – *Broken Promises*
Book 4 – *Broken Love*
Books 1-3 available on audio book

The Journey of Love Series

Book 1 – *Unconditional Love*
Book 2 – *Undeniable Love*
Book 3 – *Unforgettable Love*
Entire series available on audio book

Speed Series

Book 1 – *Ignite*
Book 2 – *Adrenaline*

YA Novels written under the pen name Ella Bordeaux

Beautiful
Forever Beautiful (Releasing October 2016)
First Kiss (Releasing early 2017)